"WRY, DELICIOUS FUN."

—*New York Times* bestselling author Susan Andersen

Acclaim for the delightful and romantic humor of Molly Harper's Nice Girls series, which *Romantic Times* calls a "must read"!

"A chuckle-inducing, southern-fried version of Stephanie Plum. . . ."

—*Booklist*

"Hysterical . . . as charming as it is hilarious."

—*Publishers Weekly*

"Sure to please fans and keep them laughing . . . one awesome story."

—*Romantic Times*

"Charming, sexy, and hilarious. . . . I laughed until I cried."

—Bestselling author Michele Bardsley

"Quirky characters . . . funny situations . . . an amazing novel. . . ."

—Romance Reviews Today

"Wicked fu n

one delicio ıs

"There a

my copy

around. .

"Chock fu

And

AND ONE LAST THING . . .

molly harper

GALLERY BOOKS

New York London Toronto Sydney

Gallery Books
A Division of Simon & Schuster, Inc.
1230 Avenue of the Americas
New York, NY 10020

This book is a work of fiction. Names, characters, places, and incidents either are products of the author's imagination or are used fictitiously. Any resmblance to actual events or locales or persons, living or dead, is entirely coincidental.

First Gallery Books trade paperback edition August 2010.

GALLERY BOOKS and colophon are trademarks of Simon & Schuster, Inc.

For information about special discounts for bulk purchases, please contact Simon & Schuster Special Sales at 1-866-506-1949 or business@simonandschuster.com.

The Simon & Schuster Speakers Bureau can bring authors to your live event. For more information or to book an event, contact the Simon & Schuster Speakers Bureau at 1-866-248-3049 or visit our website at www.simonspeakers.com.

Designed by Renata Di Biase

Manufactured in the United States of America

10 9 8 7 6 5 4 3 2 1

Library of Congress Cataloging-in-Publication Data

Harper, Molly.
And one last thing . . . / Molly Harper.—1st Gallery Books trade paperback ed.
p. cm.
1. Divorce—Fiction. 1. Title.
PS3608.A774A84 2010
813'.6—dc22

2010010292

ISBN 978-1-4391-6877-6
ISBN 978-1-4391-6878-3 (ebook)

For my mother, who let me grow up to be the person I was meant to be.

acknowledgments

This is my first book that doesn't involve people with fangs, fur, or magical/psychic powers. I want to express my gratitude to super-agent Stephany Evans and my editor, Jennifer Heddle, for letting me try something different.

Thanks go to my brilliant, loving, self-proclaimed "trophy" husband, David, who can say without a doubt that he is the inspiration for Monroe. That's right, ladies, he's all mine. A big thank you to Jennifer Sacharnoski, who was willing to let me pick her devious legal mind. To J. C. Hutchins, my horror Yoda, thank you for teaching me the fine art of not being a dang Care Bear. To Brandi Bradley, whose bad influence on me is now recorded for all time. To my parents, who never flinch, thank you.

1

The BumbleBee and the Stinger

If Singletree's only florist didn't deliver her posies half-drunk, I might still be married to that floor-licking, scum-sucking, receptionist-nailing hack-accountant, Mike Terwilliger.

That's not to say I blame Cherry Glick for bursting my little housewife bubble with her badly timed, incorrectly addressed floral offering. Hell, I don't even blame the aforementioned receptionist for my husband's "misstep." I put the blame where it's due—on my floor-licking, scum-sucking husband.

To put this all in perspective, I'll take you back to that fateful Wednesday morning, when Cherry, stinking of plant food and blackberry schnapps, ambled up to my front steps with the biggest, gaudiest arrangement of peachy-orangish roses I had ever seen.

The card read, "To my BumbleBee, Happy Anniversary, With all my love, The Stinger."

"The Stinger?" I read aloud, checking the name on the envelope. Sure enough, the card was addressed to "BumbleBee." Mike had never called me that. In fact, in eight years together, Mike had never given me a nickname. And it was nowhere near our anniversary. We got married on August 1, not in the second week of June.

"Cherry, honey, I think you got this delivery wrong!" I called, chasing after her with the floral albatross.

Cherry lived perpetually south of buzzed, just drunk enough to avoid thinking about the fact that she'd been married to a very handsome, asexual man for twenty years, but not too drunk to drive her delivery van. She looked over her delivery list and muttered to herself.

"Nope, it's right," she slurred. "Right here, it's says 'Rose Romance Special Deluxe' from Mike Terwilliger to . . . oh. This is supposed to go somewhere else. This is supposed to go here."

She took an envelope out of her back pocket and handed it to me. She swayed slightly against her van and shook her head. "Wait, no, both of them are supposed to go . . ."

"W-where are they supposed to go, Cherry?" I stuttered.

"Um . . ." Cherry looked away from me, her eyes not quite able to focus anyway.

"Oh, for Pete's sake," I snapped and tore the billing envelope open. Mike was listed as the ordering party. Next to "Rose Romance Special Deluxe" Cherry's assistant had scribbled "Terwilliger-Office."

My stomach clenched, ice cold. Somewhere, in a rationalizing corner of my brain, I clung to the hope that maybe Mike was planning to bring those roses home to me this afternoon as a surprise . . . and that he was planning on giving me the nickname "BumbleBee."

Oh, God. My husband was having an affair. With a woman who called him "The Stinger." And that's when it hit me. BumbleBee.

Mike's receptionist was named Beebee Baumgardner.

"Sorry, Lacey, I'm so sorry," Cherry murmured, climbing into the van.

She knew. Soused, silly Cherry Glick had figured out my husband was having an affair before I had. Oblivious to the fact that my front door was standing open, I tugged my keys out of my pocket and ran for my Volvo. I tossed the roses into the passenger seat and, for some reason, took the time to secure the vase with the seat belt.

The next thing I remember was sitting in my car outside Mike's new offices on Spring Street, watching through the picture window as Beebee answered phones. She'd worked for Mike for a little over a year, replacing old Mrs. Keach after the secretarial dinosaur literally died at her desk. I had a healthy respect for the sunny, girl-next-door exterior God had given me, but Beebee scared me with her stunning good looks, the kind of fine features that made me feel like my face was drawn with a crayon. Her hair was so dark it seemed to absorb the light around it. It fell in soft, careless waves around her face, the kind I was always aiming for but ended up with crazy blond Shirley Temple curls instead. But I couldn't even complain that Mike only hired her for her face . . . or her perfect heart-shaped ass . . . or the boobs she was still financing. She was very professional, had excellent typing and filing skills, was great at handling the clients. She answered the phone with a smile on her face. And she even made better coffee than I could manage.

It was odd that Mike and Beebee seemed to be alone in the office. Mike had two accountants working under him, the associates in "Terwilliger and Associates." He complained that all they did was hang around the lobby, ogle Beebee, and plow through pastries. Still, it was possible they were out on client visits.

I sat there in an idling Volvo, feeling very stupid. Nothing was going on. I'd been sitting there for thirty minutes and Mike hadn't even come out of his office. I was about five seconds from hauling the roses inside, explaining Cherry's funny, schnapps-fueled mistake and having a good laugh with Mike when I saw him emerge from his office door. He grinned at Beebee and she smiled back with a familiarity that sent a little twinge through my chest. I tamped it down, ashamed of my disloyalty. I told myself it was nice that Mike had found someone so friendly to fill the receptionist spot. I was glad he enjoyed being around someone he had to share office space with for eight hours a day.

And lots of people give their secretaries affectionate shoulder squeezes, I told myself, watching after he crossed the room to rub his hands under her blouse, across her bare collarbone. It was borderline inappropriate, but not an indicator of an affair. And lots of people drag their secretaries out of their chairs like a character in a tacky romance novel. Lots of people kiss their secretaries . . . with tongue.

Especially when they're having an affair with them.

Sweet merciful crap, they were going at it in front of a huge window, apparently not caring who could pass by and see. Hell, his wife was sitting less than twelve feet away from them and they hadn't noticed me.

A whimper stuck in my throat, gagging me. How long had they been doing this? Who else had seen them? Who else knew? How many people would be chewing this over with their dinner tonight? My hands didn't seem to work right. They wouldn't close around the door handle so I could march into the office and toss the vase at their heads. I took a few deep steadying breaths, but instead of opening the door, my hands put the car in gear and steered toward home. I don't remember much about the drive, except that at one point I saw a vinyl sign advertising Terwilliger and Associates with Mike's stupid smiling face on it. And I ran it down.

When I got home, I braked hard to avoid running the car into the garage door. The roses bounced onto the floorboard, vase and all, spilling stems and plant water all over. I rushed into the house, the door still standing open, and grabbed some paper towels. Mike was crazy about keeping the cars clean. A dirty car's resale value fell by forty-five percent.

I tossed the empty vase and the flowers into the garbage can. Kneeling, the hot concrete scraping my knees, I wrapped my hand in toweling and started blotting. The sickly sweet smell of wilting flowers and plant preservative rolled off the upholstery and hit me like a blow. I ran into the grass, doubled over, and threw up until tears and mucus hung in long threads from my face. I fell on my knees and waited for the second wave.

"Lacey, you all right, honey?" Our neighbor, Mrs. Revell, yelled from her yard. She gave me a knowing wink. "Ginger tea and saltines help with that."

Mrs. Revell thought I was pregnant. Great. By the time Mrs. Revell stopped making calls, not only would I be poor Lacey Terwilliger whose husband had the bad taste to have an affair with his secretary, I would be poor Lacey Terwilliger, whose husband had the bad taste to have an affair with his secretary after he knocked up his unsuspecting moron wife.

2

Worst Case Scenario

Every women's magazine I've ever read says there are five signs a man is cheating on you. All married women, hell, all women in a committed relationship, know them by heart.

Repeat them, if you will, ladies. Diminished sexual appetite. Finding reasons to work late. Cutting you off from his communications—leaving the room when his cell phone rings or changing an e-mail password without explanation. Unexplained charges on the credit cards. Finding fault with you because it makes him feel justified in cheating.

In my defense, the age-old standard didn't exactly help me. I'd always felt so safe, so stupidly smug in the security of my marriage, I never even thought of them. Again, because I'm a moron. Mike's sexual appetite had never been exactly ravenous. He regularly worked ten-hour days, twelve to fourteen hours during the January to April tax season. So many of his phone calls dealt with clients' financial issues that it was normal for him to take business calls in another room. I never saw our credit card statements because Mike handled all of our bills. And he hadn't found more fault in me than he had when we first got married, which wasn't really a compliment to either of us.

As I was vomiting on the lawn, this list of cheating signs bounced through my head like a Buddhist chant. With more purpose than I could fathom, I cleaned up the car mess and ran into the home office. Mike and I had separate e-mail accounts, again for business reasons. When I logged on to the quickmail.com server, believe it or not, he was dumb enough to have left thestinger@quickmail.com in the user box and checked "Remember this address."

Mike's e-mail password had always been a combination of my phone number from college and my middle name: 6410agnes. But it was not working. I tried it three times and made sure the capslock was off.

The son of a bitch had changed his password. Honestly, where was the trust? I tried combinations of his birthday, his middle name, my birthday, the street we lived on, our wedding anniversary. Nothing. Finally I tried "Bumblebee."

"Please tell me this isn't it," I muttered.

"Welcome!" the monitor yelled, showing me a list of Mike's new messages. I thunked my head on the desk and sobbed, "Damn it!"

Mike and Beebee must have had complete confidence that I was far too stupid to figure out Mike's new password, because his in-box was a treasure trove of divorce court exhibits. First up, we had several digital photos of Beebee, who was apparently very proud of her recent purchase of lingerie and her new tattoo. Her poses were enthusiastic and . . . detailed. Then there were several messages outlining their plans to meet at the Royal Inn outside town on nights when Mike was supposedly meeting with clients or attending dinners with the Rotary Club. Other postrendezvous mash notes described what they'd done, where they'd done it, and how good it felt. One charming missive detailed the night Mike returned late from a romp with Beebee and slipped into bed with me, reeking of her perfume. The phrase "She doesn't suspect a thing" was repeated enough to prompt another vomiting run.

Well, at least he'd left a paper trail. I managed to keep it together enough to print out copies of everything and hide them in the bathroom drawer where I kept my feminine supplies. Mike was almost clinically phobic of Tampax. I also forwarded the entire contents of his in-box to my own e-mail address. Including the pictures. That done, I ran for the newly retiled comfort of our shower and huddled there, the spray burning needles into my numb skin until the hot water ran out. Waterlogged and shivering, I bundled into my ratty old blue robe and crawled under the covers. I just couldn't seem to warm up.

It felt like life had thrown a pie right in my face. And that pie was full of bricks.

Across the room, there was a bank of matching silver picture frames on a table that had been Mike's great-grandmother's—a happy blond couple on vacation in the Bahamas, at a Fourth of July barbecue, sitting in front of a Christmas tree. In each of them, I'm smiling blithely into the camera, secure in my position in a life where nothing could possibly go awry.

How could he cheat on me? Was Beebee his first . . . was "girlfriend" the right word? Had there been others? Did he even think about how this might make me feel, or was I even a consideration before he unzipped his pants? Was she better in bed than me? Did she know special tricks?

How dense could one person be? I didn't even bother asking about his Lions Club or Rotary meetings anymore. After hearing "Oh, nothing new" so many times, I just assumed he wouldn't want to talk about them. I never questioned how many nights he was spending away from home. He came to our marriage bed with her stink on him. And I didn't see (or smell) any of it.

I was the stupidest woman on the planet.

I slipped off my wedding ring set and stared at the tasteful solitaire. My hand felt so light without that empty circle, that hideously appropriate symbol. I laid it on the nightstand and wondered if Mike would notice that I wasn't wearing it. Our wedding portrait had been sitting on the nightstand for so long, I'd almost forgotten it was there. For the first time in a long time, I looked, really looked, at the pretty blue-eyed girl in the white dress and the handsome man smiling down at her. She seemed so bright and full of promise. Capable, confident, just a smidge sassy. What the hell happened to her?

I was someone in my own right before I married the Tax King of Hamnet County. I had plans. I was going to be a newspaper reporter. As my Gammy Muldoon always said, everybody has a story, the trick was finding a way to tell it that didn't bore the hell out of people. (Gammy was a colorful woman.) I loved finding the story. And I was good at it. I even won a couple of minor awards writing for my college newspaper. Right after graduation I was supposed to take over a general assignment position for the local newspaper, the *Singletree Gazette.* But I got so wrapped up in planning the wedding that I agreed when Mike and Mama suggested I should just wait until after we were married to start working at the paper. Daddy was an old golf buddy of Earl Montgomery, whose family had run the paper since 1890. Earl agreed to keep the reporting job open for me until after the honeymoon. And then we bought the house and Mike said we should finish moving before I started working. Moving became renovating, renovating became redecorating, and Earl finally told me that he'd had to fill the position while I was waiting for wallpaper samples to be shipped in from Tulsa. I was disappointed and embarrassed, but I understood. And soon it didn't matter, because Mike's business took off and he finally admitted that he didn't want me to work because none of his friends' wives worked and it would be "uncomfortable" for him.

So I stayed home. I never considered myself a homemaker because that always made me think of those scary ladies who organized the baking competitions for the county fair. I was Mike's at-home support. I joined clubs, women's organizations, charitable boards. I approached planning benefits and auctions like it was a career. My job was to live and breathe the image of a happy wife of a successful, capable accountant so that people would bring their finances and tax problems to said accountant. I worked full-time to make sure Mike's accounting firm seemed as prosperous and thriving as possible, even before it was prosperous and thriving.

At work, Mike was the ultimate go-getter, motivated and energetic, meticulous to a fault. But when he came home, he shut off. He honestly believed that because he paid the bills, I should have to handle all of the messy details of our life together. He just wanted to show up and be there—like when he used to live with his mama. I took care of booking Mike's dental appointments, vacation plans, shopping for gifts for his parents. Mike didn't want to get a pool or a dog because it was too much maintenance. He had halfheartedly broached the subject of having a baby, but seemed relieved when I put him off for reasons even I couldn't explain. This turned out to be a good thing as I would hate for our children to currently be witnessing Mommy's snot-coated, terry-cloth-wrapped breakdown.

What was especially ironic was that part of what had attracted me to Mike was his plans, this unrealized potential that I found adorable and anchoring. When we were in college, he would talk about traveling and seeing the world together, about the family we would raise. When we were married, he made promises about putting shelves in the garage or putting a rose bed in the backyard. Neither of those ever materialized. He was always going on about his boat, this little sixteen-foot wooden sailboat that he had been building for the last five years. When we were at parties or holidays or any gathering where there were more than two people, he waxed poetic about his connection to the water, how a man could only master a vessel he'd built himself, until I wanted to gouge my ears with a shrimp fork. He spent thousands of dollars on tools and materials, despite the fact that he'd never completed so much as a birdhouse. So far, he had the basic structure of the hull, which he'd assembled in the first year. He hadn't added anything to it since. So pardon me if I no longer believed his boat was going to be anything more than some sort of nautical dinosaur skeleton in his workshop.

Unless it related to the business, these things never seemed to get done if Mike was left to his own devices. In fact, even though it *was* for the business, Mike couldn't be bothered to write his monthly office newsletter. Every month I dutifully wrote it, laid it out on seasonal stationery, and trudged down to the bulk mail office to ship it to hundreds of Mike's family, friends, and clients. Part public relations, part brag sheet, part actual business correspondence, it was chock-full of vital information, such as "Lacey is learning to crochet, badly. She's either making a tablecloth or a very large potholder." For some reason, our friends and family seemed to love the fact that I made fun of myself while promoting Mike's firm.

I'd suggested that we switch to an electronic format to save paper and postage. I'd even gathered the vast majority of the recipients' e-mail addresses in a spreadsheet and loaded them into E-mail Expo, an online marketing service that allowed users to design mass messages using ready-made templates. It would have meant the difference between my spending two hours or two days every month on the newsletter. But Mike was afraid of alienating his older, less techno-savvy clients, so I just kept buying that stupid themed stationery. It became another thing I was expected to do to make Mike's life easier.

He loved the idea of the report. He loved the friendly personal touch with the clients and what it did for the business. He just didn't want to have to do it himself.

It was now 4:24 p.m. Mike was due home in an hour. I had a roast in the oven and it would dry out it if I didn't check on it in the next ten minutes. But the idea of getting out of bed was a mountain I was not prepared to climb.

"Get up," I muttered to myself. "Get up."

But my limbs stayed where they were, leaden, tired, stubborn. Maybe I would lie here long enough to die and Mike would have to explain the soggy, woebegone corpse in his master suite.

After convincing myself that I didn't want to be found dead in my bathrobe, I crawled back into the shower, running it on cool to try to take the swelling down in my face. I looked into the little shatterproof shaving mirror and swiped at my eyes, which seemed to be a little less puffy. I didn't like having the mirror in our shower because the suction cups left weird little soap-scum circles on the glass door. But Mike insisted that his mornings would be much easier if he could just shave in the shower, so I'd spent the better part of an afternoon hunting down the best mirror I could find. Just like I'd spent countless afternoons doing countless stupid little errands because they were important to Mike. I'd wasted most of my twenties doing his stupid little errands.

Somewhere in my stomach, the tight, miserable little ball of tension bubbled to my lips in the form of: "Asshole!" I screamed, yanking the mirror off the door and throwing it against the wall. "How could you fucking do this to me, you miserable, dickless piece of shit!"

I picked up the mirror again and brought it crashing down on the floor, stomping on it, doing my best to break it. But the damn thing was shatterproof. I was just making noise, empty, stupid pointless noise that no one would hear. I slid down the tile wall, collapsing in a heap on the floor.

I wasn't going to cry anymore. I was tired of making empty noise.

I blew a shallow breath through my teeth and pushed to my feet, putting my face under the cool spray. I wondered how close Mike was to the house. Was he actually coming home tonight or did he have another "meeting"? Either way, I didn't want him to find me like this. I needed time, to think, to decide, to plan. I needed focus to keep myself from knocking him out the minute he walked through the door and supergluing his dick to the wall.

"Get up, you giant cliché," I said, my voice stern, cold. "Get *up*. Get your ass out of this shower and stop re-enacting scenes from every *Lifetime* movie ever made. Get up. Get up. Get up!"

I sat up, brushing the wet, snaggled hair out of my face. "Now brush your damn teeth."

• • •

I am an emotional person. It's one of the reasons Mike said I would never make a decent accountant. (That and needing a calculator to perform long division.) Mike was always in control of his emotions. Though, not apparently, in control of his penis. He would not expect me to remain calm, cool, and unaffected in the face of his pantsless office hijinks.

So I got up, got dressed, and waited. I smiled when Mike managed to make it home for dinner and served him pot roast. I told him about my Junior League meeting that morning and acted like the problems we were having printing this year's charity cookbook were the biggest worries on my mind. And I slept beside him, having to concentrate hard to prevent myself from smothering him with the pillow.

It was the last thing he would see coming. The calm thing, I mean, not the smothering. Though he probably wouldn't see the pillow coming either.

In my weaker moments, I considered forgetting this whole thing and staying with him. For one thing, you can't discount eight years of history. My parents were very fond of him. My parents and his parents seemed to enjoy spending time together, a rare and precious coincidence that meant I never had to split my holidays. And Mike was safe. He was stable. Apart from the receptionist-screwing, he had been a decent husband to me. I didn't have to worry about bills being paid or him drinking too much or watching an alarming amount of SportsCenter.

We'd made a life together. It wasn't perfect, but I was proud of what we'd built. Even if he'd smashed it all to hell by betraying the unspoken rule I thought we'd both agreed to—don't have sex with other people.

And at other, angrier moments, I found my hands gripping the edge of the kitchen table as I stared at my husband. Mike had retained the blond, boyish good looks that had drawn me to him when we were seniors in high school. The sun-streaked sandy blond hair that curled just at the ends. The guileless brown eyes that crinkled when he smiled. The little cleft in his chin that his mama called "God's thumbprint."

Mike was equally tense. He wouldn't look me in the eye. His knee was bouncing steadily under the table, a sure sign he was nervous about something. He didn't even complain about our dinner menu of blackened catfish and Mama's "Light Your Fire" cheese grits. Mike hated spicy food with a passion. He treated Taco Bell like exotic third-world cuisine.

I said I was trying to behave as normally as possible. I didn't say I was a saint.

Finally, he cleared his throat and asked, "Honey, did Cherry Glick stop by here with some flowers a few days ago?"

So that's why he was wound so tight, I mused. He'd been stewing for days, wondering where Beebee's anniversary flowers had ended up. "No." I said, concentrating on every muscle and nerve in my face to keep it a pleasant, blank mask. "You sweet thing, did you order me flowers?"

He paled ever so slightly as he stammered, "N-no, one of my clients lost his mama. I sent an arrangement, but I don't think it arrived at the funeral service in time."

Well, that was a far more interesting lie than I would have previously given him credit for. I gave a breathy little gasp. "Oh, no, whose mother died?"

I watched him squirm as he searched for the right answer. "Oh, nobody you know," he said, picking at his plate. "It's a client over in Quincy."

"Oh, well, it was so thoughtful of you to send something. I can call Cherry and double-check whether it arrived."

"No! No, I'll take care of it," he said, far too quickly.

"I don't mind," I told him, willing my lips not to curve upward.

"It's okay, really. Don't worry about it," he assured me.

"All right," I said, shrugging blithely.

His shoulders relaxed and the tense little lines around his mouth disappeared. He was comfortable again, sure that I was still in the dark. My fingers gripped my fork, my teeth grinding ever so slightly as I imagined jabbing the tines right into his forehead.

"So, um, how's the old monthly report coming?" he asked around a mouthful of catfish. "Remember, we have to get it out by next week. You only have a few days left to mail it out."

I hadn't looked at it in a week. And somehow I just didn't think descriptions of Mike's golf game and repainting the office were going to cut it this month.

"It's fine," I lied.

"Be sure to mention the condo. And call down to the office and talk to Beebee," he added before downing half of his glass of water.

I dropped my fork. But considering my usual level of clumsiness, he didn't notice. "What?"

"It might be nice to put sort of a getting to know you interview thing in this month's letter," he told me. "She's been with us for a while, but some of the clients haven't met her yet."

My mouth dried up. He actually *wanted* me to talk to the woman he was screwing behind my back? Did he have no shame? Didn't that make him the least bit nervous at all? Apparently he trusted Beebee enough not to spill everything to me. Or he trusted me to be dumb enough not to pick up on any hints Beebee might drop.

"What do you want me to ask her?"

"Oh, the usual stuff," he said, shrugging and returning his attention to his food. "You'll figure it out."

I smiled, my lips stretched so tight, I sensed the coppery sting of blood welling up into my mouth. "Oh, sure, just let us girls sort it out."

3

The Magic and Mystery of Beebee Baumgardner

I sat in the lobby of Mike's office, peering over the top of a year-old copy of *Redbook* and watching Beebee make appointments over the phone. And trying to make her head explode though telekinesis.

I'd waited until Mike had gone to lunch to come by the office for her "interview." Oh, I had a whole list of questions for her, like, "Who the hell do you think you are?" and "Do you have a history of sexually transmitted diseases?" But I doubted I would be able to use the newsletter as an excuse for those.

Watching her, I bounced between wondering how I was expected to compete with someone as outrageously sexy as Mike's secretary and thrilling at every little fault I could find, like a weirdly shaped mole at the base of her neck or the fact that one of her eyebrows was slightly longer than the other. How could Mike cheat on me with someone who drew her eyebrows on and still got them asymmetrical? I knew that when it came down to it, a man didn't give a damn about eyebrows when you had a butt they could bounce a quarter off of, but it helped me cling to a shred of superiority.

Beebee had caused quite the stir when she arrived in town. The fact that Mike had hired an unknown was highly unusual in the first place, as knowing someone who knows someone is half the battle of the Singletree employment market. The only reason Singletree parents joined churches and bridge clubs was to guarantee that their children could move out of the house one day.

Beebee had charisma, this aura of intimidation that had the local women talking about her at the gym, at the grocery, at our club meetings. Because, basically, the people I know never left high school and Beebee was the cool new girl that scared us. At the office she dressed in pencil skirts, leopard prints, and Mamie Van Doren sweaters. It was edgy and sexy but managed to keep her just outside kissing distance of tacky. It was like someone had told her "Leave them wanting more." Tragically, that person failed to tell her "less is more" when it came to tanning and tooth whitening.

My first face-to-face interaction with Beebee was about two weeks after Mike hired her. I finally worked up the nerve to see if she lived up to the hype and made an excuse to visit Mike at the office. When I walked in the front door, she was facing away from me and she was lecturing someone named Leslie about dating the wrong kind of man.

"Sweetie, you're never going to move out of that double-wide if you don't start thinking with parts of your body above the waist," Beebee snorted as I walked through the door. Her back was turned to me as she twisted the phone cord around her fingers. It was the first time I'd heard Beebee's real accent, a far cry from the melted sugar tones she used when I called the office. Her natural voice was lower and sort of harsh, like crinkling aluminum foil. "You can't keep dating these guys. They're no good for you. They don't take you any place nice and then they always expect you to put out at the end of the night . . . I don't care that you would do that anyway. You could at least go after someone with a nice clean office job. Someone who will spring for a place with cloth napkins. I mean, at the rate you're going, why not just marry a carny and be done with it?"

"No. No, you can't date both." She grunted. "That's the thing with these white-collar, middle-class guys, they need to think that they're the only ones or it's no fun for them. And if you're going to get knocked up—"

Unfortunately, this was the moment Beebee checked over her shoulder and saw me standing there listening. She dropped the phone in the cradle and greeted me in that sweet, fake voice. That was the first time I realized Beebee was not nearly as dumb as she looked.

What really killed me about this whole situation is that the affair was the second thing Mike and Beebee had pulled over on me. On August 23 of the previous year, I'd turned thirty. When Mike asked what kind of party I wanted, I suggested something low-key; maybe going up to our little cabin at Lake Lockwood with friends and family and having a nice weekend together. But while my brother sent a dozen candy-pink roses and a gift certificate for a seaweed wrap, my birthday came and went without so much as a card from my husband.

So I held a twenty-minute pity party, ate half a fat-free cheese-cake, and allowed spa technicians to wrap me in a detoxifying kelp burrito. That Friday, Mike said he wanted to take me out to a nice dinner to make up for not having time to get me a present.

He took me to the Singletree Country Club, where about one hundred fifty people jumped out at me and yelled "Surprise!" I was surprised, all right. I didn't know who the hell these people were. I recognized my parents and Mike's parents, and that was about it.

"Happy birthday, honey!" Mike yelled, kissing me on the cheek with a loud smack.

Through a tight smile, I asked, "Mike, what is this?"

"It's your birthday party, silly," he whispered under the guise of kissing my cheek again. His voice rose as he said, "I bet you thought I forgot, didn't you? I know you said you didn't want a big fuss, but you only turn thirty once. And I thought a surprise party would be fun."

I looked around the room at the smiling, expectant faces. You couldn't really tell this was a birthday party. The reception room, one social step down from the sacrosanct "for weddings only" banquet room, was tastefully decorated with votive arrangements of white roses. A piano player played low jazz tunes from the corner. There was an open bar and a beautiful buffet set up with seven different kinds of shellfish, all of which would make me break out in hives as I was allergic. It looked like a really nice cocktail party for a humane society or something.

"Mike, who are all of these people?" I asked quietly.

"Our friends." Mike shrugged, sipping champagne.

"None of our friends are here," I said through my smile, waving at an elderly woman in the back of the room who seemed to recognize me. Or she could have been trying to flag down a waiter. "In fact, I don't recognize anybody. How did you manage to host a party in this town without inviting a single person I know?"

"They're clients, Lacey," he said in a low tone. "And potential clients. I thought this would be a good opportunity for us to get to know them on a personal level, to show them that we appreciate their friendship."

"What about Scott and Allison? Or Charlie and Brandi?" I

asked, naming two of Mike's best friends and their wives, both of whom were our designated weekend barbecue buddies.

"There wasn't room on the guest list."

"Okay, where's Emmett?" I asked, looking around the room. My brother loved all birthdays, though the roses and spa certificate were among his tamer offerings. On my twenty-eighth, he had his friend, Tony, the only working drag queen in the county, dress up like Marilyn Monroe and sing "Happy Birthday" to me. While Mike's grandma told Tony he was a very talented girl, Wynnie and Jim Terwilliger sat there stone-faced and left right after cake.

Mike shrugged. "Beebee said he didn't RSVP."

"You didn't call him?" I asked.

"I just figured he knew he would be uncomfortable and didn't want to come," he said. "Besides, I don't think he'd make a great impression on the guests."

My eyes narrowed at Mike. He had never been comfortable around my brother. He always tried to make conditions and restrictions on the time we spent with my family because he didn't think he should have to put up with Emmett. He would go to Easter at my parents' house as long as Emmett didn't bring a date. He would go on a golfing weekend with my dad as long as Emmett wasn't invited. It was like he thought the "gay" could rub off or something. "I thought that this was a birthday party for me. I told you I just wanted something small, something with my family—"

"Why would we want something small, when I've given you all this? Why can't you just say thank you?" he said, gesturing across the room to his scantily clad secretary. Stunning in an off-the-shoulder black cocktail dress, Beebee was carrying a clipboard and intently instructing the waitstaff on the placement of an ice sculpture swan. "Beebee and I worked really hard to set this whole thing up and it wasn't easy after just coming off the end of the fiscal year. Why can't you just enjoy this?"

"Because I didn't ask for it." I poked my finger into Mike's chest. "As usual, you just—"

I felt my mother's arm slide around my waist and heard her tinkling laugh as she announced she was taking me to the ladies' room to "freshen my lipstick." Apparently, I'd chewed all of mine off.

"Why didn't you tell me about this?" I demanded the moment Mama shut the door behind us. She waited until she checked under the stall doors for feet to answer me.

"I thought you knew!" Mama exclaimed.

"But I told you about the lake thing; I even asked which weekend would work for you."

"I thought you were trying to get information out of me," Mama said, tutting sympathetically as she dabbed my lips with one of the dozens of lipsticks she kept in her handbag, organized by time of day and occasion. My brother and I were younger reflections of our mother. Age hadn't dulled the china doll blue eyes, but careful maintenance had kept the thunder out of her thighs and the gray out of her wavy blond bob. She said she'd give up and go "scary and natural" after her sixtieth birthday. Until then, she was coiffed, calorie-conscious, and carried an emergency makeup kit in her purse. "I thought you were playing dumb."

"Obviously it wasn't an act!" I hissed, blotting dutifully when she held a tissue to my mouth.

"Well, it explains your outfit," she said, peering down her nose at my peridot-colored cotton sundress and high-heeled sandals. While bright and breezy, the ensemble was not exactly country-club caliber. My hair was in a ponytail, for God's sake.

"He said a 'nice dinner.' For Mike, that means D'Angelo's, for which this outfit is perfectly appropriate. And of course he didn't think to warn me that I might want to dress up a little."

"Still," she said, tsking gently. "This green is not your color—"

"Mama! Focus!"

"Right, I'm sorry, baby. I thought you would like a surprise party," Mama said, wrapping her arms around me and squeezing me tight, but somehow managing not to wrinkle her beaded peach suit. "A little bit of fuss over a girl's birthday never hurts."

"It's not what I asked for," I said, grinding my teeth as I leaned against the wall. "As usual, Mike didn't listen to me. He didn't really care about what I wanted. He's using my birthday as an excuse to schmooze clients. He's going to write my birthday party off as a business expense."

Mama gasped. "Is that who all those people are?"

"And why isn't Emmett here?"

"I don't know," Mama said, her own coral-coated lips thinning. "I thought it was strange that he didn't mention anything about it, but I thought that was because Mike was throwing the party and he couldn't find anything nice to say about it."

My parents were as politically conservative as the next Southern Baptists, but woe to the person who teased the gay cub in front of my Mama Bear. Carla Gibson still avoids Mama at the Piggly Wiggly after trying to ban Emmett's "Salute to Cher" from the senior talent show when we were in high school. Mama never complained about Mike or his family or how they treated Emmett. Well, she never complained *directly* . . . she did, however, wonder aloud why Mike couldn't try a little harder with Emmett, why his parents always clammed up whenever Emmett was around. This was, of course, a hint for me to do something about their behavior. But I'd never figured out what that was supposed to be.

"He'll be sorry to have missed the chance to make fun of the outfits in there." Mama smirked, dusting powder across her nose. "Did you see that blue thing Penny Frensley is wearing? What was she thinking?"

"This is just so typical of Mike," I groused. "And he didn't even plan the damn thing. He let his secretary do it."

"Well, she did a good job; it's a perfectly nice party," Mama conceded. When she saw the glare I was giving her, she added, "Which is entirely beside the point. You're absolutely right. Mike was wrong, wrong, wrong."

"Thank you."

Mama gently brushed powder across the bridge of my nose. "You might want to do something about your jaw, honey. It's clenched awfully tight."

"Because I'm planning on chewing on Mike's ass when I go back out there."

"Lacey, I know that I taught you better than to have a tantrum in public," she said, patting her hair purely for dramatic affect. "It reflects badly on me as a mama. Of course, I also taught you when somebody screws you over, even when that someone is your husband, you don't just lie back and think of England."

"I haven't done anything irrevocable yet, have I?" I asked.

"No," she assured me. "It was a very quiet hissy fit, barely noticeable. I only swooped in because you were doing that frozen beauty queen smile and that means you're about five seconds from Chernobyl territory." I laughed. She squeezed my shoulders. "I know my baby."

She turned me toward the mirror to show me she'd painted my mouth a bloody-murder red. "The question is, what do you do from here?"

With what Mama called my "scary-pleasant hostess face" on, I floated across the room and very loudly, very sweetly thanked Beebee for putting together such a wonderful party for Mike.

"Oh, don't think anything of it," Beebee said, blushing to the roots of her hair. She kept looking over my shoulder for some sort of escape route. At the time I thought she was just uncomfortable being caught between her boss and his pissed-off wife. Now I think she was nervous that I'd figured them out and was about to smack her. "Mike—Mr. Terwilliger—just wanted to make sure you had a nice birthday."

"Well, aren't I the lucky girl?" I asked, my smile stretched tightly across my face.

Beebee didn't answer, instead waving at the caterer to begin the circulation of canapés.

After Mike spent most of my birthday toast talking about the new online debt-tracking packages available through Terwilliger and Associates, I went around and introduced myself to nearly everyone in the room and asked them how they knew Mike. Including Mike's parents.

My mother-in-law was not impressed with my display.

The problem was that, once again, my performance was so convincing that by the end of the night, Mike thought I'd really enjoyed myself. He really had no idea that he'd screwed up. He seemed so pleased with himself for weeks afterward, talking about how he knew it was right to trust the whole thing to Beebee. That she'd known to pick the best caterers and the best florists (Cherry Glick, ironically enough) and then trusted their good taste. The implication was that I was a control freak who would have wanted to see to every detail myself, and look how much easier it was when you trusted the "experts."

Sadly, even then, it didn't occur to me that Mike would sleep with someone else, much less his secretary. I could believe him to be clueless, obtuse, even shamefully oblivious to the feelings of others, but never a cheater. I wanted to believe he was better than that. Or that he was too lazy to pull off an affair.

Looking back, the party probably served as an opportunity for Mike to introduce Beebee to his client list. To show them what a find she was, how beautiful and "well put together." And by contrast, what an ungrateful social misfit I was. Really, who could blame him for replacing me with a more gracious model?

"I'm sorry," Beebee said, smiling up at me and snapping me back into reality. "The phone just rings off the hook this time of year."

As I stared into the dark depths of her eyes, I saw the smallest flicker of fear. Shame or embarrassment would have disappointed me. But fear I could work with.

A clarifying sense of purpose seemed to still everything in my head. I focused my gaze on Beebee's face, her beautiful, troubled, guilt-clenched face. A sharp, sweet smile curved my lips. "So Beebee, tell me every little thing about yourself."

4

Hell Hath No Fury . . . Like a Woman with a Mailing List

It's that time of the month again . . .

As we head into those dog days of July, Mike would like to thank those who helped him get the toys he needs to enjoy his summer.

Thanks to you, he bought a new bass boat, which we don't need; a condo in Florida, where we don't spend any time; and a $2,000 set of golf clubs . . . which he has been using as an alibi to cover the fact that he has been remorselessly banging his secretary, Beebee, for the last six months.

Tragically, I didn't suspect a thing. Right up until the moment Cherry Glick inadvertently delivered a lovely floral arrangement to our house, apparently intended to celebrate the anniversary of the first time Beebee provided Mike with her special brand of administrative support. Sadly, even after this damning evidence—and seeing Mike ram his tongue down Beebee's throat—I didn't quite grasp the depth of his deception. It took reading the contents of his secret e-mail account before I was convinced. I learned that cheap motel rooms have been christened. Office equipment has been sullied. And you should think twice before calling Mike's work number during his lunch hour, because there's a good chance that Beebee will be under his desk "assisting" him.

I must confess that I was disappointed by Mike's overwrought prose, but I now understand why he insisted that I write this newsletter every month. I would say this is a case of those who can write, do; and those who can't, do taxes.

And since seeing is believing, I could have included a Hustler*-ready pictorial layout of photos of Mike's work wife. However, I believe distributing these photos would be a felony. The camera work isn't half-bad, though. It's good to see that Mike has some skill in the bedroom, even if it's just photography.*

And what does Beebee have to say for herself? Not much. In fact, attempts to interview her for this issue were met with spaced-out indifference. I've had a hard time not blaming the conniving, store-bought-cleavage-baring Oompa Loompa–skinned adulteress for her part in the destruction of my marriage. But considering what she's getting, Beebee has my sympathies.

I blame Mike. I blame Mike for not honoring the vows he made to me. I blame Mike for not being strong enough to pass up the temptation of readily available extramarital sex. And I blame Mike for not being enough of a man to tell me he was having an affair, instead letting me find out via a misdirected floral delivery.

I hope you enjoyed this new digital version of the Terwilliger and Associates Newsletter. Next month's newsletter will not be written by me as I will be divorcing Mike's cheating ass. As soon as I press send on this e-mail, I'm hiring Sammy "the Shark" Shackleton. I don't know why they call him "the Shark," but I did hear about a case where Sammy got a woman her soon-to-be ex-husband's house, his car, his boat and his manhood in a mayonnaise jar.

And one last thing, believe me when I say I will not be letting Mike get off with "irreconcilable differences" in divorce court. Mike Terwilliger will own up to being the faithless, loveless, spineless, shiftless, useless, dickless wonder he is.

• • •

I still couldn't believe I'd written it. I'd opened a new document in E-mail Expo, selected the pathologically patriotic Independence Day template and written the first thing that popped into my head: "Mike Terwilliger is a lying, whoring degenerate who would have married his mother if it were legal."

Everything was a little hazy after that.

Needless to say, talking to Beebee hadn't improved my frame of mind. Staring at her was like looking into a particularly warped fun-house mirror. Mike was ruining our marriage for her? Sex with her, spending his nights with her, was worth hurting me? It was worth wrecking the life we'd built together?

I'd never be able to trust anything about my life again. I would question everything Mike said, from his after-work plans to telling me he loved me. For the rest of my life, I would look back on the little moments in my marriage, the parts of my life that I thought meant something, and know that they'd been tainted.

If I was going down, I was taking Mike with me.

My hand shaking, I moved the cursor and clicked on send. And much faster than I would have imagined, a screen popped up, cheerfully announcing, "E-mail Expo has distributed your message!"

Distributed my message. To three hundred and two of our friends, family, and clients. Complete with dancing firecracker graphics.

There was no cancel button, no retrieve function. The genie was out of the bottle. The shit had hit the fan.

"Ohgodohgodohgod, what have I done? What have I done?!" I shrieked. I made a grab for the plug on the safety strip and yanked it out of the wall because, in my panicked brain, I thought somehow that might keep the message from spreading from my computer. But it was out—now there was no taking it back.

My eyes stinging, hot tears threatening to spill down my cheeks, I sagged back against the desk chair. It was all so useless. I couldn't go back to living with Mike in that perfect, empty house, to those pictures of him pretending to be happy with me.

I glanced at the clock. It was a little after 1:00 a.m. I had a few more hours before my friends and neighbors woke up and checked their e-mail. My stomach churning, I bounced between dreading their discovering what a blind idiot I'd been and being happy that the final layer of bullshit would drop away. All of my cards were on the table. I felt . . . free. I didn't have to smile while I lapped up Mike's stupid lies. I didn't have to pretend. I didn't have to care anymore. What was done was done.

• • •

The slow-burning fuse for this particular act of self-destruction had been lit sometime in the afternoon. After my disastrous meeting with Beebee, I'd driven straight to Goote's Jewelry Shop on Main Street and placed my wedding ring set on the counter. "How much can you give me for this, Mr. Leo?" I asked.

Leo Goote, who probably wore his jeweler's loupe into the shower, had gone to church with my parents for forty years. "Lacey, honey, you don't want to sell your wedding rings," he said, the papery skin of his hands buckling as he wrapped them around mine. I stared into his kind, clear brown eyes and something told me that he knew. "You don't want to do something you'll regret."

Gritting my teeth together and willing myself not to cry again, I gave Mr. Leo a tight-lipped smile. "No, Mr. Leo, I do. I'm going to be doing some traveling. And I need some cash."

Leo spent another forty-five minutes trying to talk me out of selling the platinum-set 1.5 carat brilliant cut that Mike's father had called a wise investment when he helped Mike select it from Leo's stock. He gave me ten thousand dollars for the set, a practically unheard of price for Leo, who prided himself on resale value.

I, did, however, use Mike's Visa to charge an obscenely large cushion-cut sapphire to replace my engagement ring. The ring itself didn't really make me feel any better, other than covering a rather disturbing groove worn into my ring finger. But imagining Mike's face when he opened the Visa bill did improve my mood.

As I left, Leo offered me a butterscotch candy, patted me on the head, and told me he would hold on to the rings for me for a while in case I changed my mind. I drove home, printed out the necessary documents from DoItYourselfDivorce.com and filed them at the county courthouse. When I returned, I found a technician from the Peace of Mind Locksmith Company waiting for me in the driveway. I'd called a service from two towns over to keep Mike from being tipped off about my plans to re-key every door in the house. The technician, a stocky guy in his forties whose shirt dubbed him "Roy," assured me this would only take an hour.

I wandered into my suddenly silly bistro-themed kitchen

with the ridiculously expensive appliances. And I felt a little lost. I was so alone. I wanted my mama. It seemed wrong to go through something like this without her. When the chips were down, my mother could be counted on to tell you you'd done something irretrievably stupid, but she loved you anyway. She was well aware of our faults, but God help the person who pointed them out to her.

My parents were out of town at Daddy's annual Phi Rho Chi reunion in Hilton Head, a bunch of old businessmen remembering what life was like when they still had hair. It was the highlight of Daddy's year. Right up there with the week he spent hunting with the Phi Ro's at a stocked lodge in Missouri . . . and the week he spent deep-sea fishing with them in the Florida Keys. Mama was a very patient woman.

I'd dialed her number on my cell a dozen times, but always hit end before it rang. As much as Daddy loved his children, he would not come home early from the reunion unless it was to bury one of us. And even then, he'd probably fly back to try to finish out the weekend. Mama had enough to deal with, pouring my dad into bed each night as the Phi Rho boys participated in the annual beer-related relay challenges. I didn't want to put her in the position of choosing between the two of us. Besides, she'd probably need to conserve her strength for the aftermath of my little publication when she came home.

I can usually count on Emmett's indignant wrath in situations like this. But Emmett was on a two-week trip to the Bahamas with his current boyfriend, a "freelance food service contractor" named James.

If this were a Renée Zellweger movie, my girlfriends would rush over here, alcohol and chocolate in hand, to assure me that everything was Mike's fault, that I was perfect and I would find a better-looking, richer, more sexually expressive man in no time. The problem was that I didn't have a lot of friends. Well, not any real friends. I knew some ladies from our Sunday school class. And I was friendly with the women in Junior League. We had couples we went to dinner with, clients that we entertained, but I didn't have any girlfriends of my own. When you're a couple, it's hard finding friends that you and your husband agree on. Generally, you try to hang out with couples so no one feels left out or weird. But maybe the husbands get along but the wives hate each other. Or the wives get along great, but the husbands have nothing to talk about. It was just so much easier to hang around with Mike's friends and their wives. It was the simplest way to get him to agree to socialize.

I let friendships with my single friends fall by the wayside because it just seemed like so much work to maintain them. Finding neutral conversational territory is a killer, especially when they're out in the world working and your biggest problem is finding drapes that complement the new sofa. Plus, I couldn't help but feel that my working friends judged my staying home, particularly when we didn't have kids. The last time I had lunch with my friend Katie, a preschool teacher with three boys, she asked me what I did all day. I rambled on about appointments and meetings for about ten minutes before I realized I didn't have a very good answer for her. We didn't have lunch again.

I sat at the counter bar, toying with an apple from the crystal bowl we'd bought on our honeymoon in the Bahamas. I hated that stupid bowl. I'd wanted to buy a painted ceramic one I saw in the straw market, but Mike insisted on something from the duty-free shop near our departure gate. He promised it would be something we'd use for years, a story we could tell our children.

Because nothing says romance and adventure to kids like tax-free breakables bought in the airport.

I didn't want the bowl. In fact, when I looked around the kitchen, I saw a lot of things I didn't want. Hideous pink rose-bud china that had belonged to Mike's great-aunt. Copper-bottom pots that I was afraid to use because they weren't dishwasher safe. Champagne flutes that we hadn't used since our wedding toast, but were kept displayed proudly in the china hutch. I ambled into the living room and saw more that I could live without. And in our bedroom, as well as Mike's office and my closet. I didn't need any of it, never needed it, rarely touched it. I could walk away from all of it.

I didn't even want the house. I knew that some divorcing women plant their feet like Scarlett at Tara when it comes to moving out of their houses. But I really didn't care. It was a horrible irony that I'd spent years decorating and redecorating the house and still didn't like the way it looked. Don't get me wrong; it was beautiful. Thanks to the help of expensive, dedicated decorators, everything matched, everything coordinated, like something from a magazine. It looked like I'd bought rooms from a catalogue called Earth Tones Your Mother Will Approve Of. And I hated earth tones. I always wanted to paint the walls Caribbean Turquoise or Lemon Meringue Pie. Mike said it would make the house look like a preschool. So we went with Terra Cotta and Spanish Moss. And I hated it. If I wanted earth on my walls, I would have lived in an adobe hut.

There was a small matter of pride, the fact that the house had been purchased with proceeds of selling our first home—the down payment for which came from my family. But I wouldn't want to live there, even if Mike handed it to me in the divorce. I didn't think I'd be able to sleep there again. I could force Mike to sell or to get him to buy me out, because if my leaving him didn't hurt him, the loss of equity certainly would. I wasn't afraid of living in an apartment. Singletree actually had a very nice complex out on Hartson Road called Pheasant Hollow, despite the fact that the only wildlife in that direction was possums. It was the cleanest, newest housing available for the town's unmarried set, though most singles had to have several roommates to afford the pricey units. Of course, Beebee lived there. Alone. On what Mike paid her.

I had a feeling I would be kicking myself for years to come over the signs I missed.

I didn't want the bowl, the china, the stupid unusable pots. But I did want the little watercolor Mike had bought me for our first anniversary. It was probably worthless, but I liked the way the blues and greens flowed together. And the quilt my aunt made for me when I graduated from high school. I wandered from room to room, clutching the items to my chest. While Roy worked on the back door, I boxed up everything that belonged to me or my family. I took all of the pictures that made me look thin. I took the clothes that I wore for me. None of the gowns I'd worn to the country club formals, nothing I'd worn to ass-numbingly dull state Financial Advisors Association's dinners, nothing Mike's mother had bought for me. This left a lot of clothes in my closet.

I didn't break anything. I didn't even throw anything out of place. I thought about leaving my vibrator in the middle of the bed, because Beebee was going to need it. As pointed and clever as that would have been, I'd worked too hard to get that thing to leave it behind.

Did you know that because Aphrodite's Palace has a strict no return policy, they give the merchandise a test buzz before you leave the store? *I* didn't.

I threw the vibrator, or as I'd come to think of it, Old Reliable, into the last of my boxes and toted them to the car. The locksmith was waiting for me at the front door, new keys in hand. "Ma'am, I know this is none of my business, but we see a lot of this sort of thing in my line of work," he said, accepting my check. "I'm sorry you're going through a rough patch, but it's company policy to tell you that unless you can show us a court order barring another occupant of this home from the premises, we will provide them with a key if they can show current picture ID listing this address as their residence."

"That's fine with me," I said, looking across the street to Mrs. Revell's front window, which was empty. "I can't lock him out of the house, but I can make it more difficult for him to get in."

Roy did not smile as he extended a clipboard toward me. "Can you sign this release stating that I have informed you of this policy?"

"You've had to give that speech a couple of times, huh?"

Roy nodded and handed me a copy of my receipt. He gave me a fatherly, somewhat condescending smile. "Whatever he did, I'm sure he's sorry."

I handed Roy a twenty-dollar bill as a tip for speedy service. "Um, no, but thanks for playing."

You know that feeling you got when you had a bad report card and you were waiting for your parents to come home to sign it? Time seems to go by too quickly, but drag on interminably at the same time? Well, waiting for your husband to come home so you can tell him you're leaving his cheating ass works pretty much the same way. I just sat on the couch and watched the minute hands move. Around six, I was sitting in the kitchen picking at a sandwich when Mike called and told our answering machine that he had to work late to prepare a proposal for a new client.

By eleven, I'd figured out that he wasn't coming home for the night. He'd had to work through the night several times in the last year, what with being so busy and all. But I stupidly had believed he was actually working. I'd felt sorry for him, packing him little care packages with clean shirts and a little shaving kit and Tupperwared meals. Mike was so touched he actually sent me (correctly addressed) flowers. White tulips, my favorite. Of course, now I suspected that they were guilty "You made me dinner while I was boning my secretary at a cheap motel" flowers. And the fact that I would question every single nice thing Mike had done for me over the last few years was not exactly conducive to sleep.

I was exhausted, but I couldn't bring myself to climb into our bed. I had no place there anymore. And I wouldn't lower myself to sleeping on the couch. It's hard to be a vengeful warrior woman when your husband comes home to find you cuddled up under an afghan watching infomericals.

Bored and restless, I sat down at the computer, fired up the internet browser, opened up E-mail Expo . . . and we all know how that turned out.

I was never going to sleep now. My house felt like a tomb, which was oddly appropriate because when Mike came home, he might actually murder me. So I drove to my parents' place. Never mind that it was 2:00 a.m. Never mind that it was highly likely that Mrs. Ferrell next door would call the cops and tell them someone was breaking into my parents' house. (The woman believed television was evil, but watching her neighbors through binoculars was perfectly okay.) Never mind that when Mike eventually did arrive home, he wouldn't be able to get into the house and the angry phone calls would begin. I wanted to be somewhere I could sleep, somewhere I could hide.

After climbing up the darkened stairs, I dropped my bag in my old bedroom and flopped back on the white canopied bed Mama couldn't bear to replace. With my shoes and clothes still on, I pulled the old pink sheets back and pulled the covers over my head. Unwilling to think about what the morning would bring, I squeezed my eyes shut and tried to sleep.

5

The Shoe Drops

I woke just before noon feeling oddly hungover. For a second, I wondered why I was in my old room at my parents' house before it all rushed back.

It wasn't a nightmare. I'd actually sent the thing.

I sat up and winced at the pain in my neck from sleeping in a nonorthopedic twin bed. If memory served, I had given up on sleeping around 4:00 a.m. and spent the wee hours of the morning signing Mike up for magazine subscriptions ranging from *Hustler* to *Knitters' Digest*. I called telemarketing agencies and left them messages to call Mike's number. Under a slightly less legal heading, I placed classified ads on Craigslist, Freecycle, the *Pennysaver*, and the *Singletree Messenger* offering Mike's brand-new bass boat for a rock-bottom price of zero dollars. He was going to be getting a lot of phone calls. A *lot* of phone calls.

Phone calls. I pressed my hand to my grainy, tired eyes. Mike had no idea where I was. He probably came home this morning to an empty, locked house and reported me as a missing person. I was going to end up another missing blond, white woman on the news.

I ran to the dresser for my cell phone and checked my voice mail. There was one message: "Hi, honey, it's me. I'm still at the office. Thank God for those clean shirts you sent me, huh? I'm sorry—"

A bubble of hope slipped up from my stomach to my spine. There was the voice of the man I married. He still cared. He was grateful for something I'd done. He was sorry. Maybe I could send a follow-up message to everyone on the mailing list asking them to delete the first message without reading it. Maybe—

"I'm sorry to do this to you twice in a row, but I'm not going to be home tomorrow night either. I've got to go to a Lions Club thing and then I'm supposed to meet Brent Loudermilk about some Little League thing he wants the firm to cosponsor. Who knows how late that could go? See you later."

The bubble burst.

Mike was so disconnected from me, from our home, that he hadn't even realized that he'd been locked out of it. He hadn't spoken to me in almost forty-eight hours and he still had plans to go out. And I sincerely doubted it was to a Lions Club dinner. I could have been actually missing and he wouldn't have noticed.

I went into my parents' bathroom and ran a scalding hot tub. They had the only updated bathroom in the house and I was in dire need of a bath that didn't involve rubber duckie nonslip decals. Peeling off my grimy, long-past-their-prime khakis and T-shirt, I slipped into the tub. The nip of the water felt good, a connection back to the reality I'd only kept casual contact with over the last few days. I sank to my chin, then my nose, letting my breath make little ripples across the surface of the water.

Now that the initial shock had worn off, I kept expecting this wave of depression to overtake me, a heavy weight in my chest that would pull me under and crush me with its force. But that precious bubble of hope had popped and I didn't feel anything: nothing good, nothing bad. Nothing. I think I was more depressed when George Clooney left *ER*. It felt like I was rooting around in my brain, probing it like a sore tooth, trying to find some hidden abscess of misery. Surely a normal person wouldn't feel like this at the end of a marriage, the destruction of a life. A normal person would feel something—

I heard my cell phone ring from my room.

Uh-oh.

I let the phone ring until it sent the call to voice mail. Then Mama's phone rang from her nightstand and Daddy's private office line down the hall jangled to life. Apparently the e-mails had landed.

Well, if I couldn't feel depressed, dread would have to do.

• • •

My voice mails were an odd and interesting mix that morning.

"Lacey, this is Jim Moffitt," was the first message on my voice mail. "I think we need to talk. I know you're going through an emotional time right now. Just call me."

Damn it. I forgot Reverend Moffitt was on the mailing list. He was a nice man and wonderful pastor, but we hadn't gotten particularly close in his two years at the church. And I was pretty sure Mike and I were well beyond a good old-fashioned pastoral counseling session at this point.

The next message was from Mike. "Lacey, baby, my mom just called. She mumbled something about the newsletter and then she was crying so hard that I couldn't understand what she was saying. I didn't see a receipt for postage. Did you mail something out without showing it to me? What's going on?"

Double damn it. I forgot to take Mike's parents off the list.

"Lacey, it's Mama, Norma Willet just called us in Hilton

Head and told me I needed to call you right away. Is everything okay?"

I really should have called my mama before I did this. Well, the next time I find out my husband is cheating on me, she'll be first on my emergency contact list.

"Lacey, it's Jeanie Crawford, I just got your e-mail, and I wanted you to know that I'm so sorry for what's happening to you. I gotta tell you, I laughed my head off at what you wrote."

Well, that was just strange.

Mike, again. "Lacey, baby, it's me. Bob Martin just called and said I need to get a tighter rein on you. What does that mean? Call me."

So apparently people were calling Mike about the newsletter but were too embarrassed to give him details. Good, let him squirm.

"Lacey, you need to call me, right now. Right now." That was the last of Mike's messages.

6

Bagels and Bitchery

I turned all phones off that afternoon after my voice mail and Mama's answering machine filled up. The one person who'd stopped calling me was Mike, whose divorce lawyer, Bill Bodine, had left a message stating that all future communications from Mike would come through him.

In retrospect, it would have been wiser to leave the phones on as that might have given me some warning that my mother-in-law would be dropping by for a visit. Instead, picking at a bagel, I opened up my mother's front door to find Wynnie Terwilliger, standing there, twitching.

This wasn't good.

While Mike claimed to be a modern man, his mom pretty much ruined him for women born after 1952. His mom didn't work as he grew up, so he was used to coming home to an immaculately clean house, hot meals, and pressed shirts. Wynnie considered dust bunnies to be an insidious threat against democracy and the sanctity of the American home.

Wynnie never missed an appointment with the colorist that had kept her pageboy the same shade of dark honey blond since the late 1970s. Today she was wearing teal pants and a jacket set off with the silver dragonfly pin she considered her "signature piece." That was strangely appropriate as Wynnie was also stick thin and had no measurable sense of humor.

We'd never had any real problems, because, in general, I met her standards for a good daughter-in-law. I came from a good family, kept a nice home, entertained beautifully, and made the family look good. In general, I did what I was told when it came to holidays and family events because I just didn't have a reason not to. It's hard to object to spending every Christmas with your husband's parents when your parents were going to be there anyway.

This didn't necessarily mean I enjoyed spending time with my mother-in-law. If passive aggression were an Olympic sport, Wynnie would have her own Wheaties box. She couldn't seem to get through a conversation without lovingly correcting me, whether it was the way I fried chicken or showing the proper reverence for the roof "her boy" put over my head. Every Christmas, she gave me clothes at least one size too small and reminded me that "Mikey has always liked his girls thin."

Wynnie honestly believed Mike was perfect in every conceivable way. So telling her that her precious baby boy suffered from cranial-rectal inversion would have done little to improve her disposition. The general lack of acrimony in our relationship left me unprepared for the venom in her eyes when I opened the door.

"Well, Lacey?" she demanded. "What do you have to say?"

I offered her a bite of my breakfast. "Bagel?"

Wynnie stuck her hands on her hips and shouted, "Are you going to stand there and act like you haven't shamed the whole family? That you haven't made a fool out of yourself in front of the entire town?"

I swallowed. "No."

She sighed, staring at me for a long moment, and tapped her foot. "Well, we can't dwell on what's been done. We just have to fix it. I think you and Mike need to go away on a long vacation. Get to know each other again. Maybe go on a cruise."

"You completely misinterpreted that 'no,'" I told her as she marched past me, into the house. "I'm divorcing him. Wynnie, it's over."

"Oh, don't be silly." Wynnie waved aside my announcement with a flick of her wrist. She pulled her cell phone out of her purse. "We just need to get the two of you out of town for a while, away from all this fuss, to give your mama and me time to smooth this all over. We'll tell people that you were playing around with a new way to send the newsletter, wrote up a funny gag version of your e-mail and accidentally sent that out to the mailing list instead of the real one. And that you're very sorry for the misunderstanding. And now you two are on a second honeymoon to try to forget the whole thing." She flipped her phone open. "I'll just call my travel agent and set this whole thing up. Do you want Jamaica or Nassau?"

"Wynnie, a cruise isn't going to fix this. The only way Mike would get on a boat with me is if I were being used as an anchor. Your son obviously doesn't want to be married to me anymore and I definitely don't want to be married to your son."

"All my boy did was play the field a little bit. Why'd you have to make such a fuss? He's just a man, Lacey. They're all just men. You're a big girl. You know what men are like. You've seen other women go through this. But what you did, Lacey, how could you? This could have been handled quietly, within the family."

"Within the family. I was supposed to tell on him? What were you going to do? Send him to time-out?"

I didn't think it was possible, but Wynnie's lips thinned even more. "You think I didn't know it when Jim took up with that waitress from the club? You think I didn't hear people suddenly stop talking when I came into church? You think going to the beauty parlor was easy when I knew they'd been talking about 'poor Wynnie Terwilliger' the second before I walked in? But I held my head high. I didn't roll around in the mud, making a fool of myself. I never even told Jim that I knew. Because at the end of the day, he came home to me, to our family, and that's what mattered." She sniffed. "And before you climb up on that high horse, I think there's something you should consider, that maybe if you'd kept Mike a little more occupied at home, he wouldn't have strayed."

I narrowed my eyes at her. "I think there's something *you* should consider. Beebee could be your next daughter-in-law. She and her cleavage will make a lovely addition to the family Christmas card photo."

Wynnie turned an exquisite shade of tomato red. "There's no reason this has to come to divorce. That won't improve anything. My boy knows the difference between the kind of girl you bring home and the kind of girl you just play around with. He wasn't thinking of marrying her. He was just thinking . . ."

"With Little Mike," I suggested.

Wynnie glared at me. "If you would just be reasonable, talk to him. A good Christian wife would know how to look past this and forgive him."

"Well, I will start looking into Buddhism as soon as possible."

"This isn't the time for your inappropriate jokes. I don't think you appreciate your position here, Lacey," she said, her tone sweetening to a wheedle. "When I was your age, Jim had no idea whether I knew about his little dalliances. He was always so guilty, so nervous that he'd be caught, that I had whatever I wanted without even asking for it. I always knew when he'd been with her because he'd bring me home flowers, a sweet little piece of jewelry, or he'd take me on some wonderful trip to make up for it. For my fiftieth birthday, he took me to New York City to see *Cats*. Do you think he would have done that if he wasn't cheating on me? And Mike's already been caught! He's got that much more to make up for. You could end up with an entirely new wedding set or maybe even a car!"

I stared at her. "Are you on medications that I'm unaware of?"

"Are you listening to anything I'm saying?"

"Yes, you think I should let Mike humiliate and betray me repeatedly for the sake of the presents."

"Well, if you're going to think about it that way, I'm not going to be able to help you," she grumbled.

"I think you need to leave now," I told her.

Wynnie could whip up tears in a second's notice. Her eyes glistened. Her lip trembled. She fished around in her enormous teal handbag for a monogrammed hanky. "I can't believe you. I can't believe how ungrateful, how unfeeling you're being after all these years. I can't believe you're being so hard-hearted. This isn't the Lacey I know. I'm ashamed of you. You're not the girl I welcomed into my family."

Under normal circumstances, that kind of disapproval would have sent me scrambling to make up for whatever I'd done. I would have apologized automatically. Wynnie was looking at me with the kind of contempt my father reserved for straight-ticket voters. She was probably angrier with me than, well, arguably anyone, had ever been in my life. And the world wasn't ending.

I was fine. My stomach wasn't churning. I wasn't tearing up. My hands weren't even shaking.

I'd spent so much of my time worrying about whether I was liked, whether other people were happy with me. I took stupid, mind-numbingly tedious assignments at club meetings because women with bigger shoulder pads told me gathering twelve different kinds of coleslaw recipes would be "just perfect" for me. I let Wynnie keep a key to our house, because Mike said it would hurt her feelings if she didn't feel free to let herself in, even if we weren't home. People had certain expectations of me and I rushed to meet them, because if I didn't . . . Well, I didn't know. I never figured out that it wasn't the end of the world if I disappointed someone or made someone angry.

Honestly, how much worse could it get? What was Wynnie going to do? Ground me? It's not like I was going to be married to her son for long. I didn't have to worry about getting her approval or making sure Thanksgiving went smoothly. I didn't have to swallow "that's just the way she is" because that made Mike's life easier.

I was free. So I shrugged and said, "Okay."

"I don't ever want to see you again," she said, obviously confused when her proclamation of shame failed to induce wailing and gnashing of teeth on my part.

"I understand."

Wynnie stared at me, bewildered. Finally she flushed red and ground out, "When you can stop being hateful—when you can find it in your heart to be a good and forgiving wife to my son, I'll be willing to talk to you."

Wynnie stormed out of the house. It would have been a much more effective exit if she hadn't slammed the door on her purse strap, forcing her to open it to extract herself. She scowled at me as I struggled to keep a straight face. "You just stay here and think about what you've done!"

I watched her stomp out to her town car and screech out of my parents' driveway. I sighed. "I'm going to miss her most of all."

• • •

A half hour later, the doorbell rang again. I jerked the front door open, yelling, "Wynnie, I told you I'm not going on any damned cruise!"

"Well, that's good to know," Mama deadpanned, her arms full of luggage, her elbow firmly planted against the doorbell. "Because given the circumstances, I don't think you deserve a cruise."

"Mama." I laughed. My mother set her bags on the floor and held out her arms. I folded into them and for the first time since sending the e-mail, cried in earnest.

"Baby," she murmured against my hair. "I'm so sorry."

I sniffled, my tears forming a seal between my cheek and her neck.

"I'm going to strangle that little—" Mama grunted, patting my back. "I knew I should have said something earlier, but I thought you knew about Mike and Beebee."

"You knew? *You* knew?" I cried, pulling away from her. "Why didn't you say anything?"

"I didn't *know* anything," Mama said, throwing up her hands. "I heard rumors. I suspected something was going on, but I thought after that birthday party, so would you. I thought you were just trying to put on a brave face. To keep your head up while you sussed out how to hit him where it hurts."

Mama led me into the kitchen and poured me a cup of coffee. She forced me to sit at the breakfast bar, searched in the cabinet for Bisquick. "So when you finally figured out you were married to a clichéd little man, you didn't think to call me?" she asked, her tone mildly exasperated. "Instead, I get phone calls in Hilton Head telling me to come home as my youngest child has clearly lost her mind."

And suddenly I was four years old again, with her pinking shears in one hand and the remains of my curls in the other.

"I may have sent out a little divorce notice," I said, measuring "little" with my fingers.

"In the form of a brag letter?" Mama asked, beating Toll House chips into pancake batter a little harder than was necessary. "Lacey, I'm all for healthy expressions of your feelings, journaling, creative ceramics— If you'd wanted to, we could have made a Mike-piñata and beaten the living hell out of it. But we probably wouldn't have sent pictures of the piñata party out to every person we know."

"I know, I know. It was a crazy thing to do. But I just—it was the only way I knew how to hit back. To hurt him as much as he hurt me."

"Well, Rissy called me in Florida and read it to me. I'd say you did a good job of it. I know I'm wired to think anything you write is fabulous, but after I got over the initial shock, I laughed my butt off."

"Wynnie says that all men stray and I should suck it up and stick around for the fabulous prizes," I said, sipping my coffee.

Mama slapped a ladleful of batter on a heated griddle. "Honey, I've kept my mouth shut for years, but now that divorce is on the horizon, I feel perfectly comfortable in telling you that Wynnie Terwilliger is an idiot."

"But I thought you two always got along! You did all those walkathons together and the bridge club and the holidays."

"Well, what was I supposed to say, 'No, I don't want to spend the holidays with your husband's family'? That would have seemed unfriendly."

"You should have told me this years ago, a fat lot of good that will do us now. I did the right thing, didn't I?" I asked. Mama winced. "The newsletter aside, I did the right thing. I couldn't stay with Mike."

Mama flipped a pancake without even looking. "I can't judge. How could I tell you what to do in this situation until I'd lived through it?"

"So you never had to worry about this with Daddy?" I asked, not quite sure if I wanted to hear the answer.

"Oh, honey, no!" Mama laughed, wrapping her arms around me and holding me tight. Unfortunately, she had the batter ladle in her hand and there was now unfinished chocolate chip pancake dripping down my back. "No, I never had to worry about this with Daddy. Haven't you ever wondered why I let Daddy drag me along with him on these silly fraternity trips?"

I nodded. "Every time you go."

"Well, if I learned anything from my mama, it was that if you don't want to be with your man, there will always be another woman willing to take your place," she said. "So I go on these trips and I watch your daddy make a complete fool of himself, because, for one thing, it's funny, and because there are plenty of miserable Phi Rho wives there who would be more than happy to upgrade to your daddy if they had the chance. I've said the thought of having an affair probably wouldn't occur to Daddy, but I really don't give him a chance to think of it."

"So this is my fault?" I asked. "I should have seen this coming?"

"No! Well, of course, you did miss a lot of signs." Mama said, flipping the pancakes onto a plate and coating them in butter and syrup. "But you didn't know what to look for. Mike probably saw this growing up."

"You knew about Mike's daddy and the other women?"

Mama snorted. "Wynnie doesn't suffer in silence nearly as well as she thinks she does," she said. "I'm sorry your marriage turned out the way it did. You deserved better. I'm proud that you stood up for yourself, proud that you refused to just roll over and die. Though you could have done it a little less spectacularly.

"For now, I want you to focus on something besides getting back at Mike. I don't want you to become one of the bitter women in my bridge club, counting every alimony penny as if making Mike suffer will make your life better."

"Yes, ma'am," I said. She sprinkled powdered sugar over my plate. "Oh, good, because I was just thinking, this isn't sweet enough."

She nudged the plate toward me. "Lacey, eat."

"Yes, ma'am," I said again, now dutifully forking a bite of pancakes. My stomach roiled at the thought of putting it in my mouth.

"Good girl," she said, giving my forehead a smacking kiss. When she turned her back to wash the griddle, I wrapped several bites into a paper napkin and tossed them into the trash.

There was a knock at the door. My eyes widened. "Don't answer it. It will be my mother-in-law with a tranq gun and two tickets to Cancún."

Mama rolled her eyes and opened the door to find a well-dressed young man with an envelope in his hand.

"Lacey Terwilliger?" he asked, looking past Mama to me. He placed the envelope in my hand and slunk back out of striking range. "You've been served."

Mama snatched the envelope out of my hand and tore it open. I padded back into the kitchen. "It's probably his divorce countersuit, Mama. It's nothing to get excited over."

Mama exclaimed, "Lacey, he's suing you for character defamation and libel!"

"Well, I can't really say I'm surprised," I snorted, taking the papers out of her hand.

"I can't believe he's actually suing you," Mama said. "It's just so . . . tacky."

"Oh, let him," I snorted. "Let him try to prove it's not true."

Holding up Mike's countersuit, Mama deadpanned, "And look, he got a two-for-one deal with the process server. His lawsuit and the divorce papers. His grounds for divorce are abandonment!"

"Abandonment?" I said, taking the papers from her. "Oh, what fresh hell is this?"

"Well, you did leave the marital home without warning or taking half of what you deserve," Mama said. "Honey, you might just want to calm down and reassess your situation. You don't want to get into a big legal battle here. Mike's like a cat."

"Emotionally unavailable and fond of licking himself?" I asked.

"I was going to say he always lands on his feet."

7

Swimming Lessons with Sammy the Shark

Despite agreeing to take my divorce case, Sammy "the Shark" Shackleton hadn't had time to meet with me yet. His office, however, had time to cash my retainer check. Given our newfound financial relationship and Mike's recently filed lawsuit, I had no qualms about calling Shackleton and Associates and asking for an emergency consultation.

I twitched a little as I waited in the lobby of the law office. Despite the elegant, minimalist décor, it still felt like the principal's office. Here was the one person who would probably yell at me about the newsletter thing and his opinion would actually hold some sway. What if Mr. Shackleton decided that my case was too weird and sent me on my way? The closest decent divorce lawyer (that didn't play golf with Mike's daddy) I might be able to get would probably be in Louisville. And that meant my piddly ten thousand dollars cash reserve would be spent in no time.

It was almost disorienting to be outside of my parents' house after hiding for so long. But frankly, the constant ringing of the phone was driving me crazy. The question was, what does one wear to meet with her attorney after ridiculing her husband's sexual abilities in a public forum? I didn't want to look like Betty Draper or the woman wronged. I wouldn't show up wearing my typical khakis and twinsets. I wanted to look like someone else, someone braver and bolder. I put on a black tank top and a pair of my skinny jeans, which fit better than ever thanks to my stomach churning for the last three days.

Mama suggested that she come to the meeting with me, but somehow I didn't think bringing my mommy would reinforce my stance as a responsible, emotionally mature, noninsane person. I twisted my purse strap round and around my fingers, staring at the clock. Shackleton was running five minutes late.

A young woman clipped through the reception area, wearing a crisp gray pantsuit and shuffling through several files.

"Excuse me, do you know when Mr. Shackleton will be ready to see me?" I asked in my polite-customer tone. "I'm a little anxious."

The woman's lip twitched. "Aren't we all? Why don't I take you back and I'll see if I can find him for you."

I followed her into the surprisingly light and airy office marked "S. Shackleton, Attorney-at-Law" and quirked an eyebrow as she circled the desk and sat in her boss's chair. She extended her hand over the desk and shook mine. "Samantha Shackleton."

I wouldn't have had any idea this woman was a lawyer, not because of any preconceived sexist notions, but because she looked nowhere near old enough to have attended college, much less law school. Samantha had sharp aquamarine eyes and a long nose, set in a face completely devoid of makeup. Her skin was deeply tanned in that genuinely healthy way, like she'd spent all weekend hiking. She looked like she'd just walked out of an advertisement for trail mix.

"Well, I am deeply, deeply embarrassed," I said, chewing my lip.

"So I take it you didn't put a lot of research into your quest for a divorce attorney?" she asked.

My cheeks flushed hot. "I'm so sorry. All I've heard about you is that you got Mimi Reed's husband's . . . well, you know."

"The junk in the mayonnaise jar story?" she asked, grinning. "Well, that's been slightly exaggerated in the telling and retelling. And I can't really comment on it, because I protect my clients' privacy, as I will, of course, protect yours. Let's just say that if your wife supports you and cares for you while you recover from testicular implant surgery—and pays for the surgery using a recent inheritance—you shouldn't leave her for your nurse."

I gasped. "She really did take them back?"

"I can't really say," she said while nodding. "So let's get down to business."

She opened my file. "Well, you're probably one of the more interesting clients to walk through that door, mayonnaise jars aside," she observed drily. "I think you should know that I've received forwarded versions of your e-mail from a dozen or so of my colleagues under the heading of, 'Well, at least, we're not representing her' or similar."

"So I've gone viral?" I asked. "Great."

"Of course, they didn't realize that I *am* representing you. I'm not afraid of the challenge, Lacey. Believe it or not, you're not my first client to do something rash when faced with the betrayal of a spouse. I have a prepared speech I give to these clients; would you like to hear it?"

"I don't feel I'm in a position to refuse."

She cleared her throat and in a professional monotone, she said, "I understand that you are very upset. It's natural to feel hurt and betrayed when your spouse has left you for someone else. In the heat of the moment we sometimes do and say things that we normally wouldn't. If you'd shown your e-mail to my mother, she would have told you to put it in a drawer for three days and then decide whether you wanted to send it. Obviously, the genie is out of the bottle now—okay, I'm sorry. I'm breaking from protocol. I've had clients change their outgoing messages to invite callers to press two to leave messages for 'the cheating bastard.' I even had one client start a blog called TheMillion-WaysKevinIsAnAsshole.com. But I've never had someone abuse the internet the way you did. I have to ask, what the hell were you thinking?"

I probably deserved much worse than that, so I took her bemused, exasperated tone with a grain of salt. "I may have gone a little too far, comparing Beebee to an Oompa Loompa," I conceded. "I can't say thinking had a lot to do with it. Mostly it was a reaction fueled by rage. Can I claim diminished mental capacity?"

"Well, you certainly deserve it more than most of my clients, but I don't think that would help. Professionally required scolding aside, I did think it was pretty funny. Just don't ever, *ever* do it again. At least, don't put your name on it, if you do. You're just inviting threats to your legal/financial/physical health."

I handed her a file folder containing copies of Mike and Beebee's e-mails and photos from Mike's inbox. "It was just a one-time thing, I'm sure. Do you need me to sign something to that effect . . . ?"

Samantha quirked her lips. "I don't think that will be necessary. Well, the good news is that there is precedence for judges, as in the case of the angry blogging ex-wife, to rule that these types of publications are protected by the First Amendment."

"That's good!" I exclaimed, letting out a shaky, relieved breath.

"Of course, in other cases, the courts have stated that these communications are inappropriate and the author should, in one judge's words, 'Shut the hell up and show some class.'"

"That's bad."

She cleared her throat. "Now, on to the questions I ask every client: You need to decide how far you want to go. Do you want to get even? Do you want to recover some dignity? Or do you want to slink away and hope we can depend on the common sense of the court and win the defamation suit?"

"Can I have some of column A and a little of column B? I don't really want to skin him," I admitted. "I just want what's fair. Hell, half the stuff in that house, even the house, I don't want it. I don't want the condo. I don't want the cars or the bass boat. And I could care less if he ends up paying me alimony. In fact, I don't think I want monthly contact with him, even if it's just through a check. I just want—I want enough to start over, to get on with my life."

Samantha smiled. "I take it you just happen to have detailed financial records for the entirety of your marriage?"

"Um, no. I know this is going to sound pretty cliché, but Mike took care of all of our finances. He was an accountant. I trusted him. It just made sense at the time."

"Let me guess, when it came to loans, bills, and tax returns, you just signed where he told you to?"

I nodded, staring at the twisting hands in my lap.

"Don't worry about the records, Lacey. The discovery process makes my clerk feel useful. The first thing we're going to do is make sure that Mike's house is in order, that there's nothing illegal or unethical going on. And if he's up to something illegal or unethical, we'll do what we can to make sure you aren't liable for any of it. Then we use it as leverage."

I chewed my lip as I considered that. "As much as I would relish the idea of Mike showering with his back against a prison wall, I don't think you're going to find anything but above-board business with Mike. He's ambitious and materialistic, but also dull as a box of mud and straight as an arrow. Frankly, I didn't think he had the guile to carry off an affair."

"You'd be surprised," Samantha said.

"I'd really rather not be surprised again," I muttered.

"The fun part is that we can ask for every piece of financial information Mike has handled since your wedding. You have every right to see it and searching for it will be a gigantic pain in the ass for Mike and his lawyer. And if you want to have some real fun, we can demand that every cent Mike spent 'entertaining' Beebee be paid back to the marital pot. We might even get the judge to consider her salary part of his maintenance of the affair. We'll have my associate go over every receipt and credit card charge, pick out all expenditures, like two thousand dollars spent at a jewelry store or three days at a resort. If you don't remember getting a diamond anklet or a weekend getaway in Hot Springs, then we assume that Mike spent that money on Beebee, and not, say, his mom."

"Yes, let's do that, please. But you should know his mom is also a strong possibility."

"Ew."

I nodded. "Exactly."

We talked for another hour or so and I found it oddly therapeutic, even if Samantha mostly kept her head down to take a copious amount of notes. She nodded. She grunted. She occasionally muttered something in Latin.

We finally came to the subject of the newsletter, how I'd found the information, how I'd written it. When I told her I'd forwarded the actual messages to my account, her smile was a mile wide. Samantha assured me that even if Mike had deleted the e-mails from his account, that her forensic computer analyst would be able to prove the messages were sent from Mike's IP address at work, where I didn't have access.

Sammy went on to explain that the lawsuit would be handled separately, but she would handle both cases. Apparently, in the course of her divorce court experience, she'd handled quite a few defamation suits—which made me feel a little bit better. She assured me that as long as information in the newsletter was proven to be true, there was nothing the court could do to prevent the publication or punish the author.

"We shouldn't have a problem then, because it was all true," I told her. "Everything I wrote was based on finding those e-mails. Wouldn't the pictures alone be enough to just cancel this whole lawsuit thing?"

"Well, no, you would have to respond to the suit either way, particularly since Mike and Beebee's complaint states that the e-mails were spam and Mike has no idea who they're from. They're claiming that the woman in the photos isn't Beebee, that this is a horrible case of a nosy wife who found bad information while snooping and wreaked havoc with it. They're saying you've defamed both of their characters, have damaged Mike's reputation/earning potential, and harmed Beebee's standing in the community."

"Oh, what standing in the community?" I snorted. I opened the file folder with the e-mailed photos. "Besides, you can tell it's Beebee, just look at this . . ."

I sifted through the photos, tamping down the flare of rage

ignited by seeing them again. But as I thumbed through, I realized that none of the pictures showed Beebee's face. I gasped. How could I not have realized that I never saw her face?

"Crap," I moaned.

"Exactly," she said. "These pictures are more anatomical in nature."

There were no face shots.

"He's going to win, isn't he?" I sat back, deflated. For the first time, I realized that as scared as I was, up until that moment I sincerely believed that I was going to come out of this unscathed. My marriage couldn't be saved, obviously, but I honestly thought I would be able to emerge from this ordeal able to carry on a normal, productive, not-working-as-a-french-fry-technician life. I wasn't aware I was even capable of that kind of optimism, so I wasn't willing to let it die just yet. "Wait!" I snatched up one of the pictures. "Look! The bumblebee tattoo. Beebee has a bumblebee tattoo on her inner thigh. Can you subpoena her thigh?"

"Not as part of the divorce action, but to defend you from the lawsuit, yes. We can ask for an inspection of her thighs as proof of identity," Sam said, examining the photo. "That's a good catch on the tattoo. Even if she tried to remove it before the suit goes to court, it would still show up.

"But for now, do me a favor," she said. "From this point on we need you to appear to be the brokenhearted discarded wife, not the angry, possibly crazy, woman scorned. Do not discuss the newsletter with large groups of people. If you see Mike or Beebee in public, do not cause an ugly scene. Do not call, e-mail, write letters to, or otherwise contact Mike or Beebee without contacting me first to see if it's a good idea. When you do appear in public, try to look sort of, well, beaten and tragic."

"That shouldn't be difficult, thank you."

"In fact, if you're comfortable with therapy, you might start seeing a counselor," she suggested. "It will help establish the psychological trauma Mike has inflicted on you. Since you obviously enjoy writing, it would also help if you started a journal to document your hellish, slow recovery from said trauma. How is your current financial situation? How are you getting by day to day?"

I shrugged. "Actually, it's okay. I don't have a lot of living expenses. I'm staying with my parents, which I don't think can last much longer. I'll probably have to find an apartment soon. But I have a little savings cushion. If the case drags out, I have some investments I can cash in if I need to."

"I'll be honest, you're probably going to need to," she told me, pinning me with those frank seawater eyes. "It all depends on how contentious negotiations are going to be. And I doubt Mike is going to be forthcoming or cooperative with us. I've had some cases that only took sixty days. Then again, I'm still involved in negotiating a canine custody agreement that has dragged a divorce settlement out for almost three years."

"Canine custody agreement?"

"Both parties want sole custody of Bobo the Pomeranian. Lacey, I can't say that your literary aspirations are going to help us in court because some judges around here are pretty old school. But I have to tell you, I thought it took a huge pair of Spaldings. A lot of the people who come through that door are just so caught up in being a victim that they can't see straight. It's part of the job, but it's pretty damned annoying. It's refreshing to meet someone who's not helpless. You are not what I expected."

"You're not what I expected either, Ms. Shackleton." I rose and shook her hand.

"If you need anything, you call me."

"By that, do you mean, 'It's eleven p.m. and I just need to talk' or 'It's three a.m. and I need bail money'?" I asked.

Samantha grinned. "Um, neither of those."

"Fair enough." I nodded.

"You're going to be one of those 'interesting' clients, aren't you?"

I arched a brow at her. "You're just now figuring that out?"

8

Doubly Screwed by the Fourth Estate

It was starting to feel crowded at the old homeplace.

Daddy returned from his reunion a few days after Mama and he was less thrilled to have one of the baby birds back in his empty nest. Other than repeated inquiries as to whether I would need extra boxes when I moved out, he refused to discuss anything with me. If I came into a room, he left it. If I happened to catch him long enough to ask him a question, he answered it in as few syllables as possible. I'm pretty sure the only reason he ate at the same table as me was that Mama refused to serve his meals anywhere else. Daddy was smart enough to know he couldn't survive on his own cooking.

Daddy was never what you'd call a hands-on father, but he'd never been so distant. When he was disappointed in us, his usual MO was to tell Mama and have her relay the message. Even when Emmett finally, quietly, came out to my parents, Daddy told Mama to tell my brother to be careful. And that was about it.

Daddy seemed to be employing more of a scorched earth policy these days. I think he believed if he made the situation uncomfortable enough, I would give up this whole silly divorce and go back to my own house. He was particularly irritated by the way Mama had managed to insulate me from the phone calls, the insistent visitors, Wynnie's repeated efforts to talk some sense into me.

"You've got to quit coddling the girl," I heard him grumble through their bedroom door on one of my nightly wanderings around the house. "She needs to face her own music. Personally, I don't blame Wynnie and Jim for being pissed. Or Mike. Do you know what kind of jokes they're making about Mike and Beebee down at the golf course? And Lacey? I just don't understand what was going through her head when she did this. We didn't raise her to—"

"To what?" Mama demanded. "To stand up for herself?"

"To make a damn fool out of herself," Daddy countered. "How would you feel if somebody wrote this sort of thing about one of our kids, Deb?"

"Keep your voice down," Mama hissed. "And our kids wouldn't be sleazy enough to cheat."

"Well, if Emmett does cheat, he'd better not tell Lacey about it; God knows what she'd do."

"Walt, are you upset because you're embarrassed or because you want her out of the house?"

"Well, she's never going to leave if you keep stuffing her with pancakes and grilled cheese sandwiches!" he cried.

"Oh, she's not even eating them," Mama said. "She doesn't eat anything. She doesn't sleep. She just wanders around the house all night, which is why you should keep your voice down!"

I backed away from the door. I didn't want to hear any more. I was going to have to leave the house, soon. Besides the loser factor, I couldn't stay at my parents' house, causing tension and problems for the two of them. There were enough failed marriages in our family.

As I watched my parents' marriage from a newly enlightened adult perspective, I noticed little things about them I hadn't before. Little things, like when my dad got my mom a glass of water, he ran the tap for a while, to make sure he was getting her the coldest, least faucet-tasting water possible. Mike used to just stick a glass under the tap.

My parents had that something. Something Mike and I didn't have. I didn't know what it was and that was what was driving me insane. I'm not going to say Mike was a total monster. I mean, there was the year that he got me an air purifier for my birthday, but only because I'd mentioned that the infomercial was interesting. I shared some blame in that. We had no connection. No dependence on each other, no real intimacy. We started dating in high school because we ran in the same circles and our parents approved. We got married because that was what you were supposed to do when you'd been dating for a while and were graduating college. It seemed like the next step and we couldn't think of a better one.

There were things I didn't expect, a rush of longing when I smelled Tide detergent, a scent that would forever remind me of Mike's shirts. Not having someone to rub my cold feet against under the covers. Someone to eat my pizza crusts, which I always left behind and Mike called the "pizza bones." But I think these were signs that I needed a roommate, not Mike. Or maybe a neutered cat.

Yes, Daddy drove Mama nuts with his constant need to be around his stupid adolescent college buddies. But reconnecting, nay, dwelling, on his past kept Daddy happy. And that made Mama happy.

She compromised, she didn't settle.

• • •

I woke up the next morning to find that my car had been towed.

Mike had removed my name from the title more than a year before and I just hadn't noticed. When I called the county clerk's office to try to order a copy of the title paperwork, I found that Mike had also managed to cut off my American Express, my Visa, and my MasterCard. I was still on the phone with MasterCard when Mama came into the kitchen wearing a bathrobe, staring in horror at the morning edition of the *Singletree Gazette.*

She turned the front page toward me so I could read the headline, "Scorned Local Woman Sued for Scathing E-Mail."

"Oh . . . no," I groaned, dropping the phone on its cradle.

Reporter Danny Plum, whose byline hovered over my own personal nightmare, was an industrious little bastard. He'd found the bridal portrait we'd included with our wedding announcement years before in the newspaper archives. It was front and center, just under a smaller subhead reading "Widely Forwarded Anti-Adultery Missive Sparks Divorce, Community Debate."

Mama's face was as white as the newsprint. "Baby, I didn't mean it. I didn't know he was writing it down. I'm so sorry."

I took the paper from her shaking hands. "Unable to return to her marital home, Mrs. Terwilliger is reportedly staying with her parents, rarely leaving the house except to consult her attorney, Samantha Shackleton." I read aloud. "When contacted by the *Gazette,* Mrs. Terwilliger's mother, Deb Vernon, insisted that many wronged wives would follow in her daughter's footsteps, 'if they thought of it.'

"'Everybody thinks Lacey's gone crazy, but that's not true.

She knew what she was doing,' Mrs. Vernon said in a phone interview. 'She was just pushed too far. And yes, she overreacted a little bit. It happens to the best of us, but I don't want to comment. Of course, if Mike didn't want to be publicly embarrassed, he shouldn't have run around town chasing some hussy like his pants were on fire . . . but I don't want to comment. I just wish people would mind their own business. Really, I have nothing to say.'"

My mother cringed as I made a sound somewhere between a groan and call of a dying crane.

"I *declined* comment! Declined!" she cried. "And he's twisting what I did say all around! I'm going to strangle that little weasel reporter!"

I picked up the ringing phone without thinking about who could be calling. Samantha's voice, frustrated and weary, came through the receiver. "I know I didn't specifically tell you not to have your mama defend you to the press, but I thought I made it clear that you needed to keep a low profile."

"Mama says she declined comment," I told her, giving Mama an exasperated look.

"Did she say 'off the record'?" Samantha asked. "Those are the magic words. Unless she said, 'off the record,' anything she said, even in passing conversation while she was declining comment, can be quoted. You should know this stuff. I thought you had a background in journalism."

"Yeah, the ethical kind, where reporters don't screw people over when they say they're not interested in being quoted. She didn't mean it, Sam. Mama couldn't stop him from writing a story, but she wasn't trying to make it any worse. Of course, it would have been helpful if she had told me she talked to a reporter in the first place."

"I didn't want to upset you," Mama whispered. "I was trying to screen your calls!"

"Why would they want to write about a divorce case in the first place?" I asked. "Don't I have the right to privacy?"

"When Mike filed suit, this became a matter of public record. This is not good, Lacey," Samantha said. "Mike is made to look like the injured party. And he managed to decline comment, through his lawyer, so he seems to have some sense . . . and tact. Your mama, as well intentioned as she may be, made it look like you don't have any remorse and that you feel justified in what you did. You're the harpy first wife. It's not exactly a sympathetic role. This probably won't improve our position in court."

"Well, I'm not really remorseful and I do feel justified in what I did," I said.

"That's fine; you just shouldn't tell anybody that!" Samantha exclaimed. "Look, this could just die down. But considering that the newsletter is supposed to be 'widely e-mailed' I doubt it. In case it doesn't, and by some horrible whim of fate you manage to get the attention of other media outlets, you don't even speak to decline comment, you just walk away. In fact, you don't talk to anyone you don't know, got it?"

"Lacey!" Mama called. "I think you need to come see this."

I carried the cordless phone into the living room, where Mama stood in the window, watching a news crew setting up on our front lawn.

"What?" Samantha asked.

"Um, a camera crew from Channel Five." I told her.

"And Channel Seven!" Mama called.

"And Channel Seven," I told Samantha.

Samantha groaned as Mama snapped curtains closed. And if I wasn't mistaken, I could hear her banging her head against her desk. "Do you have somewhere you could go lay low for a while?"

"I'm thinking maybe Timbuktu," I muttered, padding back into the kitchen.

"Funny," she snorted. "I want you to leave town for a while and I don't want you to talk to anybody. Keep your cell phone on. Tell your parents if they get any media calls to refer all questions to me."

After a few more curt instructions from my lawyer, I hung up and banged my own head against the kitchen counter.

"This is just not good," I moaned. "I'm going to end up a punch line on *Jay Leno,* like that Runaway Bride girl with the crazy eyes."

Mama sighed. "You should have thought of that before airing your laundry." When I gave her a stern look, she shrank back a little. "Too soon?"

"Samantha says I need to find a place to lay low for a while."

"Maybe you should head up to the cabin," she said. "Hide out there for a while. Even if someone told the reporters where you were, I doubt they'd be able to find you."

I lifted my head, taking a Post-it note with "milk, eggs, bread" written on it with me. I swatted it off of my forehead. Why hadn't I thought of the cabin?

Mike and I hadn't been to the cabin on Lake Lockwood in months. Gammy Muldoon left the cabin to me just before we got married, with the understanding that Emmett could use it whenever he wanted to. But Emmett was religious about protecting his skin from damaging UV rays, so he never wanted to use it. Mike and I went up for weekends sometimes, but we'd fallen out of the habit unless it was Memorial or Labor Day.

Despite the fact that his boat-in-progress was housed there,

Mike didn't particularly enjoy our time at the cabin. It wasn't as nice as our friends' places and he didn't feel like we could entertain properly there. He hated the rattling old window-unit air conditioner, the shabby, splintering porch swing, and the sprung chintz couch in the living room. One of the biggest fights we'd ever had was over Mike's listing the house with a Realtor to gauge the market viability of the property without telling me. He argued that we never used that "run-down old shack" and it would be much smarter to sell it and put the money toward a place in Lighthouse Cove. I called the Realtor, canceled the listing, and went out and bought new outdoor furniture, a hammock, a new couch, and a laundry list of other things to fix the house up. I maxed out my Visa for that month, but at least Mike couldn't complain about the damn couch anymore.

The good news was that along with its lack of a prestigious address or central air, Mike deeply resented the tax liability the lake house represented. So, when we got married, it stayed in my name.

Mike's being a tightwad had finally paid off.

9

First Impressions or *Pride and Panties*

The cabin was only about an hour from Singletree, but it might as well have been an ocean away. It wasn't much to look at, one story of aging gray cedar set two miles back from the nearest access road. The water of Lake Lockwood was always freezing and smelled faintly of fish, but some of my best childhood memories were rooted in that cabin.

My maternal grandma, Gammy Muldoon, made no apologies for designating me her favorite grandchild. She wasn't cruel or hurtful about it. She gave thoughtful Christmas and birthday presents to Emmett. She took him out for special outings and called him her "little monkey." But I was Gammy's special girl . . . because I stood still long enough to listen to her stories.

Gammy was a pistol. She cheated viciously at rummy and drank a steady stream of daiquiris after 4:00 p.m. Many people say she's where I get my special unladylike mastery of "bluer" language, which my Grandma Vernon never managed to cure. Gammy and Grandpa built the family cabin almost fifty years earlier, back when even the richest of the rich didn't have air-conditioning. Going to the lake was the only escape from the sticky, humid heat. The whole house was decorated in early American Coca-Cola. Old signs, posters, glasses, plaques, everywhere you looked there were rosy-cheeked young citizens trying to sell you the most delicious caffeinated beverage known to man. It was either kitschy or within kissing distance of serial killer territory.

The closest thing to a town near Lake Lockwood was Buford, a tiny tourist trap that depended on summer traffic to keep stores open during the year. As I drove my mom's car through town, I had to dodge RVs and boat trailers as tourists with very little experience driving either negotiated the streets. We had a local woman, Mrs. Witter, who kept the place up for us. She came in once a month to check for storm or pest damage, gave it a good annual spring cleaning, and closed the place for the winter. It was obvious she'd given the place a thorough once-over after I'd called her that afternoon. The floor was freshly scrubbed and the living room still smelled like lemon Pledge and Windex. As usual, she'd left a plate of her famous snickerdoodles for me on the table.

I carried in my suitcase, my laptop and a couple of bags of "on the lam" groceries. Dropping it all on the kitchen counter, I stared at my new home. I'd never realized how small the cabin was. Or that it had a weird old refrigerator sort of smell. Or that the floor slanted slightly when you walked back toward the bedroom.

"Stop it," I told myself sternly. "Stop it, right now. Stop finding fault and freaking out. It's going to be— Oh, for crap's sake, I've been living alone for five minutes and I'm already talking to myself."

Right now the only thing the cabin had going for it was that the phone wasn't ringing off the hook. The reporters that had been calling, visiting, and just plain camping outside my parents' house had proved themselves to be resourceful little buggers. My first order of business was to unplug the phone. I did, however, leave the cord in the outlet because I was going to need it for slower-than-Christmas dial-up internet access.

For an hour or so I managed to occupy myself with mundane little moving-in tasks, but you can only rearrange your toiletries so many times. I tucked my suitcase under the bed, threw the boxes in the burn barrel, and fixed a turkey sandwich, which I couldn't eat. I just stared at the plate until the edges of the meat got sort of dry and crusty. I threw it out, dropped onto the couch, and rubbed at my chest, where my stomach acid rose with threatening velocity.

I had no idea what to do. Even when I "stayed at home" before, I had a daily to-do list. I had lists of lists. Grocery shopping. Committee meetings. Hair appointments. Yoga classes. Picking up dry cleaning. Planning dinners for friends. Waiting at home for the carpet shampooers, the exterminator. Writing endless thank-you notes to people I barely knew, waxing poetic about their participation in the Junior League Fall Festival or their donation to the Ladies Auxiliary Golf Tournament. My hand could practically write, "Thank you so much for your generous contribution" on autopilot.

What would I do all day? What would keep my racing mind occupied?

I didn't even have cable. My only TV options were videotapes that had been at the cabin since my grandmother owned the place. She refused to watch movies made after 1950, so her collection was comprised of black-and-white movies featuring actresses she called "broads" in the fondest manner. When I was little, I would come up for special weekends and she would French braid my hair and lecture me about how Joan Crawford was considered a free-spirited flapper before she harnessed the power of her eyebrows. When I theorized that dear old Joan and Bette's shoulder pads were like substitute testicles, she nearly wept with pride.

My grandmother would have been ashamed by what I'd become. If she were alive, she would have watched me cry for about two minutes, slapped some sense into me, and told me to show some backbone. I was a Muldoon, damn it. And Muldoons didn't just roll over when someone kicked them. We stood our ground. We fought back. And we stole your good liquor on the way out the door.

Well, that was probably just Gammy.

Sighing, I picked up Gammy's favorite, *The Women*. Somehow, it felt appropriate—a movie about infidelity, divorce, and vindication where not a single male character was shown. Perfectly in keeping with my new "no penis policy." I pulled the worn purple quilt from the bed, snuggled up on the sofa, and let myself get swept away to a world where everybody is beautifully lit and has blistering retorts at the ready.

• • •

My movie marathon didn't work out as well as I'd hoped. I forgot at the end of *The Women*, Mary throws away her pride and goes back to her husband. It didn't exactly put me in a drowsy place. I ended up watching a few movies where Rex Harrison pretended to sing and John Barrymore pretended to be sober. I wrapped up with *Rebecca*, a movie about a first wife who was such a vicious bitch that her mere memory eventually drove everyone around her kind of nuts.

I found that message a little more cheerful, but I was still awake at 5:00 a.m. and not sleepy in the slightest.

I hadn't been awake to see the sunrise in years, so I decided to go out to the front porch and enjoy it. I settled into an old cane rocker with some juice and propped my feet on the porch railing. I loved the quiet time at the lake in the mornings, before the birds started chirping or the boaters and the Jet Skiers started their wake wars. The water reflected a bright coppery light that made you feel cleaner and somehow healthier and more virtuous just for being outside in it. Even the gentle lapping of the water seemed muted and kinder.

I might have worried about the fact that I was wearing just an old Wildcats T-shirt, panties, and a surprisingly chipper expression. But the only cabin within sight was the old McGee place, about fifty yards down the shore.

The McGees had been friends of my family for generations. They were sweet people who cohosted decades of Fourth of July barbecues with my grandparents. But the tradition had died with Gammy Muldoon. My parents preferred entertaining at their house and I hadn't quite graduated to hosting family holidays yet. I was still doing "hostess training wheel" events like baby showers and bridal teas. Besides, Harold McGee was getting older and no one had opened up the house for years. I thought so right up until the front door opened and my new neighbor stepped out onto his porch.

"Gah!" I yelped, tumbling off of the chair in a panty-baring heap. If there was one thing Mama drilled into my head, it's that you never have a second chance to make a first impression. And I had just made a first impression on my new neighbor with my ass in the air. Lovely.

Maybe I could commando-crawl into the house without him realizing I was even there. I peeked over the porch railing to see him staring at me, openly smirking. "Morning."

Maybe not.

"Morning." I said, standing and trying to pull my shirt down as far as possible. I stood behind the rocker, hoping it at least would cover my bare legs.

My new neighbor, hoo boy. I will admit that the only reason I own the X-Men trilogy on DVD is that I have an unnatural fixation with Hugh Jackman. And here I was living next door to Wolverine personified. Old battered jeans, black T-shirt, bare feet, a lot of dark wayward hair and sideburns that desperately needed a trim. Sharp hazel eyes and sharper cheekbones, and a wide, generous mouth set in a grim line. He raised his coffee cup in mock salute and padded back into his house.

"I usually wear pants!" I called.

• • •

Later that afternoon I sat at the scarred maple breakfast table, my hands on my chin, staring at a Saran-wrapped Bundt cake. It was my special Ugly Cake recipe. Chocolate cake swirled with a cream cheese and dark chocolate filling. Once baked, it was about as attractive as homemade sin. But it was a really good ice-breaker, even if it was "Sorry you started off your day being confronted by my airborne ass" ice.

And yes, I do consider cake mix and cream cheese to be essentials when I stock up on survival groceries.

Normally, baked goods wouldn't pose such a heated internal debate, but I was absolutely mortified by the whole panty-baring welcome. That whole incident had thrown me off-kilter. I came to the lake for solitude. I didn't particularly want to be on friendly terms with my neighbor. But here I was, having lusty feelings for the Wolverine lookalike, which could not be healthy in my present emotional state.

"Oh, screw it," I muttered, scooping the cake off the table and bounding for the door. "It's just cake."

I shoved the screen door open just enough to pop my new neighbor in the nose before I realized he was standing there. "Gaah!" he yelped, clutching his free hand to his face.

"Oh!" I cried. "I'm so sorry!"

"You are reedy bad at meeding people, ared't you?" he groaned, blood trickling out from under his fingers. In his other hand, he held a key ring.

"Come in," I said, chucking the Bundt and grabbing a handful of paper towels. I pressed the paper to his nose. "I'm so sorry."

He tilted his head back. "I brod you some keys that Mrs. Witter left for you," he said. "I did not expect a door to the face."

"I'm so sorry. I usually don't assault my neighbors. And I'm wearing pants. Look, see?" I said, indicating the very covering jeans I was wearing.

"Very nice," he muttered, blotting at his reddened nostrils. He extended his other hand and shook mine. "Lefty Monroe."

"Seriously?" I said. "You tell people that?"

He gave a brief flash of gleaming white teeth, then tucked them back away. It was the first time someone had smiled at me and then taken it back. Interesting. Lefty? And to think I was embarrassed that I was going to call him Wolverine.

"Lacey Terwilliger," I said, extending my hand. I shook my head and corrected myself. "Lacey Vernon."

"New alias or multiple personality?" he asked, arching a brow, not shaking my hand.

"Newly separated. I'm taking my maiden name back," I said primly. I didn't think guys with prison nicknames should throw stones. But I did just hit him in the face, so . . .

"Sorry," he muttered, his eyes immediately putting up what I can only describe as "defense shields." Well, that was just fine. No matter how good he looked in worn Levi's, I planned to maintain and defend the no penis policy.

"I made you a Bundt cake," I said, handing him the plate. "But now I think I owe you another one for smacking you in the face."

"I would feel better if you kept your distance," he admitted. "God knows what you could accomplish with a cabinet door. Mrs. Witter said she would have left the keys in the house, but that she was afraid to. She told a very long story about you managing to lock yourself out of every room in the cabin in one afternoon."

"I was eight!" I cried. "This is the problem with continuing your acquaintance with people who have known you since your awkward adolescent phase. I'm expecting mine to be over just any day now. I'm really sorry about this morning. I didn't know anyone else was up here. The McGees haven't opened the house in years. I haven't seen anyone coming and going . . ."

"I'm renting from the McGees. I work from home," he said, his tone harsh and clipped. "I stay holed up for days at a time. I keep to myself."

The message could not have been more clear if he'd put up an electric fence. Stay away. Neighbors will be shot on sight.

"Oh, that's fine. I plan on being a quiet, keeps-to-herself, we-never-expected-to-find-those-bodies-in-the-deep-freeze type of neighbor, without the actual bodies." I said. "That probably wasn't reassuring, was it?"

He shook his head, turned on his heel, and walked out of the house without another word. Generally, people wait until they've known me for a while to have that sort of reaction. I stared after him as he made his way to his cabin, as much in bewilderment as to seize the opportunity to catch sight of his denim-clad butt. He seemed to walk with a slight limp in his left leg. And if I wasn't mistaken, one of his cheeks was, well, fuller, than the other. It was an ass with character.

"Well, at least that wasn't weird," I marveled as he slammed the front door to his cabin behind him.

Of course, his being exceedingly grumpy and potentially crazy didn't change the fact that I sort of wanted to see him naked. Fine. I really wanted to see him naked.

10

Meryl and Me

It was the Fourth of July, Independence Day. And I was independent—also known as alone—and it wasn't so bad. I sat on the end of the dock, dangling my feet into the lake, watching revelers enjoy some ill-advised and not-quite-sober nighttime boating. I sipped lemonade treated with just a smidge of vodka while I watched the residents of Lighthouse Cove set off fireworks down the shore. Mama would have been horrified by the notion of my drinking alone, but mostly because I was so close to a body of water. She would have told me if it could kill Natalie Wood, it could kill me, too.

In my mother's mind, cautionary tales are timeless, however tenuously connected.

I watched the lights reflecting off the water, violent blooms of color that made my eyes ache and my chest tighten. It was a little lonely, knowing that there were families out there, celebrating. It reminded me of the Fourth when Emmett and I were diagnosed with pinkeye and had to sit inside while all of the other kids ran around with sparklers. Every echo of a Roman candle taunted us.

I had never spent a single holiday alone. As much as I used to resent being summoned to my parents' house or to the in-laws', it was sort of disorienting to have nowhere to go, nothing to do. If not for the fact that my mother kept making up excuses to call and check up on me—including calling to wish me a Happy Fourth that morning—I could have been eaten by wild boars or brutally murdered by my antisocial new neighbor and no one would know for weeks.

At the same time, I didn't have to make three dozen deviled eggs or assemble some sort of patriotically themed outfit for the occasion. I wasn't responsible to anyone, for anything.

My soon-to-be ex-husband didn't seem to get that.

Mike had apparently decided that it was okay to break his lawyer's contact embargo if he needed something from me. Because he was basically a giant five-year-old. Earlier that afternoon, I'd been lounging on the couch, reading *The Stand* instead of the *Emotional Homework for New Divorcées* book Mama had insisted I bring with me. I'd unearthed King's masterwork from the front closet. I think one of my uncles had left it behind after a weekend visit. I was normally a Nora Roberts or Mary Higgins Clark reader, but I hadn't been able to put this book down. It turned out that I really liked Stephen King, or at least post-apocalyptic, metaphorical Stephen King. (I was still decidedly against child-devouring clown Stephen King.) Who knew?

My cell phone rang and, distracted by the seemingly banal, creeping evil of Randall Flagg, I answered it without thinking. There was no greeting or acknowledgment of any kind, just Mike imperiously demanding, "I need my blue suit. Where did you leave it?"

I was so stunned at hearing his voice, I almost barked out that I'd dropped it at Speedy Cleaners on Schultz Avenue. Like a trained seal.

Despite recent personal revelations, my instinct to soothe

and serve shamed me. I was so accustomed to jumping whenever Mike needed something, to catering to his whims before he realized he had them, that my response was automatic. I wasn't a wife. I was a personal assistant—one of those harried, abused ones that sold their celebrity employers' secrets to the tabloids.

Of course, my mouth didn't have to catch up to my brain while I processed this, so my response was something along the lines of spluttering, "Beg pardon?"

"I. Need. My. Blue. Suit," he said, enunciating every word as if he were talking to a very slow preschooler. "Where did you drop it off? Oh, and did you mail my Netflix envelope?"

I stared into the phone, sure I had just hallucinated what he'd said. He hadn't talked to me for days, on the advice of counsel, and now he wanted to make sure I'd returned his rented copy of *Alien vs. Predator*?

Seriously?

Pressing the receiver to my ear, I demanded, "Do you have anything to say to me? How about, 'I'm sorry. I've been cheating on you. I was wrong'?"

"Oh, Lacey, I don't want to go through this again."

"We never went through it the first time, Mike. I mean, really, could you possibly be more cliché? Nailing your receptionist? Why not a cocktail waitress? Or a stewardess? I file for divorce, and all you have to say is, 'Where is my blue suit?' What is wrong with you?"

Unused to hearing this sort of talk from me, Mike stayed silent on the other end of the line. He finally snorted derisively and said, "I think you've said enough for both of us. Damn it, Lacey, I was trying to stay civil here. But you just can't let it go, even for your own good. I know we were having problems, but

I never thought you'd be dumb enough to pull a stunt like that e-mail. Why didn't you come to me so we could try to work things out? How could you be so stupid? Nothing can fix this. Do you understand? My parents are never going to forgive you, never. I thought my father was going to have a heart attack.

"What did you expect to happen, Lacey? That you'd write this horrible, slanderous piece of garbage and send it out to all of our friends and family and I'd suddenly want you again? And did you think about what you were doing to the business? Or Beebee? She had to go home to Natchez to visit her mother, she was so upset. She's humiliated."

"One, it's not slander if it's true. And, pardon me, but Beebee has been humiliated? I'm supposed to worry about Beebee? How about me? How am I supposed to feel knowing that the entire area code knew that you were cheating on me? That you didn't at least have the respect to *try* to hide what you were doing . . . from anyone besides me? I mean, really, what did *you* expect from *me,* Mike?"

I could hear him flipping channels on the TV. He had already checked out of the conversation. I was talking about the destruction of our marriage and I still couldn't hold his attention. "Come on, Lacey, you had to know something was going on with me and Beebee. I thought we had an arrangement. We were having problems, but I thought we had some sort of unspoken agreement to keep up appearances. I thought you knew to hold up your end of the bargain."

"My end of the *bargain*?" I exploded. "I assumed my husband was a decent human being who wouldn't do that to the woman he was married to. If I missed some obvious signs, it was because I wanted to believe you respected me enough to honor our marriage vows . . . or at least not crap all over them. And if you thought we had some sort of unspoken arrangement, that's because you didn't have the balls to ask me about it and find out for yourself."

"You knew I wasn't happy. I mean, I was never home, Lacey. I was always working. And when I was home—"

"When you were home, you weren't *home,*" I told him. "You were talking about work, making calls for work, getting ready for meetings related to work, thinking about work, or hell, probably thinking about Beebee. I'm not saying I was any happier. But at least I didn't run off and sleep with some Cheetos-colored bimbo."

"You don't talk about her that way," he growled. "Beebee cares about me. She listens. She cares about what I want, what I need."

"Asking whether you want to be on top or bottom doesn't mean she cares about you. Beebee's looking for a meal ticket, Mike. She wants an easier life and, fortunately for her, you are more gullible than she could ever have imagined."

"She wants to see me sail my boat, Lacey. She even came up with a name for it. *The Liquid Asset.*"

"You don't *have* a boat, Mike."

"Yeah, but she wants me to finish it," he said petulantly. "She wants me to have a hobby, to relax. All you ever want me to do is work."

"When the hell have I ever said that?" I demanded. "When have I ever insisted that you work *more*? If you felt pressured because we had to pay for the bass boat, which you wanted. Or the condo, which you wanted. Or the truck or the Jet Skis or the club memberships—well, then maybe I could have gotten a job to help out. But you didn't want me to work. It was embarrassing, you said. My job was to keep you going, to build this perfect, stupid life for you. That was what you wanted. Don't blame me because you changed your mind!"

"Beebee's what I want, Lacey. And I'm not being fair to her. I can't keep making promises to her that I can't keep."

"Oh, you're not divorcing me because of Beebee. You're divorcing me because I managed to shame you as much as you've shamed me."

"You won't last five minutes without me, you know," he sneered. "The house, the money, the credit cards. I'd love to see how you're going to get along without my credit cards."

"Aw, Mike, I wouldn't worry about it. I recently liquidated some assets of my own, so I think I'll have some pocket money for a while. Mr. Goote really is very generous."

"Mr. Goote? Why would you go to Leo—" Mike gasped. "Your ring? You hocked your engagement ring? That was a— Do you have any idea how much that ring cost?!"

I shrugged. "Probably twice what I sold it for."

Mike growled. "I'm going to leave you with nothing. No cards, no cash, no house, no car, nothing. By the time Beebee and I get done suing you, you'll be living with your parents, working double shifts at the Sizzler—"

"Oh, go sting the BumbleBee," I sniped, shutting my phone off.

How, I wondered as I stared out over the water, could two intelligent adults end up like this? Well, one intelligent adult. Why was it that other relationships had flourished and ours seemed to have stalled and died an agonizing, horrible death? Mike and I had been given all the tools to build a good life together. Both sets of our parents bumped consistently along the glass ceiling between middle and upper class. We had good orthodontia, summer camps, swimming lessons, new cars for our sixteenth birthdays. We graduated college without student loans. We got married at the First Baptist Church and our reception was held at the Singletree Country Club. The down payment on our sweet little starter house was a gift from my grandparents.

Maybe the problem was that we never struggled. There was nothing to bond us together, us against the world. We didn't have to turn to each other and figure out what the hell we were going to do to pay the light bill or make the next house payment. We just coasted along. The thing about coasting is that it usually means you're going downhill.

I knew we were pathetic excuses for adults. I knew we should have told our parents to back off and just let us be. But it was so easy to let the hard stuff, the bills, the worrying, the minutiae, be taken care of so we could focus on getting our lives up and going.

I screwed myself over. That's the worst part. I did this to myself. I'd never lied to myself about the level of contentment in my marriage. I knew I was never blissfully happy. When I realized our newlywed life wasn't the ecstasy-fest I'd hoped for, I thought, "Well, no one is completely happy." And when I had to fight harder and harder to find the bright spots in my marriage, I thought there was something wrong with me. I had a beautiful home, a husband who provided for me, security, position within my community. Most women would have been thrilled with my life. I thought maybe I didn't feel things the way people were supposed to. Maybe my expectations were unreasonable. I even thought about going on antidepressants for a while, but we just don't *do* that in my family. Three Bloody Marys for breakfast was perfectly acceptable, but a Xanax or two showed character flaws.

• • •

To give a more explicit example, in eight years I'd never had an orgasm with Mike. Ever. Not even a promising twinge. I read somewhere that a good lover played your body like an instrument, listening for the right sounds and striking the ideal notes at the perfect time. Mike's playing style was more like "Chopsticks," hitting the same notes over and over again and nobody got any enjoyment out of it.

At first I was convinced it was because I was just too nervous that Mike might trick me into sex that I couldn't relax enough to enjoy our "we'll do everything but that *one thing*" phase. That was followed by our "let's just get it out of the way so there's no pressure on our wedding night" phase, followed by the "is that it?" phase. Just after we were married, I convinced myself that I was still too new to sex to enjoy it properly. About three years in, I finally realized that Mike Terwilliger was just lousy in bed.

By then, the mere mention that we might need to buy a book or get some counseling sent Mike into a snit that lasted two weeks. It wasn't his fault that I didn't respond to him, he said. If I would just relax and give in to some of his naughtier fantasies, I'd be having multiple orgasms in no time. Unfortunately, most of his fantasies weren't all that naughty. He really thought having sex in our tent on a camping trip was living on the edge.

I convinced myself my problem was clinical, like I had some nerve endings disconnected somewhere. I even tried talking to my doctor about it, but Dr. Metzger, our general practitioner, had been treating me since I was four and was extremely embarrassed by the conversation. He used some Yahtzee metaphor I didn't understand, something about scoring combinations and not expecting multiple Yahtzees in the same round, and then quickly left the exam room.

Of course, my self-diagnosis that I was dead from the waist down changed when I attended Genie Howett's Pleasure Chest home sales party. Genie, who Mama had always called "fast," had taken up selling various toys and lubes at home parties for pocket money. She announced this after her husband, Duke, cut up her MasterCard.

At the time, none of us were sure whether she did it because she enjoyed the work or because she wanted to embarrass Duke into opening another account for her. Three years later she was the regional sex toy queen managing five saleswomen. But this was her first party, a sort of trial run, before she launched herself on the public. While Duke was away on a duck-hunting trip, she invited about a dozen old friends to her house for "tapas, margaritas, and sex swing demonstrations."

Mike practically lay across the driveway to keep me from going. He considered the idea of me buying a vibrator a direct insult to his manhood. He seemed to think the other women in the room would know what his "shortcomings" were based on what I bought. He'd almost talked me out of attending—heck, I was almost apologizing for wanting to go—when he said, "You're not going to go spend my money on that crap." I don't know whether it was the tone of his voice or the "my money" part that pissed me off more, but I shoved about two hundred dollars from my mad money jar into my purse and slipped out of the house.

Imagine sitting in a perfectly respectable living room full of giggling women you've known since your Tumble Tots days, drinking from obscene margarita glasses and pretending not to be looking at a hot pink catalog chock-full of things you've only seen on the internet. You're expected to maintain eye contact with a saleswoman as she uses words like "clitoral stimulation" and "nipple tingling."

"Now, if you want to know whether a toy is powerful enough for you, touch it to the tip of your nose," Genie managed to say without any irony. "It's the most sensitive nonerogenous part of the body."

Despite the fact that several women gamely pressed candy-colored small appliances to their faces, I declined. After several seconds of nose-buzzing, Genie laughed and said that putting the toy to the web between your thumb and forefinger worked just as well. Despite their margarita consumption, our embarrassed, red-nosed party compatriots were not amused at Genie's attempt at breaking the ice, so she started passing stuff around the room to appease the crowd. I was handed something called the Velvet Slide, a small, blue, curved piece of pliable plastic that, frankly, looked like something a naughty dentist might use. I blocked out Genie's explanation of where exactly I was supposed to use it as the slender body jolted to life. I glanced around, but no one was looking at me. They were fixated on hardware of their own. I pressed the flat tip to the crook of my hand and felt . . . tingly. A strange, full awareness in my special places. It was primal and powerful and—

This must be what gun nuts felt like at the firing range.

I wanted this. I wanted to take this home with me right now. The woman sitting next to me practically had to pry it out of my hands to pass it to the next woman. I leaned over to Genie and whispered. "I think I want that one."

"Good girl!" she squealed, clapping her hands like an over-caffeinated cheerleader. "Your first vibrator! I'm so proud!"

I laughed, sipping my drink as I was handed a large purple latex wand with elaborate prongs and probes coming off the sides. "Dear Lord!"

"I see we've moved on to the heavy artillery," one of the other guests marveled, her eyebrows raised.

"Is it a tuning fork?" I asked, poking a finger at the little probe on the back. I was beginning to suspect it was meant to go where nothing had ever gone before. "Why are there little Greek gods and goddesses molded on the sides?"

Ever helpful, Genie reached over and turned the dial on "high."

"What the—" I cried as the vibrator started spinning and twirling like a carnival ride.

"We call it Zeus's Thunderbolt," Genie said, winking at me. "It's one of the most powerful vibrators on the market."

"Why would anyone want a Greek-themed vibrator?"

She was caught between a grin and grimace and nodded at the offending probe. "Well, you know, the ancient Greeks were into—"

"I'm well aware of what the ancient Greeks were into!" I hissed. I passed the angry-sounding device to the next woman and surrendered to an endless parade of things I could never take home. Flavored body gels, fuzzy handcuffs, some sort of rubber ring that looked like gummy candy from hell. Mike would never want to use any of this stuff. For our first married Valentine's Day, I bought him a cute little gift basket stuffed with naughty dice, a blindfold, some chocolate body paint. He looked at the little dice inscribed with "nibble" and "nuzzle" and various body parts, then rolled his eyes and asked why we would want to bring gaming equipment into the bedroom.

Genie wrapped up the party by demonstrating how the Slip'N'Slide Vibrating Shower Glove pulsated the Luxuriant Evenings massage lotion into our hands, she explained that this was a great way to wrap up a good round of "water play." I realized I'd never even had a round of water play. Citing the possibility of slipping or throwing his back out, Mike refused my repeated advances in the shower. Come to think of it, he'd also refused to have sex in our kitchen, the hot tub in the fancy hotel suite we booked for our anniversary, the guest room in my parents' condo. The only place where he seemed interested in me was in our very own bed.

So when Genie started rubbing the lotion into my hand with the textured buzzing mitten, I burst into tears and ran out of the house. When I came home from Genie's without so much as edible panties, Mike considered this a confirmation of his skills. He smirked and snarked so much for the next few weeks that I went to Aphrodite's Palace over in Dalton just to reclaim some dignity. Scary as it was, I bought the less "intrusive" version of Zeus's Thunderbolt, a scepter-themed gold number called Cleopatra's Asp, and a pack of D batteries.

The good news was that having regular, albeit solo, orgasms made it much easier to fake them for Mike. Unfortunately, it also meant I knew what I was missing. It was a double-edged sword.

I faked it. A lot. I deserved an Oscar for the performances I put on. Meryl Streep had nothing on my ass. I didn't know if Mike bought into the theory that I suddenly, without special effort on his part, pushed through my frigidity. I think he was content not to be bothered. I gave the appearance of being satisfied and that meant he didn't have to try harder.

The thing that really chaps my ass is that now that I'd read the e-mails, I knew that Mike was at least willing to try the new and different with Beebee. On the copy machine. On the couch in the office. In cheap motels. Why could he break his precious sex rules for Beebee and not me? Because I was his wife?

Because he couldn't think of me that way? Or was I really that bad in bed? I tried to respond in ways that made me feel good, but whenever I asked Mike what he wanted me to do, he'd just say, "That's fine." It felt like I was being criticized for not knowing what I was doing, but refused adequate instruction. It was like high school algebra.

Now he had to search for his own suits. And I was alone.

What would I do now? What could I do? I had no work experience. I wasn't trained for much besides journalism. And at this point, my skills were a little rusty. Besides, newspaper editors probably preferred writing *about* me than hiring me to write for them. The idea that I might not be able to support myself was depressing and terrifying. I'd never had to worry about money before. And the idea of going to my parents to ask for help made my stomach turn. It was bad enough driving my mother's car.

I leaned back, fluttering my feet through the cool water. At least this way I could figure out what I wanted, what *could* make me happy, without worrying how it would affect everybody else in my life.

• • •

Behind me, I heard the door to my neighbor's cabin open and Wolverine stepped out. (I refused to call him Lefty, even in my head.) Beer bottle in hand, he tipped his face up to watch bright blue and green light from the fireworks splashing across the sky. It took him a few minutes to realize I was there. He nodded, not a friendly gesture, really, just acknowledgment of my presence. I nodded back, then turned my face back to the light show.

Independence. Making the choice to be alone. I only hoped it didn't make *me* into a vaguely threatening, brooding psycho.

11

Nude Neighborhood Watch

A few days later, I stood at the end of that same dock, considering my mother's cautionary tale about Natalie Wood.

I didn't usually swim after dark, or for that matter, in water not surrounded by concrete. But swimming the lake had been a tradition since we were kids. Also, it was mid-July, the humidity level was somewhere around "sauna," and I had a window air-conditioning unit from 1978.

I sighed. Screw it. I wasn't drunk. Christopher Walken was nowhere in sight. I would be fine.

I ran off the end of the dock and slid into the black water headfirst. I sliced the mirror-smooth water soundlessly, with sure strokes. I'd always been a strong swimmer. Despite the fact that Emmett was three years older, I always beat him in our races from the dock. I propelled forward, the water streaming over my skin. My body remembered the distance from the dock to the buoy that marked the boat channel. My hand stretched out and touched the familiar rusted metal. The buoy bell, our traditional victory signal, echoed off the shore.

I laughed and kicked off the buoy, stroking back toward the shore. The night was clear, sending little firebursts of reflected stars off the surface of the water. The last time I'd swum here at night was about three years before. I was still trying to improve our sex life and got Mike up to the cabin for a weekend alone. It was Indian summer and still warm. The neighbors had all abandoned their cabins for the season on Labor Day. I thought it would be romantic and spontaneous to swim under the stars.

Of course, when Mike told his friends the story later, *I* was the one who had to be persuaded to skinny-dip. *I* was the one who whined about the water being cold. *I* was the one who objected to having sex on the dock because of the possibility of splinters. I remembered walking onto the Dixons' back deck at a barbecue the next weekend and overhearing Mike bragging to his buddies, "She couldn't get enough. I had to do some fast-talking to get Lacey out there, but once I got her in the water, she was begging for it."

I practically dropped the tray of drinks in Mike's lap. I slunk back into the house until the blush drained out of my cheeks. *I* was the one who had to sweet-talk Mike out of those stupid plaid swim trunks. *I* was the one had to beg and plead for him to do anything different, but he was taking credit for it.

I gritted my teeth at the memory, at the way Mike's friends smirked at me for weeks afterward. I stripped off my suit and slung it toward the dock. "Screw you, Mike."

I could do this. I could be unpredictable and bold. I could be naked outside. I was my own woman, my own completely nude woman. I floated on my back, enjoying the way my bare breasts puckered against the soft night air. I raised my hand, blocking out the full moon. I watched the water sluice down my skin. I looked down at the contours and curves of my body, marble white against the moonlight. I'd always had an above-average figure. That was one thing Mike couldn't blame his wandering for, my letting myself go.

I wasn't big on mirror time, but Mama had instilled in me a healthy esteem for my looks and the time and attention it took to maintain them. I had slim lines, good cheekbones, and, if Gammy Muldoon's complexion was any indicator, skin that would remain soft and unlined until I was well into my seventies. I dutifully went to my stylist for a trim and an eyebrow wax every three weeks whether I thought I needed it or not. I slathered on the Oil of Olay before bedtime. The results spoke for themselves. I knew the way Mike's friends and clients looked at me. And I'd always assumed that was part of my job, to be one half of the smiling all-American blond couple. How was I supposed to know that Mike found that boring?

If I wanted to, I didn't doubt that I could find another man. Heck, I'd had several offers, also from Mike's friends and clients—even an uncle of Mike's that Wynnie considered a saint—but since I'd assumed that my "unspoken agreement" with Mike included not sleeping with other people, I declined. The question was whether I wanted another man. They were such a sackload of trouble, and really, what had I gotten for it? Psychological issues that would require years of therapy and/or vodka-related self-medication.

I backstroked and slid under the surface, swimming underwater until I reached the dock. My breath stretched my lungs, a comfortable cushion against drowning prolonged by years of yoga classes. I plunged to the bottom, remembering the game Emmett and I used to play, sitting on the bottom of the lake and trying to talk underwater, relaying secret messages. Mostly they came out as "burbleburbleburble."

I was enjoying the quiet, muted world below when a pair

of lean arms wrapped around my middle and dragged me upward. Flashing on mental images of escaped mental patients and hockey mask–wearing serial killers, I struck out blind at my attacker, kicking and flailing. He grunted behind me as I glanced my foot off of his chest, grabbing my arms to keep me from swinging back at him. I broke the surface, spluttering and curling my fingers into claws and swinging at nothing. I couldn't see! A bubble of panic rising in my chest, I sank again, fighting against the instinct to draw water into my lungs.

Terror stretched those moments into an eternity, giving me time to berate myself. How could I have been so stupid? Swimming alone at night in a secluded area? Why didn't I just send up a "naked unchaperoned woman" flare for every sex predator in the county? Hadn't I been through enough? Hadn't my dignity already been smacked all to hell? Now I was going to die in some sort of horrible John Carpenter-esque slaughter. The headlines would read "Divorcee Mistaken for Co-ed by Horny Psychopath." My father would probably skip my funeral for the annual Phi Rho Chi Horseshoe Tournament. Mike would get widower's sympathy *and* get everything I owned since I hadn't changed my will yet.

I would not allow that to happen.

Grunting, I pushed up from the squishy mud bottom with all the strength in my legs. I was not going to die this way. I would survive. I would make it to the cabin and call 911. Okay, it was highly likely I was going to die this way because I could not fight off a full-grown man in a naked underwater wrestling match. But I was going to at least put up a fight. As I rocketed up toward the surface, my head bumped against my attacker's chin. I gave in to my instinct to curse and swallowed a mouthful of water. As I broke through to air, I swung at where I thought the guy's eyes were, but I hit his forehead instead.

"Ow!" Wolverine yelled. "Stop! Stop struggling and just let me help you!"

"Help me?!" I wheezed, coughing up water as he wrapped an arm around my chest and towed me toward the dock. "You're drowning me. What is wrong with you?"

My neighbor clapped a hand on the wood stairs and anchored us there. He was not dressed for a night swim, wearing jeans and an old navy blue T-shirt. I could feel his sneakers bumping against my legs as he treaded water. "Me? What's wrong with you? What are you doing out here?"

"Swimming! Now would you mind getting your hands off me?" I said, slapping at the protective arm slung around my breasts. He winced and let go, letting me slip under the water again. I considered staying there for a moment, just to prevent the conversation that would follow. But ultimately I bobbed up and got my own grip on the staircase.

"What are you doing swimming at two a.m.?" he grunted, hauling himself out of the water. His jeans dragged low on his hips under the soggy weight of the denim. He plopped down on the dock and slicked his hair out of his face.

I stayed in the water for the sake of cover, blushing as I tried to explain. "Well, I didn't count on you jumping in fully clothed and trying to drown me."

"I wasn't trying to drown you. I was trying to stop you!"

"Stop me from what?"

"From killing yourself!" he shouted.

"I'm not trying to kill myself! I'm just . . . It was too hot to sleep." I finished lamely.

"Well, of all the stupid—" He grunted as he pushed himself to his feet. "Swimming alone at night? Do you have any idea what could have happened to you?"

"My neighbor could jump in and try to kill me?" I snarked.

"Look, I know you're going through some emotionally traumatic thing right now, but I don't have time for this shit," he snarled. "I'm not going to be the guy who swoops in and saves you from yourself. I don't want your Bundt cake or your lasagna or whatever you used to make for your husband that he never appreciated. I won't be the guy who helps you get your groove back or whatever you think I'm going to do to nurse you back to health before releasing you into the wild. I don't want to spend time with you. I don't want to get to know you better. I am not interested in you. So the next time you're feeling like doing something like this—don't. All right?"

Cursing under his breath, Mr. Monroe turned on his heel and stalked up the dock. My natural tendency when faced with this sort of open hostility—well, I don't know what that would be because I'd never faced this sort of open hostility. Nevertheless, I launched myself up the ladder and stomped after him. The limp slowed him down, which meant I was able to easily overtake him.

"Hey! *Hey!*" I yelled, slapping at the back of his shoulder. Carried by my own pissed-off momentum, I narrowly avoided crashing into him when he stopped.

"I don't know who the hell you think you are or where you got such a damn high opinion of yourself, Mr. Aloof Brooding Loner Man. But maybe you should, just for a moment, consider the fact that *I'm* not interested in *you*. I didn't come up here trolling for a rebound man. I didn't come up here looking for anything but a place to hide. I am in exile, you ass. I was humiliated by a husband who couldn't keep his dick in his pants and then I overreacted, just a little bit, in an extremely public way." Monroe's lips twitched, even if his eyes were still glaring with unexpressed urges to throttle me. "I have no interest in replacing one untrustworthy male appendage for another. In fact, if I had known there was a penis within a five-mile radius of this cabin, I wouldn't have come up here. But I did and now you're just going to have to live with it. But when you go to sleep tonight, comfort yourself in the absolute certainty that I have no interest in you, or the emotional baggage you're obviously toting around with you . . . and I'm still naked, aren't I?"

Monroe looked down and nodded, the barest hint of a smile quirking his lips.

"Shit." I muttered. I didn't have so much as a towel to cover myself with, so I did my own heel turn and stalked up to the cabin. I could only hope my ass wasn't jiggling, which really would have capped the humiliation of the evening.

"Just so we're clear, we have established that we're not interested in each other, right?" he called after me. I could hear the barely contained laughter tightening his voice.

"Oh, fuck off!" I yelled, not bothering to look back at him.

• • •

The good news was that my being angry at Monroe gave me a break from being angry at Mike. It was like my ears had been ringing for weeks and suddenly it had stopped. I showered, using well water to wash lake water out of my hair, which had never made sense to me. I shampooed in anger, which is never smart as you tend to go through about half a bottle of Paul Mitchell before you realize what you're doing. I dragged on some pajamas and pulled out my laptop bag.

I sighed, staring at the blank Word document. Samantha had asked me to come up with some thoughts on the breakdown of my marriage to Mike. She said it would help her come up with the best plan of attack for divorce court. But I sat there, mocked by the blinking cursor, and couldn't come up with anything to say. After what happened with the newsletter, I was almost afraid to write anything. Where to start? When did my marriage start to decline?

If I was honest with myself, I typed, *I would say my marriage probably started to decline before it started. About three days before we got married, I woke up in a cold sweat. I marched into my parents' room and was about to tell them I couldn't marry Mike. We weren't right for each other. I wasn't ready to get married yet. There were too many things I still wanted to do. I opened my mouth and got as far as "I can't" when I saw my father's face. Whatever I was about to say, he didn't want to hear. As usual, he only wanted to hear "happy thoughts" from his youngest child. So I bit my lip. I said, "I can't find my address book for thank-you notes. Have you seen it?" And I backed out of the room with a lead weight in my stomach.*

The morning of our wedding, I woke up and vomited. And then vomited again. And part of me hoped that I was pregnant so I would have a good reason for going through with the wedding.

It turned out to be nerves.

I wrote about the pressure I felt from our families to stay with Mike, about my own feelings of obligation to Mike after being with him for so long. I wrote about losing the job opportunity at the newspaper, the shame I felt in letting myself get talked out of working, how useless I felt staying home, and how lost I was with no expectation of how I would spend every day. I wrote about how I'd networked and entertained and worked part-time in Mike's office during tax season. And yes, how I wrote his monthly newsletter.

It felt like automatic writing, like some filter-impaired spirit had taken over my typing fingers. I wrote about the first time I realized that Mike's dad was a jackass and it was likely that Mike was going to turn out just like him. About getting conception advice from eighty-year-old Margaret Mason, a fellow church member who'd decided that "enough was enough" and it was time for us to have a baby. I wrote until my fingers hurt and the space between my shoulder blades began to ache. My eyes were grainy and tired. I felt hollowed out. Nothing. No anger, no anxiety. Just empty and tired. I'd lost track of time . . . and had written almost fifteen pages. And I hadn't even gotten to the "Mike's a cheating bastard" period of our marriage.

I ran a hand over my face and saved my document. I wasn't sure how useful it would be to Samantha, but writing it made me feel . . . lighter. It was easier to move, like my joints had been unlocked. I stood, stretched high, and yawned. I looked at the little double bed in the "master bedroom" with the old purple patchwork quilt. It actually looked inviting. I stretched across the top of the blankets, keeping carefully to my usual side of the bed, the left, before I realized that I didn't have to share. If I wanted to sleep lengthwise, I could. Experimentally, I slid my feet onto the right side, stretching in a long line, enjoying the luxury of unlimited legroom. I sighed, switched off the little bedside lamp, and wondered what I would write the next day.

• • •

I woke up to a pitch-black room. I panicked for a moment, unsure of where I was or whose bed I was in. It was still an adjustment to sleep alone, even though Mike wasn't exactly an exciting presence in the bedroom, when he was there. And it was a comfort to have his warm weight balancing the mattress. Once you get used to that, trying to sleep alone feels like you've forgotten something. You lie there and wonder whether you left the front door unlocked or the stove on and then you realize, oh, there's supposed to be another person in my bed.

I was starving. I hadn't eaten anything during the literary unburdening of my soul. I foraged in the fridge and was overwhelmed with my choices. I never ate midnight snacks. Since, as my mother-in-law put it, "Mike likes his girls thin," I was pretty careful about what I ate. And despite the fact that I loved to cook a variety of dishes, so much of my meal planning and shopping revolved around Mike's finicky palate—no spices, no fish, no nightshade vegetables. The rare exceptions were when we entertained people who, say, might like seasonings other than salt and pepper. Mike suffered through those meals, and after our guests left, groaned for the rest of the night as if I'd poisoned him.

Even now, the contents of my pantry reflected Mike's tastes. White bread, American cheese, deli-sliced roast turkey. (Because smoked turkey was too exotic.) I must have shopped on automatic pilot.

So what did I want? It was so strange not to have to take anyone else's feelings into consideration. If I felt like eating pot stickers and waffles for dinner, I could. If I felt like eating pot stickers and waffles for dinner every night for the next two weeks, I could.

So what did people eat at this hour of the morning?

I finally settled for the makings of a grilled cheese and tomato sandwich and a can of Coke. I didn't bother turning on the porch light as it would only attract mosquitoes . . . and the attention of my neighbor, who was awake and sitting at his computer near his living room window. He seemed to be smiling at the screen. The tilt of his lips, the arch of white teeth, lit up his whole face. He was relaxed, happy, an entirely different person from the ass who pulled me out of the lake. It would have been nice to spend time with—

Wait, I disliked this man, intensely. "Enjoy barelylegalfarmgirls.com, you jerk," I muttered.

He stretched his long, lean arms over his head, craning his neck toward the window. He did a double take when he saw me watching him. His relaxed expression all but evaporated and with an abrupt flick of his wrist, he shut his blinds.

Asshole.

I took an overly aggressive bite of sandwich, feeling a surge of guilt at being so tense in the face of such serenity. This place was my sanctuary. I had just as much right to be there as Monroe did. I would not let him take this from me. I forced the snark to drain from my body so I could enjoy it. The sky was perfectly clear and so close to dawn that it was starless. I could hear the water gently bumping Gammy's rowboat against the dock. Somewhere in the weeds, a bullfrog tried to drown out the crickets. Across the cove, a devoted fisherman was rowing along the shore, setting gig lines, long, floating strings of hooks that you set before dawn, hoping to return for an economy-size catch. It was so peaceful. Opening my drink seemed to make an obscene amount of noise.

I yawned. The hermit lifestyle was messing with my internal clock. I doubted that postmidnight snacks involving grilled fats and soda would do much for my waistline. If I wanted to do my trainer, the Carb Nazi, proud, I would put on my running shoes and go for a jog at daybreak. But the first thing I wanted to do was get back on my laptop and start writing about Mike's mother's ability to sense every single time we were naked and call to "see what we were up to." It was like she had a chip implanted in him somewhere.

Revived by bubbly caffeine, I worked until the sun came up, describing how I felt when Mike first hired Beebee and how all the women in town seemed to have a collective fit. I looked out the window and saw that Monroe's lights were off. Apparently he'd turned in for the morning. Maybe he was some sort of nocturnal creature, only capable of annoying me after dark.

I tapped at the keys to bring up what I'd written about the morning I'd received Beebee's flowers. I had my own neuroses to deal with. I didn't have time for his.

12

Shakespeare Territory

"Come on, loser, out of bed."

Lifting my drool-stained face from the pillow, I squinted up at my brother, who was smirking down at me and waving a pint of rocky road under my nose. I winced when Emmett pulled up the shades, flooding the room with late afternoon light.

"Go away, I was up at the butt crack of dawn," I moaned, pulling the quilt over my head. "Besides, I'm in hiding."

"Well, you're doing a lousy job, love lump," Emmett chided from the other side of the bed. I felt him nudging my ribs through the quilts. "It took me all of two guesses to get your location out of Mama."

"What was your other guess?" I asked, my voice muffled by the blankets.

"That creepy old sanitarium where we used to visit Great-Auntie Myrtle."

Emmett shook my covered shoulders. "Get up or I'll eat all this ice cream myself and you will be responsible for the resulting cellulite on my thighs."

I whipped the covers off my head as he continued to poke at me. "Oh, you don't have any cellulite, you bastard. You're the only one in the family without it."

Emmett shrank back at the sight of my horrific bedhead and pillow creases. "Gah! Quick, take the ice cream before your eyes turn me to stone."

I glared up at him. Emmett was basically a male version of me. The same dimples, our father's blue eyes, the same top-heavy, bowed lips. Our hair was a matching shade of buttery blond, which Emmett insisted he dyed to look like mine. I thought he was trying to be nice until I caught him attempting to cut a sample swatch of my hair to take to his colorist.

Emmett has boundary issues.

My brother ran The Auctionarium, a brick-and-mortar business for people who didn't know how to use eBay, Amazon, or basically any online site that sold used items. He took in weird family heirlooms, antiques, and garage sale fodder and sold them online for a handsome profit. From looking at him, you couldn't tell he was a computer geek-slash-the-world's-foremost-authority-on-carnival-glass. Unless he was crawling around in someone's basement or barn searching for valuables, he favored a sort of Cape Cod aesthetic. Lots of madras and plaid. It looked like Calvin Klein threw up in his closet.

Imagine growing up with a brother who knew how to dress better than you did. It's humiliating.

"Come on, Lace, out of bed," he said, smacking me repeatedly with a pillow. "This is starting to look like something out of *Valley of the Dolls.* And not in the fun way."

"I'm coming, but only for the ice cream." I grumbled, snatching the container from his hand and wrapping the quilt around my shoulders. Emmett, who'd always had a flair for the dramatic, took the tail end of the quilt and carried it like a royal train.

"What time is it?" I asked, using the spoon he ceremoniously presented to dig into the melty chocolate.

"Around four," Emmett said. "Why were you up at the butt crack of dawn?"

"Writing," I said. "The sad story of my life. My lawyer wants my thoughts on how exactly my marriage went to crap."

"Well, it started when you married a pompous, pretentious, prematurely old man," he snorted.

Emmett loved alliteration, but he had never liked Mike. When Mike and I started dating, I thought it was normal for Emmett to treat Mike like an annoying younger brother. And after a few years, I blamed the distance between them on Mike's latent homophobia. But now I had to admit that Emmett's "ass-hat radar" was just more acutely tuned than my own.

"Hey, where have you been, Em?" I demanded, finally awake enough to be indignant. "My life has come crashing down around my ears and you can't drag yourself home?"

"Sweetie, I'm sorry, the resort was all about relaxation and binge drinking. The staff didn't allow TVs, internet access, or newspapers . . . or Crocs. It was fantastic. I had no idea what was happening until we landed in Florida and I saw you featured on the 'news of the weird' portion of *Inside Edition*. Not your best picture, by the way."

I glared at him.

"Which is, clearly, not the point. It doesn't matter, because Emmett's here now to make it all better." He dragged me into the cabin's tiny kitchen, where he proudly displayed the contents of a festive picnic hamper—several bottles of vodka, tequila, rum, and mixers in a rainbow of fruit flavors, lemons, limes, a five-pound bag of mini Hershey bars and bulk-sized box of Hostess CupCakes.

"You know, this looks a lot like the picnic you packed for my twenty-first birthday," I said, tilting my head against his shoulder.

"Well, let's see how many colors we can get you to throw up this time," he said, patting my back.

"Will you be joining me in this neon-colored hooch fest?"

"Ugh. Even I'm not gay enough to drink that swill." Emmett winced, putting a case of Heineken in my fridge to chill. He reached into the cabinet over the sink to unearth Gammy's ancient turquoise blender. "This is the one area where I proudly reject the stereotype. But I will gladly mix up a batch of my frosty, frothy cocktails for you."

As he measured out just the right amount of ice with a flourish, he gushed, "Lace, you wouldn't believe how many people are talking about you back home. It's like you're Princess Di or Britney Spears or someone more interesting and less tragic than you."

"I honestly don't know how to take that."

"Your husband moved his secretary into your house the night you left town. That's practically Shakespeare territory," he told me.

My jaw dropped. "He moved her into our house?" I repeated.

"I was going to break it to you gently," he said. "But the kindest version I could come up with involved an obscene limerick."

I shook my head. The emotional emptiness I briefly enjoyed was replaced with a dull ache in my chest. I rubbed at it with the heel of my hand. I tried to make light of it. "Oh, screw it. Let Beebee deal with the damn earth tones."

"Well, that's good to hear," he said. "Mama said I shouldn't tell you. She was afraid you were going to freak out again and do something stupid, like shave your head or give Mike's boat a Viking funeral."

The moment the words left Emmett's lips, he cringed. It was probably because of the way I stopped in my tracks, face alight with interest at the prospect of setting Mike's boat aflame. "Oh . . . no," he murmured.

I'd almost forgotten the boat was stored just a few yards away. I turned, a sly Grinch-ish grin spreading over my face as I focused on Mike's little workshop. Short of actually setting fire to Mike, burning his would-be vessel would be the best way to get under his skin. That pile of wood represented his hopes and dreams, the best imagined version of himself. I wanted to take that from him, to make him doubt himself. And, best of all, he would never, ever be able to talk about the damn thing again.

"Lacey!" Emmett hissed. "Forget I said anything! It was just a joke! You cannot possibly be thinking of setting Mike's boat on fire."

"Technically, it is on my property," I murmured, chewing my lip. I mean, it's just an idea. I mean, a joke. I'm just joking."

"You don't sound like you're joking," Emmett objected as I walked out the back door toward the workshop. "Besides, I think you need flaming arrows and a virgin for a Viking funeral."

"I just want to see it," I told him as we approached the workshop, which was difficult with him dragging on my elbows.

Emmet's voice broke into a panicked pitch. "Look, I have a better idea. We'll break into your house, take a bunch of Mike's stuff, and I'll sell it online for pennies. We'll start a website called TakeMikesStuff.com. Or hell, we'll give it away."

Emmett waved my cell phone in my face. "Mama said your lawyer told you to call her before you made any rash decisions. Call her. Let her talk some sense into you."

I forced the workshop door open and was assaulted by dust.

You would think it would smell of sawdust or pitch, but this was the dust of dead space. A damp, mildew-spotted canvas was slung over the hull frame. I swear, my mouth just about watered at the thought of lighting that first match. I could almost smell the smoke, hear the explosion as the varnish ignited. Dialing my cell phone, I shook my head as if waking from a strangely satisfying fog. I muttered, "We could say it was an accident . . . Like I tripped and the gas just spilled out of the—"

"Samantha Shackleton." My lawyer picked up on the first ring. And from the tone of her voice, I could tell I was taking her away from valuable after-hours downtime.

"Hi, Sam, it's Lacey," I said. How exactly did one broach this subject with their attorney, I wondered. "So . . . uh, that thing they say about possession being nine-tenths of the law . . . if something's in my possession, I can't really get in trouble for damaging it, right? Because nine-tenths of it is mine anyway."

"Oh, Lord," she muttered. "Lacey, whatever you are thinking of doing, first of all, don't tell me about it. And secondly, just don't. I want you go into your bedroom, get a pillow, and punch it. It will make you feel better."

"It would just be a little fire."

"Am I going to have to declare you a danger to yourself and others?" she demanded. "Lacey, I can't represent you if you're going to do things like this. Destroying Mike's property, particularly with arson, is what we call, in legal terms, *a bad thing*, all right? It won't make you feel better in the long run and it will just make things more difficult for us. Mike could get all kinds of injunctions and damages and there's the chance you could hurt someone—"

"I was speaking in the hypothetical!" I protested.

She was silent on the other end of the line.

"Okay, it wasn't entirely hypothetical," I admitted in a small voice.

"Have you been drinking?" she asked.

"Not . . . yet."

"Are you alone?" she asked. "Is there at least one sane, sober adult with you?"

I handed Emmett the phone. "She wants to talk to you."

With Emmett occupied, I wandered toward the boat. After my Realtor related hissy fit convinced Mike that I wouldn't budge on selling the cabin, he tried to talk me into replacing the dock with a huge boathouse/workshop. His buddy, Charlie, had just added something similar to his lake house. Mike figured that if he couldn't get the cabin he wanted, he would have a brag-worthy place to house his future seaborne penis replacement. While my refusal was rooted in my attachment to Grandpa's dock, I appealed to Mike's money sense. What was the point of having a waterfront cabin without a dock? How would that affect the potential resale value?

So Mike built the workshop around the dock, grousing about the added expense the entire time. He was unhappy about the cost, but got what he wanted. I was unhappy about having a pretentious faux Cape Cod mini-building ruining my view, but I got to keep my dock. And somehow both of us felt that we'd proven our points.

While I hoped that putting the workshop near the cabin would encourage Mike to want to go there more often, the cabin's location and undesirability gave Mike yet another reason not to work on the boat. And according to Mike, it was my fault, because if we had a better lake house, he'd want to go to the lake more often, and he would be finished with the boat by now.

"No problem, Sam," Emmett was saying. "I'll keep an eye on her. I look forward to meeting you, too."

"You, eat this and think happy thoughts," Emmett said, shoving the ice cream back in my hands. "Sam says you are not to be left unsupervised for at least twelve hours or until your destructive urge passes. She said chocolate should speed that process along."

Behind us, I heard the rumble of Monroe's truck as he pulled up to his cabin. I looked out the window to see him pause and watch Emmett dragging me toward liquor and, hopefully, improved sanity. Monroe rolled his eyes and began hauling his groceries into his cabin, as Emmett, distracted by the sight of my grumpy, rumpled neighbor, gasped, "Oh, my God, who is that?" He screeched to a halt and stared after him. "I don't normally go for the scruffy, taciturn lumberjack type but—wow!"

"That's Wolverine," I said, my words garbled by a mouthful of ice cream.

He grinned at me. "What?"

"That's my neighbor, Lefty Monroe," I said as Emmett shoved me onto my couch. "Despite the hotness, he's a jerk. I think he's got an internet porn addiction, possibly online gambling. In a choice between his being oversexed or broke, I think I'm rooting for gambling."

"I can work with either," Emmett said, shrugging. "Wait, did you say 'Lefty'?"

I swatted at his hand as he attempted to dig a chocolate chunk from my ice cream carton. "Yeah."

Emmett grinned. "I wonder where he got that name. Oh, the possibilities are endless."

"I don't know, but if you start to make guesses, I will leave," I told him.

"He's just got so much potential," Emmett told me. "Lacey, I think that tall drink of water is exactly what the doctor ordered."

"For what?"

"To help you banish the memory of Mike the Moron. You know what they say, 'The best way to get over one man is to get under another one,'" Emmett said, bowing his lips into a pert moue as he poured the makings of his famous chocolate vodka milk shakes in the blender. "It's a life philosophy I wholeheartedly embrace."

"That's because you're a man-whore," I told him.

Smiling sweetly, Emmett hit the frappé button. The grinding noise of the decrepit motor covered the stream of profane insults he sent my way. I could read his lips well enough to tell he was denigrating my intelligence, wardrobe, general hygiene, and ability to color coordinate a room. I let him vent. After all, he was providing the liquor.

"Believe me when I say you deserve a piece of that cranky beefcake across the way there," he said, cutting the blender off with a metallic groan. "It will be like therapy, only without the couch. Or, use the couch. That could be a learning experience for you."

"I don't think more bad sex is the solution to my problem. Besides, he could be a serial killer for all you know," I cried. "And he's a potential serial killer who has zero interest in me. He's made that abundantly clear."

"What do you mean?"

"I mean that the other night he made it very clear that he has no interest in seeing me naked ever again."

Emmett quirked an eyebrow. "Again?"

Crap.

"There's no way I'm getting out of telling you this story, is there?" I groaned as Emmett's eyes lit up.

"No," he said. "So spill before I take away the ice cream. This could be my favorite Lacey story ever."

"I went skinny-dipping. It started off as just swimming because it was too hot to sleep and I was thinking about the races we used to have when we were kids. And then it turned into a sort of a sexual empowerment, feminine ritual thing . . . Stop looking at me that way!"

"How did you go from pleasant childhood memory to naked?" he asked.

"There was a process!" I cried, which made Emmett burst out laughing. "I was swimming—"

"Naked," he interjected.

"I was swimming," I said again, ignoring him. "And the next thing I know, Mr. Monroe has his hands on special places, dragging me out of the water. He thought I was committing suicide. And when I made it clear that I wasn't, he seemed to want to kill me! He said he has no interest in me. And then I told him to fuck off."

"You dropped the F-bomb?" he gasped. "Mama would be shocked. Appalled. Why did you tell him to fuck off?"

"Because he deserved it. Among other things, I told him I wasn't interested in him either, which I'm not. I was stomping off, ass fully in view, and he said, 'Just so we're clear, we're not interested in each other, right?' with this little smirk in his voice. He was laughing."

Emmett's smile stretched a mile wide. "No, he was flirting!"

"He was not flirting," I insisted.

"He was watching you walk away naked and he made a joke about being interested in you," Emmett squealed, clapping his hands like a soccer mom whose son had just scored his first goal. "That's flirting."

"But I was kind of horrible to him."

"Oh, straight men secretly love the idea of a woman who can kick their asses. Now, this is what you have to do. Ignore him completely. Even if you see him outside, don't acknowledge his presence. He thinks you're going to seek his attention because you're this desperate woman on the prowl. He's going to look for any sign that you're coming on to him so he can continue to mock and scorn you. It will hurt his fragile straight guy feelings when you don't. And then he will start chasing you."

"But I don't want him to chase me. I'm not saying I don't find him attractive, but I can't handle any sort of relationship right now."

"Who said anything about relationship? We just want to get you laid." Emmett pulled an alarmingly long strand of condoms from his basket of goodies. "And we want you to be safe."

"What exactly do you think I'm going to be doing?" I asked as he draped the string of prophylactics over my shoulders like a boa. "Entertaining longshoremen?"

"You could be up here for months," Emmett said.

I pulled the condoms off of my neck and counted more than two dozen little foil packets. "Well, Mama always said I needed more hobbies."

13

Even Jesus Hates Miley Cyrus

I lifted my face from the pillow and immediately regretted it. Someone had let a polka band loose in my cranium.

I groaned, rubbing my hands over my eyes to shield them from the unforgiving sunlight pouring through the window. I smacked my lips, cringing at the dry, sandpapery sensation of my tongue scraping the roof of my mouth. It tasted like a small rodent had nested there overnight. Given the cupcakes and circus-colored candy I had consumed, I suspected Mickey Mouse.

I rolled on my back, exhausted by the monumental effort that seemed to entail. Something felt wrong with my head, and not just the massive hangover. It felt too light. There wasn't enough dragging weight between my head and the pillow. I gasped, reaching up to lace my fingers through my hair and finding nothing but sheet.

Cursing spectacularly, I stumbled into the bathroom and flicked the light switch. Squinting into the mirror, I screeched, "Damn you, Emmett!"

Obviously, my brother had cut my hair at some point during the evening, which he was wont to do when his sister was smashed. I should have known better. I woke up the day after my twenty-first birthday with sassy layers. I cursed the years Emmett spent dating the head stylist of The Right Tangle Salon. It had convinced Emmett that he knew more about my follicles than I did and he had just enough skill with the scissors to be dangerous. Now, instead of long curls that settled between my shoulders, I had a short, sunny cap of blond with a fringe of bangs across my brow. I looked like a pixie, a hungover pixie, but a pixie all the same.

After plying me with an indecent amount of vodka, carbs, and fats, my brother had tucked me into bed and slunk away into the night. Emmett, ever practical, had cleaned up the mess before he left. When I woke in the morning to the sound of inhumanly loud Jet Skiers whooping their way across our little cove, the only evidence that Emmett had been there was a collection of movies that he left to keep me entertained. *The Strangers, Friday the 13th, Cabin Fever, Evil Dead, Sleepaway Camp*—all movies about people who isolate themselves at cabins and end up horribly, horribly dead. Emmett said the idea of me scaring the crap out of myself appealed to his puckish sense of humor. Emmett was a twisted little man.

There was also a reminder note on the counter that read, "The best way to get over a man is to get under another one. Love, Em. . . . P.S. Stop cursing my name. Your new hair is a huge improvement over the frumpy suburban Stepford zombie thing you had going. Embrace the pretty and move on."

I didn't have the energy to process my new 'do just yet. But I did, for some reason, feel hungry for the first time in weeks. In college, I'd learned that the only way to fix a hangover was wonton soup. Fortunately, Lockwood had a passable Chinese place called Wok'n'Go. I was pretty sure their egg rolls were from the frozen food section, but they had the best sweet and sour chicken in this end of the state. Since I hadn't eaten out in weeks, I decided to spoil myself with the chicken, a double order of pot stickers, and extra fried rice. I was looking forward to a truly gluttonous late lunch followed by a nap with a cold washcloth over my face.

When I came back to the cabin, MSG in hand, I found a girl lying in my hammock, listening to her iPod and reading a copy of David Sedaris's *When You Are Engulfed in Flames.* She had about fourteen piercings in each ear, a nose ring, jeans with more tears than material, and a black T-shirt that read "Even Jesus Hates Miley Cyrus." Her long legs were crossed over the edge of the hammock, her feet encased in purple Chuck Taylors. I'd seen wine stains that weren't as red as her hair.

Was it possible that this was some castoff girlfriend of Monroe's? She looked just antisocial enough to be his type. I wasn't sure whether to get her attention or whip out the pepper spray. This wasn't an issue as she looked over the edge of her book and grinned broadly.

"Lacey Terwilliger?" she asked, sitting up and yanking her earbuds out.

"Yes," I said, stepping back and keeping the bag of Chinese up like a shield.

She let out a breathy laugh. "Wow, I'm just so glad—I drove, like, nine hours to meet you."

She seemed nice. I hoped we could still be friends after I called the cops.

"Maya Drake," she said, tucking her card into my hand. "Internet entrepreneur and devoted fan."

"Of what?" I asked.

"Of your work," she said. "A friend of mine forwarded your e-mail to my account last week. Plus, it's on like thirty different websites, a bunch of legal blogs, women's health forums. And some woman claiming to be you is doing angry readings of the newsletter on YouTube. You are the voice of pissed off, betrayed housewives of your generation."

"Well, that's both flattering and upsetting," I told her, hitching the increasingly heavy bag against my hip. "How did you find me? Seriously, doesn't anyone respect the whole 'in hiding' concept?"

"Well, I went into town and hung out at the White Hat Café until I heard someone bring you up. It took a grand total of three minutes. When someone brought your letter up, I asked where you were staying. Everybody had a different story. You'd fled to Mexico. You were holed up at a spa getting Botox. You were on your way to Vegas to be a showgirl. But then I ran into someone who was more than forthcoming with good information. Your brother says hello, by the way."

"Resourceful and very creepy." I nodded. "Look, if this is one of those lure the unsuspecting desperate divorcée into a secluded place and kill her scenarios, I feel I should warn you that I have nothing left to lose. I will take you down with me."

Maya laughed. "I don't want to hurt you. I just want to talk to you. Um, you wouldn't happen to have a few extra egg rolls you could throw my way, could you? It's been a while since that tuna melt at the White Hat."

Mama had pounded Southern hospitality and good manners into my bones since birth. Being a gracious hostess was practically a genetic imperative, like salmon spawning or swallows flying to Capistrano. So before my better judgment could win out, I sighed, "Come on in."

Fortunately, the amount of food that was sinful for one

person was just enough for two. Although I did deeply resent sharing my egg rolls, frozen or not. Over the pot stickers, Maya explained that she'd received an e-mail with my newsletter the week before and decided she had to meet me. Maya ran a greeting card company called Season's Gratings. She provided clever, customized cards for people who were getting quickie annulments, were taking time off for a nervous breakdown, or had kids come out of the closet. You know, all of life's little surprises that Hallmark didn't quite cover.

"So you came all this way to sell me some divorce announcements?" I said as I tossed the paper plates in the garbage. "I admire your tenacity, but I think most of the people I know took the e-mail I sent out as the announcement."

Maya grinned. "I don't want to sell you cards. I want to hire you. I want you to write newsletters. Hundreds of them." She opened her laptop to show me a prototype of a website called, And One Last Thing . . .

She cleared her throat and used what was obviously her "professional voice" to give me her pitch.

"This site would allow the customer to order completely customized newsletters tailored to their unique marital situation. They fill out an online form and select a number of design options. You would take the specific information provided by the client and do what you do best, write a fantastically snarky newsletter. We distribute it to a list of e-mail addresses provided by the client, routing through their personal address. I don't think it would be hubris to say that we could retire before we even started operation. I've done some test marketing on the card site and I've already got enough preliminary orders to keep us busy for the next year."

"I think you need to leave now," I told her. "But I may call you if I need some 'I've gone into hiding because I lost my mind' cards."

Maya was clearly caught off guard by my not immediately jumping on board and thanking her for such a golden opportunity. Or that such a seemingly nice person was rudely tossing her out on her ass. "You don't think it would work?"

"No, I'm sure it would make us both temporary millionaires!" I laughed. "It's crazy. Brilliant, diabolical, inspired. But there are some serious flaws in this plan."

She shrugged. "Such as . . . ?"

"We would be sued," I cried. "There would be no way we could guarantee any of what the client said was true. And I'm already being sued for the first newsletter I wrote. If I write another, my lawyer will hurt me. She's short, but I'm pretty sure she works out."

"Which is why I had *my* lawyer draw up an ironclad release form where the client swears the information is true and takes sole responsibility. We're not disseminating the information, we're just formatting it in a pleasing manner," she said. "Plus, we would be completely anonymous. We would be ghosts."

When I sat staring at her, unmoved, she grunted. "Aren't you even curious as to how I came up with the name And One Last Thing?" she asked.

"That's really not the biggest concern for me—"

"It's from the last line of your e-mail!" she cried. " 'And one last thing, believe me when I say I will not be letting Mike get off with "irreconcilable differences" in divorce court. Mike Terwilliger will own up to being the faithless, loveless, spineless, shiftless, useless, dickless wonder he is.' It was the best part!"

I chewed my lip. "That's not a tribute I deserve. In the negative or positive sense of the word."

"Promise me that you'll at least think about it," she said. "I've e-mailed the mock-ups for the website to your address."

"How did you know my e-mail address? Wait, I don't want to know, do I?"

She shook her head. "Hey, what are you doing?"

"I'm looking for the interlocking triple sixes," I said, surveying her scalp. It seemed a fairly intimate act, poking a chopstick at the head of a woman I barely knew. But Maya was so laid-back, so open, she sort of exuded this instant closeness vibe, once you got past the piercings and hair dye. She was someone I could see myself being friends with.

It struck me that I was free to have friends like Maya now that Mike wouldn't be screening them for acceptability. Mike refused to shop at the mall anymore because he couldn't stand the thought of crossing the paths of "those weirdo Goth freaks." It would have been high entertainment to invite Maya to dinner just so I could watch Mike squirm.

The weird thing was that I didn't miss Scott or Allison or Brandi or Charlie, people who were supposedly my closest friends when I was married. I hadn't even thought to call them in my post-Beebee period, and that said something. I think Mike got them in the divorce anyway.

Maya popped the last bite of sweet and sour chicken into her mouth. "Even though I feel compelled to mention once again that this venture would be incredibly lucrative, I just want you to know that I'm not in this for the money. I had something similar happen to me."

She reached into her bag and pulled out her car keys. In a

glittery black-frame key chain, there was a photo of a smiling girl with light brown hair posing with a football-player type. Her hand rested on his broad, manly chest, a whopper of an engagement ring glinting on her finger.

"Cute couple," I commented, handing the picture back to her.

"I call it my young Republican phase," she said, regarding the picture with no small amount of disdain.

"Holy shit, that's you?" I cried, snatching it back to get a closer look. Yep, underneath the thick eyeliner and the silver studs, there was the same chin, the same twinkling green eyes.

"Why does everyone react that way?" she demanded.

I grinned. "So where is the other Future Business Leader of America now?"

"Hopefully, rotting somewhere in the seventh circle of hell," she snorted. "Brock—"

"Brock? Oh, come on, his name was *Brock*?"

"Do you want me to tell this story or not?" Maya demanded. I threw up my hands. "Once upon a time, there was a sweet, simple girl named Brooke who had dedicated her whole life to keeping her parents happy. Brooke majored in marketing, because her father wished that he had majored in marketing. Brooke joined a sorority because her mother had always wanted to pledge a sorority. She wasn't particularly interested in either of these things, but she was interested in making as little fuss as possible. Telling her parents she'd rather major in graphic arts would have caused a large fuss. When Brooke arrived in that magical land known as college, she met a handsome prince named Brock in her freshman seminar. Brooke's parents approved of Brock, which meant no fuss."

"So . . . Brooke *and* Brock? I mean, the names alone would be reason enough not to get married," I observed drily. She glared at me. "Which is entirely beside the point."

Maya cleared her throat and started again. "They had the perfect, all-American courtship followed by a perfect, all-American engagement their senior year. Little did Brooke know that her prince was following that all-American tradition of banging a prettier, better-endowed girl who had no qualms about hooking up with her roommate's fiancé."

"Your roommate?!" I exclaimed. "So instead of stealing your Hot Pockets, she stole your future spouse? That bitch."

"Oh, yeah, Joanie was my maid of honor." She shrugged. "I should have known something was up when she said she didn't care which bridesmaid dress I chose, she just wanted me to be happy."

"That was definitely the guilt talking," I agreed. "So I take it that when Princess Brooke figured out what was happening, she broke the spell and made one hell of a fuss?"

"I came back to the dorm earlier than expected from spring break to find them going at it on *my* bed. I tossed Brock's clothes out the window and made him do the walk of shame buck naked down the hall. Joanie ran after him and refused to come back to our room without a campus police escort. She was always a bit of a drama queen. And Brock just didn't get why I was upset. He told me he didn't love Joanie. It was just that he was able to do things with her he couldn't do with me."

"Because he could only think of you as his future wife?" I asked. "I think Mike had the same problem."

"No, because I refused to do those things with him," Maya said primly. "Along with the 'no fuss' principle, Mama drilled the 'men don't buy the cow' philosophy right into my brain stem. And Brock told me he respected that. Of course, he respected that because it meant I wouldn't screw around on him while he was screwing around on me. Anyway, he informed me that I had no right to be angry. That it was really a compliment to me, that my skanky roommate was the girl you snuck around with, but I was the girl you brought home to Mom, the kind of girl you marry."

"And I take it you didn't see his philandering as the romantic gesture it was intended to be?" I asked.

"No, I told him to take his grandmother's ring and choke on it," she said. "This was about three months before the wedding. I'd just had my first shower, thrown by said skanky roommate. *I* had to return all of the gifts. *I* had to take my dress to a resale shop. *I* had to cancel the four-tier cake, the caterer, the hall. And he didn't have to do any of it. He didn't have to deal with people feeling sorry for him or making the 'aww' face."

I sent her a questioning look. She tilted her head, made a sympathetic noise and crooned, "Awwww."

I winced. "Yeah, that one sucks."

"My mom sent me down to the printer's to send out cards announcing the cancellation. I was standing there at the counter, in this shop where they hadn't changed the stationery samples since 1983, and I couldn't come up with the wording. I had to be so polite about it. I had to find a nice way to put it, to make sure that neither one of us came out looking bad. The poor engraver couldn't help me. He'd never had to deal with something like that. He had this helpless look on his face and kept saying that most people just call everyone on the guest list and inform them personally. But I wasn't up to that and neither were my parents.

"They didn't want me to embarrass Brock or his family by telling people what a lowdown dirty snake he was. And I kept wondering why? Why protect him? Why sugarcoat it? So I wrote my first card. It was plain white card stock, nothing fancy. Lucida Handwriting font. On the inside, it said, 'Our wedding has been called off because Brock__________' and then it had a big blank. The next sentence was, 'If you want to fill in the blank, call Brock at 555-236-8367 or my former maid of honor at 555-236-1924.' The engraver got a big kick out of it. I think he thought I was kidding at first. And then I ordered about two hundred of them."

"How did it make you feel?" I asked. "Because when I sent out the e-mail, I mostly wanted to throw up."

"About the same," she admitted. "But I went home that night and slept like a baby. My conscience was clear and I knew that Brock couldn't say the same. His family was mortified, and once they figured out that it wasn't a joke, so was my family. My grandma wrote me out of the will."

I shrugged. "Well, I don't see you as a sterling and china girl anyway."

"Oh, I was," she said, shaking her head. "For about five minutes, it was devastating. I didn't know how to handle people being mad at me. Pre-engagement me would have done anything to keep people happy. But then, after Nana stopped crying, I felt sort of powerful. I was done being polite. Not having to worry about keeping people happy was like this huge weight being lifted from my chest. I told Nana I loved her, but I didn't care whether I ever used her silver gravy boat on my very own table. I told Mama that I was moving out and I didn't know where, and I would call her when I was ready. And I finally told Uncle Herb that if he used hugging as an excuse to touch my ass one more time, he would draw back a bloody stump where his hand used to be."

I barked out a laugh. "That's a variety of subjects in one rant. Uncle Herb was lucky you didn't turn that one into a card."

"I can't believe I've never thought of that. It could be a whole new product line," she exclaimed, taking out a notebook and scribbling while she muttered. "Creepy Uncle Cards. When you care enough to say, 'Stop touching my chest.'"

"Your ability to find the incredibly disturbing silver lining astounds me," I said drily.

"Anyway, on the very long drive to my new hometown, which I hadn't selected yet, I came up with the idea for Season's Gratings, sketched ideas for cards on truck stop napkins. I chose a new name, Maya. I figured a Maya wouldn't bother being polite. And I used the money Brock's parents had given us for a honeymoon as investment capital."

"They didn't mind?"

"I think they were just glad to have the family diamond back. There was a rumor circulating that I planned on throwing it in a garbage disposal. I don't know where they could have gotten that kind of crazy idea," she said, making an ineffectively innocent face.

"And why do you carry around a pocket-sized Brock with you?" I asked, picking up her key chain.

"To remind me of how far I've come," she said. "The girl in this picture worried way too much about what people thought. It's no way to live a life, Lace."

"What about your parents?" I asked. "Because my dad seems to think the silent treatment will make me fold like a cheap chair."

"Well, they don't have any pictures of me from the last five years in the house. And when 'Brooke' comes home for Christmas, they ask if I wouldn't mind dyeing my hair a 'natural' color. I think they have as much of a relationship as they want with me, and vice versa."

"But you're happy now, right?" I asked. "You own your own business. You're a productive member of society. You obviously have a unique fashion sense. You're not still consumed by anger-slash-bitterness, right?"

"Well, not *all* of the time," she conceded. "I still have twinges, every now and again. But for the most part, yeah, living my own life makes me very happy. You're going to be okay, Lacey, I promise."

I'm pretty sure my expression was somewhere along the lines of disbelieving, because Maya let me have the last egg roll out of pity.

"So what does the future hold for me?" I asked. I cracked open my fortune cookie and read aloud, "'Your true love could be closer than you think.'"

"Sorry, you're not my type," she said, breaking open her own cookie.

"Thanks."

"You will share an incredible moneymaking opportunity with a new friend." Maya read, grinning at me.

"It does not say that!" I laughed.

"You're right," she turned the slip of paper in my direction. "It actually says, 'Those egg rolls *were* frozen.'"

14
Olive Branches

I couldn't sleep. I read. I watched endless movies. I stared out the window into the darkness, but I couldn't close my eyes.

Three days before, Maya had departed, promising to give me a month or so to think about Season's Gratings. She gave me her e-mail address, her cell number, her business phone, and her other e-mail address, just in case I wanted to contact her. I was torn. I liked Maya. It was comforting to see that someone in my situation had emerged relatively normal. Well, functional, at least. But I didn't want to rush to a decision just because I was grasping at the beginnings of an adult friendship. Also, she wasn't subtle enough not to pressure me in "friendly" communication.

The proposal package she e-mailed to my account that night was slick and impressive. Her designs ran the gamut from elegant pinstripes and monograms to her Arsenic and Bold Face package, which featured a skull-and-crossbones motif. And her prices were not cheap. If Maya's clients wanted to effectively humiliate their significant others, it was going to cost them. And as a shareholder in Maya's venture, I could work from home and be comfortable. Of course, that was assuming the whole thing didn't blow up in our faces.

Foolishly going to bed with a bellyful of doubts and Chinese food, I had a dream that I was standing at my stove in my house in Singletree, scrambling eggs for Mike's breakfast. It was like someone had hit the great cosmic rewind button and everything was back to the way it was. Breakfast, a review of our schedules, and then adjourn until dinner. I was right back where I started, only now I knew exactly how much my life sucked. I bounced up from my pillow, drenched in sweat. Furious, I swatted the bed next to me, to assure myself that it was empty. And if it wasn't, at least Mike would get a good smack I could blame on night terrors.

So for the past three days I'd been afraid that if I slept, I would wake up and find that I'd been dreaming all this time. In some sort of weird Bobby Ewing–style regression, the last few weeks had been a prolonged hallucination and I would have to go back to living my life as it had been. I'd be left wondering if Mike really loved me and live the rest of my life following him to work and looking through his e-mail and credit-card statements.

I watched every movie in Grandma's collection, and when I'd watched *The Ghost and Mrs. Muir* for the umpteenth time, I even delved into Emmett's movie collection. I got as far as watching the trees come to life in *Evil Dead* and used the remote to turn the TV off from the other room.

As soon as I could, I was going to put a serious hurt on Emmett.

I stretched, rubbed my eyes, and went into the kitchen to grab a Coke. Outside my window, I saw Monroe's lights on.

Because I had very little to otherwise entertain me, I'd decided to follow Emmett's advice and give Monroe a downright icy shoulder. If nothing else, it seemed to confuse and disorient him. And it cut off his opportunities to be rude.

For instance, the morning after the Chinese-food nightmare, a very sleepy yours truly stumbled out onto the driveway in sweats and sneakers, ready to take on the ass-busting hills of Cove Road. Thanks to the ice cream and all those damn grilled cheese sandwiches, I was having a hard time buttoning my jeans. I was definitely missing my gym time. But the closest thing in town was . . . well, there was nothing close to a gym in Buford.

I padded out to the end of the driveway, carefully stretching, as I could not remember the last time I'd exercised. Cove Road was a barely paved two-lane winding through thick trees for miles before it reached the main highway to Buford. It was easy to imagine you were the only person on the planet. There were no houses, no traffic. Just miles and miles of silence.

Running was the only sport I'd ever been good at considering it requires no hand-eye coordination. If this were the gym, I'd set the treadmill to random and zone out to my run playlist, occasionally taking time to snicker at the guys who took weight lifting way too seriously. But I'd forgotten my iPod in my flight from Mike's house, so I didn't have the elegant techno of E. S. Posthumus to keep me company as I loosened my legs on those first small dips in the road.

I had hit my stride, my legs stretching on in front of me, long and powerful. I loved that feeling, before the fatigue sets in and you feel that intangible pull of the road in front of you. The hypnotic rhythm of my feet pounding on the pavement filled my head. There was nothing but my newly shorn hair bouncing against my head and the sun warming my cheeks. No angry future ex-spouses. No slutty secretaries sleeping in my house and, most likely, listening to my iPod.

As I rounded the bend toward the highway, my footsteps

seemed to echo. I snapped my attention away from the road in front of me and looked up. Mr. Personality was running about fifty yards ahead of me. Monroe's T-shirt was soaked dark gray between the blades of his shoulders as he huffed and puffed along the edge of the pavement. His stride had a bit of a hitch but he was making good time, considering the limp. I guess he heard me, too, because as he looked over his shoulder at me, his eyes narrowed and he seemed prepared to make some disagreeable face.

Well, screw you very much, cranky neighbor man. I increased my pace, pushing my stride even longer. Hearing me getting closer, Monroe picked up his own speed, even though it seemed to cause him some discomfort.

I was on his heels in just a few minutes. I saw his shoulders tense, as if he was anticipating actually having to socialize with someone. I let myself fall into step with him for a few beats. He watched me out of the corner of his eye, his lips pressed together. He increased his pace. I matched it. We ran full throttle until we reached the incline of one of the road's steepest hills. I grinned, for his benefit as much as mine, and pulled ahead of him.

"Your shoe's untied," I panted.

Monroe stumbled slightly as he looked down to check his laces. I heard his heavy breathing and slowing footfall behind me. I streaked ahead. As I climbed the hill, I called "Made you look!" over my shoulder. Actually, it was more along the lines of, "Made" (huff, puff) "You" (wheeze) "Look!"

If I wasn't mistaken, I heard a wry chuckle behind me as I reached the crest.

Since then, I'd enjoyed myself thoroughly by pretending he didn't exist. Was it immature and more than a little petty? Yes. But it also annoyed him, so ultimately it was a wash.

At the moment, Monroe was hunched over his laptop, scrubbing his hands through his hair and looking vaguely Christopher Lloyd–ish. And he seemed to be talking to himself . . . or the computer.

Coke can in hand, I grabbed a sweater from the couch and padded barefoot to the dock—all the while muttering to myself, "I am not afraid of evil trees. I am not afraid of evil trees." While fifty years of use had left the dock a little rickety, it had also worn the planks down to satiny softness. Gammy Muldoon taught me to bait a hook on this dock, refusing to take me fishing before I could. Of course, Gammy's version of fishing was one of us grandkids rowing her rusty old rowboat while she drank daiquiris out of a thermos and threw cork floaters in the water.

In an entire childhood of fishing, I think I caught a grand total of three fish.

But the point of fishing was our talks. Gammy would tell me about the adventures she had before she got married, sneaking away to Memphis for weekends with her high school friends, serving as a nude model for art class at her college, singing in a piano bar under the name Georgia Lutece. There was an episode involving her dating identical twins from a military school up the road, but given Mama's expression when I repeated it, I don't think that I was supposed to know about it. When Gammy died, her will dictated that her whole family gather at the dock, drink daiquiris, and tell funny stories about her. It was my job to row her ashes out to the middle of the lake and "scatter her at sea." So much of the part of my life when I knew myself, when my life made sense, was spent sitting right there, watching the water swell.

So even if I didn't still have my husband, at least I kept the dock. It was nice to feel that continuity and connection as I floated unfettered on a sea of shit.

"Floating unfettered on a sea of shit?" a voice behind me mused. "That's good. Mind if I use that?"

I turned to find Monroe standing behind me with two beers.

"That was out loud? Damn it," I groused. "Look, I promise I'm not going naked swimming or boating or waterskiing or anything that will in any way place myself in danger, so you don't have to worry about jumping in and 'accidentally' feeling me up in the course of saving me."

"I just came by to apologize," he said.

I did not expect that, which was evidenced by my spluttering, "I-I'm sorry?"

He grinned, even white teeth glinting at me full force now. "No, I'm supposed to say that."

I resisted the magnetic pull of those teeth, the wide-set hazel eyes. This was obviously a trick, meant to lull me into complacency so he could mock me again. "I thought we were each going to pretend the other didn't exist. It's been working out so well."

He grimaced. "I'm sorry about that. I've been rude. I just—You have no idea how many times I've had to escape from an apartment in the dead of night because a newly divorced person has moved in next door."

I groused, "We're not diseased, you know. It's not contagious."

"No, but the drama is," he said. "I've been threatened by angry ex-husbands just for living within a mile of their exes. One woman told her kids that I was going to be their new daddy—before they even finished unpacking their stuff. But the worst is when they decide to make you their replacement husband."

At my confused expression, Monroe's voice rose to a flirty

soprano. "I just don't know anything about garbage disposals and I was hoping you could come over and take a look at it. In return, I would be willing to cook you a nice candlelit dinner." He groaned, his voice returning to normal. "Next thing I know, I've got some woman breaking into my apartment with a baseball bat to tell me that if I don't appreciate her sorting my sock drawers for me, she'll go find someone who will."

I giggled, tried to stop, and ended up giggling more. I hadn't laughed like this since, well, a long time before the Beebee revelation. It felt so good, like I was using muscles I hadn't stretched in months.

"It's not that funny!" he rumbled, drinking his beer.

"How many times has this happened?" I asked.

"Four!" Monroe exploded. "One of them was sixty! She kept mixing me up with her husband and calling me Herbert."

"So that certainly explains why your entire face shut down when I said the words 'newly separated,'" I said, wiping at my eyes. "And why you've been, well, sort of a prick."

"I shouldn't have reacted that way. And I shouldn't have yelled at you the other night. I just saw you in the water and thought it was some bizarre nude Ophelia thing. And I thought, 'Oh, God, it's starting again.'"

I sniffed, giving my eyes one last swipe. "But you still jumped in after me. So you do have a little bit of a rescuer's complex."

"I debated it for a few seconds," he admitted.

"Well, that's because you hate people."

Monroe seemed offended. "I don't hate people."

"Well, you do a remarkable impression. Okay, so you're not a misanthrope. Then why the seclusion? Why live up here in the middle of nowhere? I mean, I'm up here because I'm not fit for interaction with normal people. What's your story?"

"I live up here because it's quiet, the rent is cheap, and I like the view."

I waited a beat to let him say more, and when he didn't, I said, "That is disappointing. I had this whole ex-con, porn addict, possible serial killer persona built up for you." At his aghast expression, I added, "I have a vivid imagination."

"I thought maybe if I was rude enough, I could just destroy any romantic chances you thought there might be between us. And then you'd move out and leave me alone in peace."

"You really do think a lot of yourself, don't you?" I said, shaking my head at him.

He leveled his gaze at me. "Four times, Lacey."

"You really thought you could chase me off just by being rude? What was your backup plan? Rattling chains in my attic and making me think the cabin was haunted?"

He shrugged. "I thought about something like that, but infestations of flies are too hard to round up at the last minute. Plus, there's no outside access to your attic."

"I'm going to choose to believe you're just joking and that you didn't actually check," I told him. "So what has changed your mind about me not being a total pariah?"

Monroe took this as an invitation and sat next to me, easing his feet into the water. "Well, beyond the nude swimming, you seem pretty normal. You've had visitors and they haven't commanded me to take care of you, threatened me to stay away from you, or otherwise approached me. And you don't seem to want anything to do with me."

"So because I don't want anything to do with you . . . that makes you want to get to know me?"

"Basically."

"You are contrary."

"Yep," he said, grinning. He pointed to my head. "You have something different going on up here."

I retorted, "You don't know the half of it."

"No, your hair."

I ran a hand through it. "Yeah, my brother got me drunk and cut it. It's sort of a thing with him."

Monroe pursed his lips. "Interesting. Did that girl with all the cranial accessories catch up to you?"

"You saw Maya?"

"She was hard to miss," he said, gesturing to where Maya's piercings were. "She came to my place first and I told her where to find you."

"Okay, new rule—when strangers with face piercings come looking for me, don't tell them where I live," I said as I accepted the beer. I laughed, took a sip, and winced. "You know, there's a reason I only drink booze with fruit in the title. I'm not good at the casual beer drinking."

"Would it help if I chanted *chug chug chug*?"

"So you're trying to peer pressure me? Haven't you heard? Emotionally vulnerable divorcées are easy pickins, we don't need drunkenness as an excuse. We throw ourselves at every available man to prove we're still sexually relevant."

He took a moment, I prefer to think, to make the blood go back to the appropriate places. "Okay, I deserved that one."

"And, please, the moon glittering on the water, gentle waves lapping against the shore, cold beer, clever innuendos. This is a terrible seduction scenario." I paused to take another drink and then added, "Amateur."

He sighed. "I'd really like to sidestep all the weird tension stuff and just be two people who happen to live near each other. You seem like a nice person and it takes up too much energy to try to ignore you. You're unignorable."

"Fine. I agree I will not break into your house and bake for you without permission," I swore, holding up my hand. "If you will promise not to make suicidal gesture your first guess if you see me do something weird. Maybe suicidal gesture could be your second or third guess."

He reached out and shook my hand. "Agreed."

15

You Don't Choose a Nickname, a Nickname Chooses You

It turned out that Monroe was a very pleasant neighbor when he wasn't convinced I was out to seduce him against his will.

We still kept our distance. Monroe generally stayed inside, working at his computer, unless there was some pressing reason for him to come out. I was careful not to be the reason he had to come out. But now, instead of glaring at each other from across the yard, we smiled and waved. Monroe wasn't pressured into socializing, which made him happy. And I was getting fewer dirty looks, which made me happy.

And apparently there were heretofore unknown advantages to Mike being so anal-retentive about money. It had taken him and his lawyer very little time to turn over his financial statements.

Samantha called to say she would be "coming by" to discuss Mike's financial disclosures. She made it sound like it wasn't a big deal to drive fifty miles of back roads to visit a client, but I was paying for her time . . . and mileage. Hmm. I think she wanted to check out my living arrangements and make sure I wasn't writing "Die, Mike, Die" on the walls.

It felt sort of weird to see her in my natural habitat, because my natural habitat involved me wearing sweatpants, but no makeup, at 3:00 p.m. I was sitting on the porch, reading over my "how my marriage died" statement, when I heard her car pull up.

My big bad divorce attorney had her hair drawn up into a ponytail, her jacket slung over her arm, and was hefting an oversized picnic hamper along with her briefcase. Her sleeveless silk blouse was rumpled and wrinkled. She looked about twelve years old. Her voice was stretched very thin as she said, "Hi."

"Long day?" I asked, offering her a glass of iced tea, which she downed in a few gulps.

She flopped into the wicker chair across from me. "Do you know what it's like to spend six hours with two grown adults fighting over custody of Star Wars action figures?"

I shook my head, pouring her another glass. "No, I honestly do not."

"Well, count your blessings."

"One by one," I agreed as she took a manila file out of her briefcase.

"Did you know Mike organizes your credit card statements by year, month, card, and the color of the card?"

Sadly, I didn't know that, because I never looked at the statements.

She handed me the folder, which seemed sort of scant. "The bad news is that we didn't find anything illegal or even slightly shady. As advertised, Mike is as dull as a box of mud, but clean as a whistle. The good news is that you don't have any joint debts that you weren't aware of. He hasn't bought a house in another state or mortgaged the one you have without telling you. The interesting news is that you own both of the Hardee's franchises in town and the Baskin-Robbins. They are turning a handsome profit, by the way."

"And to think I've been paying for my frozen yogurt all these years," I muttered.

"The iffy news is that there are no suspicious charges on your personal credit cards. No jewelry receipts, no out-of-town restaurants, no hotels. But his lawyer, Bill Bodine, is giving me grief about handing over the cards for the accounting firm, so I'm thinking that's what he used."

"You're probably right," I told her. "He went on a golf weekend in Destin with some friends a few months back. There should be a charge on one of our personal cards for that. And in February he went to a bachelor party for a college friend. There should be a charge for the restaurant in Nashville, plus a hotel stay. I don't see anything here. And you're right, it makes sense that he might consider money spent wooing a staff member a business expense."

"Nice," she chuckled. "Just give me a little time. It shouldn't take too much persuasion to get those statements."

"Why?"

"Because otherwise, we will reproduce every e-mail Mike ever sent Beebee, blow them up to poster size, and review them in open court. Where Mike's mother will see them."

I narrowed my eyes at her. "So we're using the I'm-telling-your-mom! strategy in court?"

She nodded solemnly. "I didn't go to a fancy law school for nothing."

"So I finished my version of events." I said, handing her one hundred and twenty typed pages. "My characterization is not at all balanced. I come out looking naïve, but brave."

Samantha snickered. "Wow. You had a lot to get off your chest."

"Yep. And I skimped on my 'vengeance' period."

She read over the front page and grinned. "Well, keep going. If nothing else, it's good therapy. And it's evidence of your frame of mind. Oh, yeah, any idea why a Maya Drake has been calling me, begging me to 'give you the encouragement you need' but refusing to tell me what that means?"

"Because she's resourceful and incredibly creepy," I told her. "She wants me to go into business with her . . . in a way that would not make you happy."

"You should stop there, so I have plausible deniability," she said, holding up her hand in a Diana Ross–ish gesture.

"Agreed."

Samantha lifted the picnic hamper with a grunt. "Also, this is from your mother."

"My mama sent me a care package through my divorce attorney. I'm going to have to hand you my grown-up card when you leave." I opened the hamper to find carefully wrapped parcels of fudge, banana bread, cookies, divinity, hummingbird cake, molasses cookies, and a cheesecake. "Apparently Mama wants me to emerge from this divorce weighing four hundred pounds. Want some fudge?"

"No, but I'll take a brownie," she said. I tossed her a Saran-wrapped lump of chocolate-frosted future cellulite. "Don't worry, my mother expresses emotions exclusively through carbs. It's why I was the only freshman on my floor to drop fifteen pounds as soon as I moved away from home."

"So how goes the lawsuit?" I asked.

"Well, through some fairly impressive legal maneuvering, if

you don't mind my saying so, the lawsuit has been postponed until we're finished with the divorce case," she said.

"You subpoenaed her thigh, didn't you?" I asked, grinning, feeling suddenly superior in my legal knowledge.

"No, but I convinced a judge that it would be a waste of the court's valuable time to pursue a libel lawsuit if we could prove in the course of the divorce case that Mike did, in fact, have an affair with Beebee. The judge prefers fishing to presiding over the court, so it wasn't a hard sell."

"Using a man's laziness against him; that is impressive," I admitted.

"It's a gift," she said. "Now we just have to *find* the documentation proving Mike had an affair with Beebee, but that's nothing to worry about. So how is life in exile? Do you need anything?"

I shook my head. "I'm doing pretty well. I'm enjoying the writing. I'm learning to appreciate slasher films. My neighbor doesn't seem to hate me anymore. Apparently, the way to get a man to stop sneering at you is to follow a gay man's advice."

She chewed thoughtfully. "There's background here that I am unaware of, isn't there?"

• • •

It was 3:00 a.m. and I was just nodding off when the storm struck. I started awake as thunder rumbled right overhead. The cabin was dark. The clock face was blank and the air conditioner was stonily silent. I jumped as another bolt of lightning shook my walls. My heart hammered in my chest. Still bleary, I crawled out of bed and checked the backyard.

It was normal for a sudden squall to kick up over the lake in late summer, though that didn't make it any less startling to be jolted awake by atmospheric conditions. When I was a kid, Gammy would take advantage of the spooky atmosphere by lighting candles and telling me ghost stories. Ghost stories that would scare me so much I forgot how badly the storm scared me.

Clearly, this was where Emmett got his dark streak.

I stumbled to the window. The glass was so distorted by raindrops that the world outside looked like a dark, impressionist painting. Sheets of rain were falling over the lake. Windblown tree branches batted violently against each other. I was caught between conflicting emotions: the rising anxiety in my chest and the strange urge to go outside and feel the wind and the rain on my face. Where the old Lacey would have gone running for candles and a weather radio, some perverse little pocket of my post-Beebee soul was fascinated by the potential for destruction. The storm was a living thing, angry and hungry, rippling with unrestrained power.

Opening the door a crack, I saw that my dock had come unmoored. The ancient wood was pitching and rolling in the storm-tossed waters. I slipped into a pair of sneakers. I doubted I could save the dock, but the rowboat was tied to it, bobbing frantically. I didn't want to lose it. A lot of memories were tied up in that boat.

I figured I had only a small window of opportunity to go after the boat before the black waves swallowed it whole. I stewed for a few seconds as my rational brain tried to send "Are you insane?!" messages to control my limbs. But I overcame common sense and self-preservation, throwing on a jacket as I dashed out into the rain.

My tennis shoes squishing and slipping in the mud, I skidded down the hill toward the water. I squealed, falling on my butt with an undignified splat at the water's edge, my feet sliding into the mud and slime. Groaning, I pushed up with my hands and sprinted down the dock. It felt like some sort of *American Gladiators* challenge, the wood bobbing and bucking under my feet with every step, soaking my feet to the ankles. My shoes were so slick, I almost went flying off the end of the dock when I tried to stop. Lightning split the sky just across the shore, striking a tree.

"Great," I muttered, barely able to hear my voice over the roar of the storm. "Water, metal boat, lightning. Nothing can go wrong here."

My soaking wet clothes plastered to my skin, I struggled to unravel the wet rope from the docking post. The boat clanged against the dock under the force of the waves, adding another layer of noise to the already deafening storm. It was taking on water, making it that much heavier to drag along the side of the dock toward shore. The wet nylon cut into my hands as I struggled to pull it. My shoes slipped out from under me and I had already prepared for the plunge into the icy, black water, when those now familiar hands caught my shoulders and stopped my skid.

"What the hell are you doing running around in this!" Monroe yelled. "Are you crazy?"

"I think I've made that abundantly clear!" I shouted. He laughed, shook the soaking wet hair out of his face like a shaggy dog, and took the rope from my hand. With him pulling the rope and me pushing the bow, we managed to drag the boat to the shore and pulled it far up out of the water.

"Thanks! Sorry for putting your life in danger, again!" I cried, making a break for the house.

"Come on over," he yelled. "I've still got power."

Sure at first that I'd heard him wrong, I hesitated. But he pulled on my arm until I followed him to his well-lit cabin. He even held the door open for me, so I had to assume he had actually invited me in. Monroe shrugged out of his jacket and shook the water out of his thick black hair like a dog. "Wanna beer?"

"Please. I don't think I've ever seen a thunderstorm get this bad up here. Hey, why is it that I lost electricity and you didn't?" I asked, sliding out of my sodden shoes and jacket. My jeans were soaked, but I was not going to ask him to borrow a pair, because a beer and an implicit offer not to hate each other does not a pants-borrowing relationship make. "Totally unfair; you're a renter for God's sake."

"I've got a backup generator," he said. "The McGees warned me about the thunderstorms."

"Oh, sure, bring logic and forethought into it," I grumbled.

"It's clean, I swear," he called, tossing me a towel from the bathroom. I made an "uhff" sound when it hit me in the face. He grimaced. "Sorry."

"Don't worry. I've got bad reflexes. And a beer would be great, thanks," I said, studying what he'd done with the McGee place. Not a lot. The furnishings were the same, clean and old and worn. I'm pretty sure the blue rag rug in front of the fireplace was older than me. But there were new bookshelves lined with several editions of every title by a crime writer named F. Monroe, plus a smattering of Carl Hiaasen, Edgar Allan Poe, and Mickey Spillane. On the walls, there were a couple of posters touting upcoming releases of *Dead as Disco* and *Drunk Tank Duets*, both by F. B. Monroe. Editorial memos from an S. Taylor of Fingerprint Publishing were neatly stacked next to his laptop.

"Either you are F. B. Monroe or you're doing a damn fine job of stalking F. B. Monroe," I called.

I heard Monroe grunt in response. I'd read Monroe's first book, *Cross Creek*, years before. He'd been touted as the emerging author of 2002, penning the tale of two teenage boys fleeing a foster home to hitchhike cross-country and find their wayward parents. It was heartbreaking and haunting, and passages still came floating back to me on occasion years later. Unfortunately, I bought it from the superdiscount table of my local bookstore, because despite a massive marketing push by his publisher, the book failed miserably.

It felt like there were tumblers in my head, falling into place. It was bizarre trying to reconcile my mercurial neighbor with the gentle storytelling I'd enjoyed. I felt like I'd been inside Monroe's head, that I'd invaded his privacy somehow . . . beyond what I was doing at the moment by inspecting the contents of his desk and walls.

From what I'd read, it took Monroe two years to write anything else and then, when his next novel was finally picked up by a publisher, he refused to do any press for it because he didn't want to talk about *Cross Creek*'s gigantic failure. He refused to have his picture on the dust jackets, even when his quirky, absurdist crime stories became huge hits. It was as if he was rejecting the public before they could reject him again. Or he was just a hermit who hated attention. Now that I'd met him, I realized either option was plausible.

Wandering along the edge of the room, I studied the pictures of the people I assumed were Monroe's family, smiling dark-haired brothers with their arms slung around a grinning Monroe. It was strange to see him with short hair and under-control sideburns. He looked . . . happy, which was kind of off-putting.

There was a framed picture with a bunch of guys in police uniforms posing with a uniformed Monroe. And in another shot, the same cops seemed to be mooning the camera in a hospital room. Stacked in a pile on one of the bookshelves, I found a half-dozen awards and plaques honoring a Sgt. Francis Bernard Monroe of the Louisville Police Department with special service awards.

"Your real name is Francis Bernard?" I asked as he handed me a beer. "I would want to be called Lefty, too."

"I didn't exactly want it," he grumbled, taking a plaque out of my hand and putting it back on the shelf. "But you can't stop cops from giving you a nickname when you get shot in the ass stopping a liquor store robbery. I got off better than my buddy, Uniball, though. I got home that night and I am grateful for it."

My jaw dropped. "You got shot in the ass?"

Well, that explained the limp. And now I was thinking about his butt again.

"Left cheek." He nodded, taking a long pull of his beer. When I laughed, he got indignant. "You know, some people have died from being shot in the ass."

"Well, I can't call you Lefty, especially not now that I know how you got the name. Can't I just call you Francis?"

"Nobody calls me Francis," he growled, flopping on his couch.

"Wolverine?" I suggested.

"Huh?"

"Never mind, I'm just going to stick with calling you Monroe," I told him, carefully sitting so my wet jeans didn't rub against his upholstery. We were sitting in opposite corners, as far from each other as humanly possible. It was like a first date, only he'd already seen me naked, which served as an incredible ice breaker. There was no way I could be further embarrassed after that.

"I read your first book," I said.

"So you're the one," he snorted.

"Tragic coming-of-age tales are a hard sell these days." I shrugged. "But I liked it. I've never spent time with a homeless teenage boy before, but somehow I feel like I've known one. Besides, you can't be too bitter; you seem to be doing really well with your sardonic crime stuff."

"People love inept criminals."

"It's more than that, Mr. False Modesty," I teased. "The *New York Times* called you a softer Elmore Leonard. It says so, right on that poster."

He made a face, but I could tell he was pleased that I'd noticed. "I hate that quote. It's irritating as all hell. Just because I don't write about drag queens getting dismembered with a hatchet doesn't mean I'm soft."

"I said soft*er*."

"So I take it you're adequately impressed?"

"Oh, no, I haven't read anything you've written since *Cross Creek*," I assured him.

"Well, thank you for your support," he muttered.

"It's just that the crime books seem so macho, I guess," I said. "I thought about buying *Karma Collects*. But then I saw the cover and didn't know if I would like it."

"I knew it!" he cried. "I knew the puddle of blood shaped like a peace sign was too much. I told my editor I didn't like it, but, no, he said it fit the market."

"Sorry," I told him. "Loan me a copy and I'll read it, I promise."

He grumbled. "Now you're just humoring me."

"A little bit," I admitted. I grinned at him. He smiled back. Monroe wasn't really such a bad guy when you got to know him. He was actually very funny and helpful and . . . Gah! No penis policy. I had to remember the no penis policy. I would think of something else. The ocean? Too subliminal. Wombats? Well, that's just weird. Johnny Depp? No, that won't help matters. Um, Leslie Nielsen . . . He's not exactly my type. He was in, uh, *Tammy and the Bachelor, Prom Night. The Naked Gun: From the Files of Police Squad!* Naked Monroe. Damn it!

Monroe was waving his hand in front of my face, trying to snap me out of my trance. "Not used to being up this late, huh?"

"Here, lately, I've had to get used to it. Why are you up at three a.m.?" I countered.

"Because I have a rare genius that works best when I'm the only person on the planet who's awake. Your being awake is obviously what's throwing me off. So what's your excuse?"

"Oh, that's easy—I'm insane," I said. "Every time I close my eyes, I'm afraid I'll fall asleep."

"That tends to happen when you close your eyes . . . in bed . . . at night."

"Yeah, but if I fall asleep, I'll dream," I told him. "And if I dream, I'll dream that I'm stuck in an unfulfilling, endless hamster wheel of a life with financial stability and security, but no love life to speak of, bad sex, and an inability to trust men not to screw me over."

Monroe absorbed that with the stunned expression of a fish that had been dynamited out of the water. "Wow."

I laughed, running my hand over my face. "I've ruined your life. You had time to yourself, quiet. I wrecked your whole Fortress of Solitude thing."

"Oh, now you did it, there's nothing as sexy as a woman

who knows her Superman." He grinned. "I liked the solitude, don't get me wrong. It was easier to work when it was just me. I didn't have to worry about being sociable or answering questions. I didn't get distracted by bottomless ladies parading around on the front porch. But it's kind of nice to know there's someone more screwed up than me right outside my door."

"Well, you're not wrong about that," I said primly. "But I didn't parade. I never parade."

"And you're not crazy," he said. "Your whole life's been turned upside down. And you've isolated yourself by coming up here. And you're just processing all this information. I went through the same thing after I got shot."

"In the ass?" I just liked throwing that out there as much as possible.

He glared at me. "After I got shot, in the ass," he conceded. "The administration couldn't clear me for street duty anymore. I was still walking around, but I couldn't sit in the car for long periods, couldn't pass the physical fitness exam. I was looking at early retirement or a permanent desk job. So I picked retirement, holed up in my apartment, and stared at the walls for days at a time. I didn't eat. I didn't sleep. I almost ordered something off a Tony Robbins infomercial, for God's sake. That was the low point. Eventually I got out my special doughnut pillow, turned on my computer and started writing."

"So you think I should order something from Tony Robbins?" There seemed to be a pregnant pause in there somewhere. "You think I should write a book?"

"You have a strong voice," he said. I arched my brow. "I read your e-mail on The Smoking Gun."

"Of course you did."

"You just need to find the right idea and run with it," he said.

"Just so you know, writing your first novel can also drive you crazy."

"So you're saying . . ."

"If I see you typing, 'All work and no play makes Lacey a dull girl' over and over again, I'm running like hell."

I snickered and sipped my beer. Writing a book was an idea I'd toyed with off and on for years, but I'd figured everybody *thought* they had the next *Harry Potter* bouncing around in their heads. I never got past the first few pages of any story. There was always some committee meeting, a fund-raiser, something else that needed to be done. Okay, those were excuses. I just didn't want to finish them and become another failed, frustrated novelist. But at this point I was already a failed, frustrated housewife, so what the heck?

I nodded. "That seems fair. So tell me something about yourself. Something not glib."

"I'm not glib."

"If glib were a country, you would be its king," I informed him.

He seemed to search through his massive memory bank of secrets. "Okay, I was engaged once."

When I made my own stunned face, he asked, "You don't think a woman would want to marry me?"

"No, once you stop cursing and scowling at a gal, I'm sure she's putty in your hands. So what happened, did she hook up with Uniball behind your back?"

His voice was flat, serious as he said, "No, she's dead."

I gasped. "Oh, my God, I'm so sorry."

He let me stew in my own embarrassment before bursting out laughing. "I'm just kidding, Lacey."

"Asshole!" I yelled, slapping his arm.

"I'm sorry, you're just so gullible," he said, dodging the pummeling that rained down from my fists of fury.

"Yeah, it's a character flaw."

"Sarah was, is, a really nice girl. She was an emergency room nurse. We used to take a lot of crazies, drunk and disorderlies, to her hospital. I finally worked up the nerve to ask her out and that was it. There was nobody else for me. We were together for five years. We were about six months from the wedding when I got shot . . . and she just shut down. She thought she could cope with it. She was used to seeing people in crazy situations, seeing people hurt. But seeing me in her hospital, laid up with a bullet wound to the ass, was more than she could handle. The idea of waiting up each night, wondering if I was coming home, freaked her out."

"She hadn't thought of this in the course of five years?"

"Some people need to be smacked in the face with reality before the possibility even occurs to them," he said, shrugging. "Had you thought Mike was capable of boffing the receptionist?"

"Point taken." I shook my head. "But let's not bring my ex into this. If we're going to refer to him, let's give him a code name like Satan or He Who Should Not Be Named. So, she gave you back the ring?"

He nodded. "And we parted as friends."

"Oh, come on," I whined. "She broke your heart, say something that lets me hate her a little bit."

"She was half Canadian," he offered. "She was a smoker. She had never seen a single episode of *Saturday Night Live*."

"You suck at this," I told him.

"Well, pardon me for being able to let go of my hatred and bitterness."

"I don't hate my ex," I protested. "I just want him alone, broke, bald, impotent, toothless, fat, and wailing and twitching in a twisted tiny ball of spastic misery."

He shuddered. "Wow, that was visual."

"You seem fine now," I conceded. "Somewhat socially maladjusted, but fine."

He smiled cheekily. "'I spent so many nights thinking how she did me wrong. But I grew strong. I'll learn how to get along.'"

"Fine. Make fun of me. In case you're wondering, this is why people don't like you."

"I'm not making fun," he insisted, though he couldn't cover his impulse to snicker. "But do you see how that damn song gets into your head?"

16

Creative Differences

Nothing cements friendship like beer and eggs.

I ended up staying at Monroe's until the morning. The storm wasn't letting up. Monroe couldn't sleep either. We sat on his screened-in back porch and listened to it rain while we ate scrambled eggs and some of Mama's banana bread. We talked about our hometowns and our families, how Monroe got published, and why exactly I was willing to risk my neck for a rowboat that predated the Carter administration.

I learned that other than naming him Francis, Monroe came from a nice, normal family. He had two brothers, both of whom were doctors. He had loving parents, also doctors, who proudly purchased a police scanner when Monroe was hired by the Louisville department. And now his father walked around the hospital with a copy of Monroe's latest book under his arm, just waiting for someone to ask him about it.

I found out that Monroe's first crime novel, a story about a neo-hippie whose dark past catches up with him in the form of poisoned patchouli oil, stemmed from a writing exercise he did based on "the story you like to tell at parties." He was a newly graduated patrolman called to Mall St. Matthews on a disturbance call involving a man named Raintree Feldman who had chosen to "meditate against the war" in the middle of a city fountain.

"Well, that's not a capital offense, is it?"

"He preferred to meditate naked. Well, there was some liberally applied body paint. And some sort of yoga diaper thing."

I grimaced. "I hope they drained and bleached the fountain."

"That'll teach you to interrupt."

While I shuddered, Monroe told me that Mr. Feldman didn't appreciate being cited for trespassing, public indecency, and disturbing the peace. The whole time Monroe was filling out the citations, Mr. Feldman railed about how Monroe's karma would be ruined from that point on, that anything bad that happened to Monroe would be traced back to his persecution of Mr. Feldman.

"Over and over and over, karma karma karma," Monroe said, buttering a toasted slab of banana bread and handing it to me before making one for him. "He actually filed a complaint against me with the local branch of the ACLU."

"That would be a rather sad ending to that story, but I can tell by the twinkle in your eye that there is more," I said solemnly, spearing fluffy scrambled eggs on my fork. I'd never had beer with breakfast before, but I have to say it was a nice complement to the fried potatoes. At this point, a little alcohol was the only thing that was going to help me sleep when I went home.

"Well, let's just say Mr. Feldman kept right on protesting around our fair hamlet. His next meditation exercise took place in the elephant enclosure at the zoo. He didn't think it was right that the recent addition to the elephant family was born into captivity when baby Raja deserved to be running free with all the other little elephants. Turns out mama elephants get downright cranky when strangers get too close to their babies."

"Well, they do carry them for two years . . ."

"Mr. Feldman found himself on the wrong end of pachyderm maternal rage. The business end, you might say."

I groaned. "The elephant sat on him?"

He nodded. "The vegan animal rights activist was smothered by elephant ass cheeks. If that's not ironically bad karma, I don't know what is."

I was very glad I'd swallowed my banana toast because I would have choked on it when I busted out laughing. Monroe looked very pleased with himself. "And from all that, you got a book about an annoying eco-warrior who buys the farm in the middle of a corrupt natural foods store?"

"I thought the elephant story was a bit too grim. Didn't exactly paint the elephant in the best light. I killed Feldman's character in many horrible ways before I settled on patchouli poisoning," he said. "In my first draft, he choked on bulk-priced mung beans."

"Ouch." I scrunched my nose. The flickering of my porch light caught my attention. I watched as the lights of my cabin surged back to life. "Oh! I have power!"

"And you seem awfully excited about it," Monroe said drily.

"It takes several small appliances to keep me looking this good," I told him as I gathered the empty plates from the table. "I'm not going to lie; there's a belt sander involved."

"You don't have to do that," he said. I looked down at the dirty dishware. My cheeks flushed. I'd cleared the table without even thinking about it.

"You're going to do the dishes?" I asked.

Monroe chuckled, taking the plates from me. "Yeah, you're a guest. Didn't your mother teach you that guests don't do the dishes?"

"Yes, but she also taught me that you don't swim naked, alone, at night, less than thirty minutes after eating. Obviously, I'm a slow learner," I said as I carried dirty cutlery to the kitchen.

I couldn't remember the last time someone washed a dish for me. In fact, when I left town for an aunt's funeral, I came back after four days to find Mike had left me a full sink. Somehow, the idea of Monroe up to his elbows in suds was even nicer than the whole wet shirt thing.

Dang it. I really did have crush-y feelings for him. That was a problem.

"Well, thanks for breakfast. Without your kindness, I'd probably still be swimming in the lake, trying to drag my boat to shore. Or possibly just eating cold cereal. The banana bread's all yours, by the way."

"Any chance of you making more of that, even if it requires you hitting me in the face with another door?"

"I didn't make the banana bread. My mother would have to hit you in the face in order for you to get more."

"I'm willing to consider it," he said, chewing his plump bottom lip in consideration. "This was good. I think my social skills needed some airing out. My agent says she can tell when I've been alone too long, I start responding to her e-mails within five minutes. Did you maybe want to do it again sometime?"

"Mmm, let's not start making plans, or developing routines, just yet," I said, in an exaggerated aloof tone. "I'd hate to wake up one morning to find that you'd had to move in the middle of the night."

Monroe grimaced. "So, uh, how long will you be holding that against me?"

"For a while," I admitted as we walked to the door. "Thanks for breakfast."

"Yeah," he said, shaking his head. As I carefully negotiated Monroe's wet steps, he called out, "I meant what I said, Lacey. Start writing. It doesn't matter what you write or whether it's any good on your first try. Just start writing."

And since I was already awake and my laptop had a full charge, I did just that. After throwing my stiff, air-dried clothes into the washer and changing into some PJs, I fired up my computer and stared at the screen expectantly.

Nothing.

The problem was I didn't have any idea what I wanted to write now that I'd finished my divorce book report. I'd had daydreams, but most of them centered on Christian Bale in the Batman suit or revenge fantasies involving putting Mike's precious golf clubs in one of those machines that cubes cars.

Something that Monroe said came back to me. He'd killed Mr. Feldman in many horrible ways before choosing how to kill his character in *Karma Collects.* I didn't have any ideas for a book, but I did have several ideas for horrible fates I wished on Mike. I could kill him over and over again . . . in a totally hypothetical, nonbinding, legal manner. Of course, I would destroy said document so it wouldn't be used against me in court should anything happen to Mike. But not before I found the most painful, humiliating way to bump him off.

"Let's start with death by syphilis . . ." I said, opening a Word document and typing: *Mike stumbled into his tiny, mildew-ridden bathroom, clutching at the elastic of his worn boxers. He gasped at his reflection, carefully prodding the itchy pulsating sores that had sprouted from his lips while he was sleeping . . .*

Repeatedly killing Mike on the page was incredibly therapeutic. I hit him with a gas tanker truck while smoking. I let him fall into an abandoned septic tank and drown. And I wrote about him being crushed by a falling pallet of Tampax while wandering through a Sam's Club. It was like writing a prolonged Mr. Bill sketch.

I read back over the "Mike gets blinded by rabid squirrels" scenario and giggled until I had tears running down my face. I sighed, "I must be very tired."

I rested my head against my arms, sure that I should just turn off the computer and go to sleep. While cruelly ironic and cathartic, none of these little exercises really got at the root of why I was so pissed at my soon-to-be ex-husband.

Mike had replaced me. Moved another woman into my territory and expected me to just take it with that quiet dignity I used to cover up when I was really pissed off. He'd moved another woman into our home and hadn't expected me to make a fuss over it. Beebee was sleeping in my bed, using my shower, applying her makeup at my vanity table. I thought maybe I could have handled it if he'd given me some warning, some choice. If he'd come to me and said, "I want someone else," I would have been hurt, but I would have eventually accepted it. But feeling disposable, like an afterthought, was too cruel. And when I struck back, I was the bad guy. I was the one who humiliated Mike. I went too far. If I was smart, I would have found a way to hurt him by proxy.

And suddenly, the right words sprang to mind. I sat up, my eyes open and my mind cleared. I opened a new document and typed:

Greg had always loved the house, with its vaulted ceilings, the sun nook, the gently sloping staircase that led to the second floor. He'd fought tooth and nail for it in the divorce. So it made a certain poetic sense when the house opened up and swallowed him.

I stopped, read the words on the screen, and ran with it.

Laurie had been packing all night after Greg served her papers at work. Somehow, he'd managed to convince the judge that she was dangerous, a threat to his safety, and should be removed from their marital home. Laurie had, in Greg's words, "twenty-four hours to get your shit and leave." Of course, the real reason he wanted her gone was that his girlfriend, Patricia's, lease was up at the end of the week, and he wanted her to move in.

Laurie tore through the house, gathering clothes, pictures, books, anything she could get her hands on, and tossing them into garbage bags. Greg dogged every step she took, snatching things he'd decided were "marital property" out of her hands and generally being a pain in the ass. If he'd shown this much effort around the house when they were married . . . well, he wouldn't have had so much time to devote to banging the manicurist he was moving into their home.

Laurie snarled at him when he took back a little china bulldog that had been a wedding present from her grandmother. "Stop it, Greg. Just go into another room. I'll be done in a minute and then I'll be out of your way.*"*

Greg sneered. "I don't want you running off with anything you're not entitled to in the settlement."

"You hate this stuff!" she yelled, waving at the little glass knickknacks, the dust-catchers and special touches she'd added to their bedroom over the years. "You used to spend hours bitching about what I paid for it and now you're going to take a damn throw-pillow inventory?"

He followed her out onto the landing, stepping around and stopping at the top of the stairs to keep her in her place. "Because it was my job that paid for everything. Your measly little salary wouldn't keep the heat on in this place. I worked for everything here. It all belongs to me. You're not walking away with anything that's mine."

"Well, I hope you and your things and your whore are very happy here," she shot back, screaming, "Now get out of my way!"

Greg's eyes widened in alarm as some unseen force shoved his shoulders, sending him reeling off the top of the stairs. The staircase seemed to flex, tossing him through the air. He flopped, boneless, as he thudded against the wall opposite the staircase. Laurie blinked furiously as the steps rippled back into place, sure she was imagining the old varnished wood moving as sinuously as snake scales.

"Greg!" she shouted. His shoulders were stuck to the wall, holding him on his feet like a fly caught in a web, even as his body sagged. He shook his head, dazed.

"What the hell did you do, you crazy bitch?" he demanded as she scrambled toward him.

"Nothing!"

"Help me up," he growled, pushing against the wall.

"You are up," she retorted, grabbing his hands. He wouldn't budge away from the wall. Laurie pulled harder.

"Stop kidding around, Greg."

"I'm not. I can't move." His voice was getting fainter, higher. His back looked . . . wrong. The drywall behind him wasn't cracked, but somehow the fall had pushed him inside of it. He'd been absorbed into the wall, Laurie thought, staring at him, a particularly rotten piece of fruit suspended in a Jell-O mold.

She had to bite her lip to keep down a hysterical giggle. There was always room for Jell-O.

"I think I should call an ambulance," she said, backing away.

"No, don't let go of me," he pleaded. "Laurie, I—"

"Just hold on, okay?" Laurie ran into the next room, hoping maybe she could shove him back through the wall from the other side. But there was nothing to push. There was no damage on the other side of the wall.

From the hall, there was a dull, cracking sound, stalks of celery snapping. She heard Greg scream. She scrambled back to the hall to find him doubled over and sucked back into the wall, his face folded against his shins. She yelped and fell back against the stairs.

"Help me," he wheezed, his lips wet with blood. "Laurie, help me!"

She reached out to take the arm stretched so unnaturally over his head, and then hesitated. She tilted her head and asked, "Why?"

Comprehension skittered across Greg's features. "You fucking bitch!" he screamed and was pulled farther in. His head twisted at an odd angle and the rage drained from his blue eyes. There was a series of crunching noises, like chewing, that twisted her stomach. She winced and squeezed her eyes shut. The hungry snapping stopped.

Laurie opened her eyes. And saw nothing. There was no damage to the wall. No blood. No trace of anything that had just happened. She fell back against the steps and convinced herself for half a second that she'd imagined the whole thing. That she was going crazy . . .

And for the next few hours, I just wrote. I didn't know whether it was a dark fantasy or an extended plea for counseling. I just knew I liked it. Of course, I could have been completely nuts.

Given that I'd just made a house eat a thinly disguised version of my husband, I was going with nuts.

They say you should write what you know. And at the moment, I knew what it was like to have your whole life turned upside-down by a man who couldn't control his urges. Some strange part of me wanted to share that with people, to show them how it felt—the dizzying tumble of humiliation and hurt, the soul-sucking effort it takes to pick yourself up and keep going. Maybe a woman who had been through the same thing would read what I'd written and feel some sort of justice had been done.

Sam's notes for my divorce case could have translated very easily into a hyperbolic comedy. But something made me want to stick with this new dark direction. It felt a little hypocritical, considering I couldn't sit through most of the horror movies Emmett had given me. But divorce was a scary thing. And losing control, losing your options, those were elements in any horror story. This was what I knew.

There would be no shocking first-chapter revelation for my poor protagonist. Well aware of her husband's "extracurricular activities," Laurie had chosen to ignore the affairs, to hold her head up and pretend she was fine. She couldn't bring herself to admit she married the wrong man. The fact that he was cheating wasn't nearly as shocking as the fact that Greg expected Laurie to step aside. She'd been trapped, by pride, by embarrassment, by mortgage payments she wouldn't be able to make without Greg's income. But when she was replaced, kicked out of her home, her home fought back.

I wondered if it would be too much of a stretch to make the house eat Greg's girlfriend, too.

17

Wax Wings and the Pun Police

Grizzled, greasy, and smelling permanently of Skoal chewing tobacco, Hap Borchard took care of all manner of odd jobs for Buford locals and the long-established summer people. A jack-of-all-trades/master-of-Budweiser, Hap was honest to a fault, but tended to get distracted by his own long, winding stories or shiny objects if you didn't keep him on task . . . which was why I was in my sweats, wrestling fifty-year-old waterlogged dock wreckage to Hap's flatbed.

Unfortunately, my yard was still soaked from the deluge, so I was ankle deep in mud, trying to drag heavy timbers uphill. I can't say I was thrilled when I heard Monroe's voice as I slipped in the muck and fell on my butt.

"So many 'dirty' joke opportunities here," he said, shaking his head and stretching his hand out.

"I am not above throwing a fistful of this at you," I told him as he pulled me to my feet.

"Why do you think I'm helping you instead of going for my camera?" Monroe asked, taking the wet, damaged timber and tossing it onto Hap's flatbed.

Without being asked, Monroe just started working. He was

not afraid of getting his hands dirty, or his shirt, his jeans . . . We were both pretty filthy by the time Mr. Borchard finished collecting bits and pieces of the dock from the shoreline. He seemed thrilled at the prospect of meeting Monroe, because here was a person who had not yet heard his story about catching a fourteen-pound large-mouth bass on his grandson's Snoopy reel.

"Mr. Borchard, this is my neighbor, um, Mr. Monroe," I said as Monroe shook Mr. Borchard's hand. "Mr. Borchard helped my grandfather build this dock when he was eight years old."

"Her granddaddy paid my brother and me a quarter a day, plus lunch. Hector blew his on Bazooka and comic books, but I saved up all summer."

Monroe grinned. "What did you buy?"

Hap looked insulted. "I didn't buy anything. Saved it all, probably still have it in a coffee can somewhere."

"Mr. Borchard doesn't trust banks," I told Monroe, who nodded in sage agreement.

"Sad to see this old thing go," Hap said, swiping his forehead with an old red bandanna he kept in his back pocket. "Back then, we didn't know to put foam floaters underneath, so the dock would just float up if the water rose. It's been swamped so many times over the years, the water flushed it right off the bottom during the storm.

"Miz Lacey, have you given any thought to replacing it?" Hap asked. "Doesn't make any sense to have a house on the lake and no dock."

"Why don't you put an estimate together for me and we'll talk about it," I said.

Sensing a sustained job to keep him busy through the fall, Hap offered to put the estimate together that very minute. I gave him a legal pad and a glass of iced tea and he settled into the porch swing to start scribbling.

"Shouldn't you be up there with him?" Monroe asked when I found a reason to help him round up bits and pieces of wood.

"No, if I stay up there, he'll start telling a story about a fish he caught in 1972 and six hours from now I'll have no estimate and a profound death wish. I've been through this before, the summer we had to replace the window screens. I learned more about gig lines that I ever thought possible."

"Well, surely that knowledge will come in handy someday."

"Kind of doubt it," I told him. "I appreciate the help, by the way. It was mighty neighborly of you."

"Well, when I see an attractive woman doing solo mud wrestling, I've got to get a closer look," he said as he rubbed drying mud from my jaw. The warmth from his fingers seeped into my skin and it was all I could do not to lean into the caress like a cat. "The good news is you'd probably pay fifty bucks for this at a spa."

"Gross," I groaned, wiping at the itchy patch of skin to cover the shiver that wracked my spine.

"No, wait, I'll do the other side," Monroe said, holding his own grimy hands up as if he was going to swipe them across my face.

I laughed, backing away carefully as he advanced. "Stay away from me, you lunatic, or I'll injure your good butt cheek."

"Oh, come on, it's all-natural," Monroe said, lumbering toward me like Frankenstein's facialist. He caught me around the waist as I struggled to keep my face away from his muddy hands.

"No! Police brutality! No!" I squealed, laughing my head off as my upper body slid out of his grasp and toward the mud. I scooped up a handful just before Monroe righted me on my feet. I cocked my hand behind my head. "You will pay, Monroe!"

"You wouldn't; you're too nice a girl." He grinned as he held my arms at bay. My face was dangerously close to his, the scrape of beard stubble just grazing the tip of my nose. We stopped laughing, our heads cradled together. I was fixated on the white curve of his smile, the warm flow of breath on my cheek. He tilted his mouth toward mine and—

Behind us, I heard someone clear his throat. I looked up to see my brother smirking down at us. I glared at him. Chagrined, Monroe let go of me but managed to wipe his hands on my back. I snickered and smacked at him.

"So you must be Lacey's neighbor," Emmett said, barely able to contain his grin.

"Monroe," he said, reaching out to shake Emmett's hand but drawing it back for a wave when he saw how dirty it was.

"I was so worried about you up here all alone with that thunderstorm," Emmett told me. "But obviously you've had plenty to keep you occupied."

"This is my incredibly ill-mannered brother. Don't worry, he's adopted." I assured Monroe. "Emmett, Monroe was helping me clear away the dock. It sank. And you're just in time not to help us, so I'd suggest you zip it."

"Oh, honey, I wasn't worried enough to actually lift something," Emmett said, shuddering. "So, Monroe, tell me all about yourself. What have you been doing with our little Lacey? She looks so relaxed . . ." Emmett sighed.

"Leave now," I told a bemused Monroe. "Make your escape while you still can."

"I guess I'll go clean up. Let me know if you need help

getting Mr. Borchard off your porch," he told me. "It was nice to meet you—"

"Run, man, run!" I hissed. Monroe took one last opportunity to pat me on the back, leaving muddy handprints. He nodded to Emmett and then sauntered off.

"I don't want to hear it," I told my brother when Monroe was out of earshot.

"Hmmm." Emmett said, linking his arm through mine as we made our way back up to the house. "It seems we aren't as committed to the convent life as we thought."

"Shut it," I told him.

"I like him," Emmett said. "Anyone who laughs at our jokes has my blessing to bone my sister."

"Nice."

"And he made eye contact with me, which is more than I can say for Mike," Emmett said drily.

When we reached the porch, Hap handed me one sheet of paper estimating that it would take what could only be called a "crapload" of money to replace my dock.

Ouch.

"And I took the liberty of drawing up a list of things that you could stand to do around here, Miz Lacey, especially if you plan on staying up here this winter. Your storm windows and insulator need replacing. Your roof needs new shingles in a few places. It might take me a little bit, but I can finish up before the cold sets in."

As long as Hap wasn't allowed to talk to anyone, I conceded, that was probably true.

"Well, you just let me know," Hap said as I handed him an envelope full of cash for the dock removal. Hap didn't like to leave a paper trail.

"You're not really thinking of staying up here year-round, are you?" Emmett asked as we went inside.

I shrugged. "I don't know."

"It's because of Monroe, isn't it?" Emmett gasped as I poured us iced tea. "I knew it! You've been tearing up the sheets with Wolverine!"

"Okay, that's it, you're going to pun jail," I told him. "No, I'm not sleeping with Monroe. We're just friends."

Emmett's lips twitched. "Friends who wrassle in the mud and make out?"

"We were not making out!" I insisted. "We were just—"

"Face snuggling?" he suggested brightly.

I groused, "Shut it."

"So if it's not Monroe keeping you, why would you even think about wintering up here?" Emmett asked.

"It's just that it seems to be working out pretty well. It's cheap. It's quiet. I don't have to deal with Mike or anybody else."

"Oh, honey, I don't think people care about you anymore," Emmett said. "Some woman in Texas locked her cheating husband in a dog kennel and posted pictures of it on the internet. By contrast, you're downright conservative. They haven't made fun of you on the radio in weeks."

"On the radio?" I repeated. "When did that start?"

Emmett ignored me. "The citizens of our fair hamlet have had more to chew on than your sorry tale as Beebee is stepping on some toes. The humiliations have been public and spectacular. Beebee has become the talk of the town . . . again . . . for completely different reasons. She's like the slutty secretarial Icarus. She's flying so high that she can't see how far she can fall. Beebee has lost all of her sense. Ruby Huddleston overheard her telling everybody down at Sassy Nails that since you didn't work, she wasn't going to work. She is now a full-time, stay-at-home hussy."

"What exactly does that entail?"

He grinned. "Oh, shopping for trashy lingerie, going to the gym, scrapbooking the milestones of her adulterous relationship, getting permanent liner tattooed on her eyelids, networking lunches with other hussies. She's spending money like water, redecorating the house like something out of a magazine . . . that magazine being *Weekly World News.* It's nothing but hunting prints in the living room and tropical fish in the bathroom. It's a collection of the world's worst decorating themes all in one house."

"I know I shouldn't be enjoying this, considering that she's pretty much destroying my former home," I admitted. "But I am."

"And from what I hear, Beebee's not ascending to the social heights she'd anticipated," he said. "She's been wait-listed by the Junior League. And they haven't wait-listed an applicant since 1975. Remember Maude Littleton? She tried to pass off Knox Gelatine recipes as her own in the church bazaar cookbook and it marked her for years. Anyway, Beebee has been semiblackballed there. Mike can't add her onto his membership at the country club as long as he's still legally married to you. Beebee has been grudgingly accepted into the Ladies Auxiliary, but not selected for any of the important committees. She's been stuck on the solicitation committee for the spring carnival. The lowest of positions in the Auxiliary's hierarchy," Emmett added with a bitchy snicker.

"All because of me?" I asked.

Emmett burst out laughing.

"What?!" I cried as he rolled on the couch. "Okay, so I'm overestimating my importance to my friends and neighbors."

"It's self-preservation," he assured me. "The women of Singletree realize that introducing Beebee into their circles and more important, to their husbands, puts them all at risk. Even if Beebee doesn't make plays for their husbands, seeing Mike and Beebee together might give their husbands the idea that they could trade their wives in for newer models. Beebee is like a social pathogen, contagious, virulent, and surgically enhanced.

"Wynnie blames you for this debacle, of course, to anyone who will listen," Emmett said. "And that's becoming fewer and fewer people. She keeps saying you should be ashamed of yourself for 'running off' on Mike and abandoning him. I don't think she's even embarrassed by the e-mail any more. She's just pissed at you for losing Mike to someone so much worse than you."

"Wow. Thank you so much."

"People *are* asking about you," Emmett said, looking contrite. "And not with that condescending, smirky look in their eyes. You could be welcomed back into the fold before you know it."

"Oh, screw the fold," I muttered.

"Why are we talking about this boring stuff?" Emmett asked. "I want to hear more about your friendship with Monroe. If you didn't notice, Lacey, the word 'friendship' was in quotation marks."

"There's nothing to tell," I said.

Emmett patted me on the head. "Well, let's just go ahead and declare you dead from the waist down, huh, peaches?"

• • •

After helping me buff the remains of my muddy adventures from my face, Emmett made himself scarce. I think he wanted to hit the road before further manual labor became necessary. To be honest, I was more than happy to see him leave as I was suddenly bursting with ideas on the aftermath of Greg's bloody disappearance. And I wanted to make some notes on what would happen when Greg's girlfriend reported him missing and the cops questioned Laurie.

I was just starting a new chapter when Monroe came back to make sure that Mr. Borchard had left. Then he told me I was welcome to come over for dinner as he was smoking sausage.

"Either that was the world's most bizarre come-on, or you feel far too comfortable around me," I said, squinting at him.

He flushed slightly, protesting, "No, seriously, I have kielbasa."

"I'm sure you— I'm sorry, this is just too easy. And weird."

"I agree," he said, giving a small shudder. "I don't know whether to feel aroused or harassed."

"You're the one who brought up phallic meat products. If anyone should be creeped out by the boundary-crossing flirtation, it's me," I told him.

"When I flirt with you, you'll know it," he muttered.

There was an unusually long conversational pause.

"Awkward," I commented.

He nodded. "I've never had a girlfriend before. I don't know if this is okay. I mean I've had a girlfriend, obviously. But I've never had a girl who was my friend— Oh, for God's sake, I sound like I'm in sixth grade." He scrubbed his hand over his face. "Please, help me get out of this conversation gracefully."

"There is no graceful way out of this. This is the conversational Thunderdome." I shook my head sadly. "Look, I need to finish up a few thoughts. And then I would be happy to come over for dinner. I'll even bring a cake that doesn't involve you getting smacked in the face. I will leave the inappropriate sausage innuendos at home."

"I would appreciate that." He nodded toward my computer. "So how's the writing coming along?"

"I am channeling my angst into a chapter in which Laurie's husband appears as a gory apparition while she's in the tub," I said. "Sure, she gets to keep the house, but seeing her broken, bloody husband skulking around the place is going to suck the fun out of it."

"I must admit, I'm thinking of putting you on a strictly Nicholas Sparks diet. I don't think I've been a good influence on you, violence-wise."

I smirked. "It's therapeutic."

"Just remember my theory on gore: 'less is more.' The only field where 'more is more' applies is porn."

"I'll try to keep that in mind," I promised.

He peered over my shoulder at the screen. "Are you ever going to let me see it?"

I snapped my laptop shut. "It will take more than kielbasa for that to happen."

He grimaced. "And now it's awkward again."

When Monroe left, I couldn't help but wonder at the weirdness that was our friendship. Female friendship was a precious thing I had been lacking for quite some time. And besides my relationship with Emmett, I had never had anything resembling camaraderie with a man. If this experience had taught me anything (besides pay more attention to your husband's e-mail account) it was that I needed more friends, of either gender.

If I was able to choose my own friends, and I was pretty sure

I could now, would I choose someone like Maya? Strong-willed, independent, slightly off center. Or would I choose someone like Sam? Someone smart, successful, and poised? Or could I be friends with both women? If the chips were down, I think I'd want both of them in my corner. Sam seemed like the type that carried bail-ready cash around with her. But how exactly did a grown woman ask someone to be her friend? Was there an exchange of woven bracelets involved?

And Monroe. I had never been more confused by my feelings for one person. There was no doubt that I was attracted to him physically. I kept expecting those mad adolescent crush feelings to fade as we spent more time together, but with every conversation, I just looked forward to seeing him again that much more. It wasn't love. It was a meaningful friendship with someone who happened to be ridiculously good-looking.

It was really going to suck when I moved on to whatever my next step was and moved away. Or we had sex and *he* had to move because it was disastrous and it would just be too weird for him to stay at the lake.

I was pondering those cheerful thoughts when my cell phone rang. The caller ID showed it was Maya. I chuckled as I hit OK. This was going to be interesting.

"Hey, I was just thinking about you. And not in a weird way."

"Hey Lace," she said, her voice bright and clear over thrumming guitar riffs in the background. "I want you to go to your door in four . . . three . . . two. . . . one. *Now.*"

Curious, I got up and found a FedEx truck pulling into the driveway outside my door.

"How do you do that?" I asked as the deliveryman climbed out of the truck with a large purple shipping box.

"GPS tracking systems," she said cheerfully. "I've been

monitoring the delivery progress. I wanted to hear your reaction when you opened your present."

"You are a frighteningly clever girl," I told her as I signed for the package. "And you really don't have to send me presents."

"Well, I can't lure you to the dark side without bait," she said. I opened the box to find a gift basket inside, topped with a lurid purple bow.

"The First Wives Club. Enough. Sliding Doors." I read the covers of the DVDs nestled inside. "And a mix CD entitled *Music for Angry Chicks."*

I sifted through the bottom of the basket, which was lined with typed statements from women from all over the country. Texas, Mississippi, Washington, Delaware. "What's this on the bottom?"

"You might call them case studies," Maya said. "These are some of the clients who have expressed interest in newsletters from And One Last Thing. . . . I thought you might like to read some of their stories. You've got husbands who left their wives for their receptionists, babysitters, dry cleaners, golfing buddies. One woman's husband slept with her identical twin. He tried to tell her he didn't know it was cheating."

"So you lure me in with girl power movies and then you sucker punch me with women crying out for vengeance?"

"I don't like to think of it as sucker punching," Maya said. "I prefer to think of it as setting a mood."

"You're the devil," I told her as I skimmed over some of the statements. Maya's clients were from all walks of life, all over the country. The one thing they had in common was an unfaithful husband and an overwhelming need to get their dignity back. They could suffer the loss of love, the life they thought they had, the luxuries of a two-income household, if they could just hold their heads up when they went to the Walmart. And they seemed to think they could get that back if I helped them. The problem was helping them meant repeating one of the more reckless things I've ever done and directly disobeying my attorney, whose patience I did not want to test.

"Just read over them and get back to me," Maya told me. "And enjoy the movies. I've been where you are right now. You're hitting that two-month lonely stage when you start to question what you did. Your friends' sympathy is starting to wane, because they've never been through something like this and they think you should be over it by now. So you're up all night, alone, watching bad television. I thought I might help remedy that. And the CD is mostly Pink, post-divorce."

"Actually, I'm doing okay," I told her. "I'm not really that lonely."

"Have you met someone?" she moaned. "Damn it."

"And why would that be a bad thing?"

"Because if you're all dewy with the first blush of new love, you're not going to want to help wronged women get revenge," she griped. "You're in the middle of nowhere. How could you possibly meet someone there . . . Oh, wait, the hunky neighbor. The plot thickens."

"Yeah, he remembers you, too," I commented drily. "And I'm not dewy with anything. I just made a friend."

"Well, every time you start to feel all giddy with hormones, I want you to read another one of these letters and remember what it feels like to have the rug pulled out from under you by a man."

"I'll try," I promised.

"Are you still at least considering my proposal?" she asked.

"Yes," I said. "I am. I've just been sidetracked by another

project. I'll try to give you a decision as soon as possible. And thanks for the movies. I'll e-mail you."

"And listen to the angry music!" Maya called as I started to hang up. "We've got to stick together on this, Lacey. I'm sending you more movies. And some books. And some—"

I pushed END and batted packing peanuts out of the way as I examined my new movies. "Strange girl. Brilliant, but strange."

18

Workshopping Without Anesthesia

It took me a few days to work up the nerve to show Monroe what I'd written. And then I took it right back. Several times.

"I changed my mind," I said, snatching the papers out of his hand before his eyes could focus on the page.

"Okay, if you keep doing that, I will not be able to read it. Also, I will get a headache. And then I will be annoyed."

"All right, fine." I shoved the stack of pages at him.

He glared up at me. "You're going to take it away again, aren't you?"

"Just one more time," I promised, but as I grabbed for it, he pulled his hand out of my reach. I gasped as he pulled away the title page and settled into his chair. "You're going to read it now?"

"Yes."

When I reached for the paper again, he gave my hand a light smack. I bit my lip. "You're right. I needed that."

He flashed a grin at me. "Now, the question is, are you going to sit here while I read it. Or do you want me to wait until you're home?"

"Which would you recommend?"

"Here, let's make it even," he said, handing me a manuscript called *Two-Seven-Zero*. "You show me yours, I'll show you mine."

"But—" Without looking up from my opening page, Monroe pointed to a chair by the fireplace and pressed a finger to his lips. Slightly disgruntled, I sat and flipped past Monroe's title page. I looked over the edge of the paper and watched his face. I dreaded hearing what he thought, but desperately wanted to know. What if the newsletter was a rage-fueled fluke?

Monroe was distressingly straight-faced and silent as he read. Seriously, he couldn't twitch or something?

Without looking up, he called, "Read, Lacey. Read and breathe."

I cracked the manuscript and got lost in the story of a patrolman who gets sent to a routine burglary and meets a seemingly normal woman who then pulls the full-on Glenn Close routine. The numeric title was based on the police code for dealing with a crazy person.

I was so wrapped up in Monroe's description of the stalker showing up at the cop's house with a caterer to discuss the couple's upcoming wedding that I'd almost forgotten that Monroe was reading my stuff. No, wait, there was the paralyzing anxiety again. A few minutes later Monroe announced that he was finished. I resisted the urge to bolt out of the front door.

"This is my professional hat," he said, pointing at his head. "Nothing I'm about to say is personal. This is just one man's opinion—"

"Quit stalling and get on with it," I told him.

"Obviously, you're going to go through a couple of drafts, but I think it has potential. You have a strong voice, a good ear for dialogue, and there were some truly horrible, disturbing images in there."

"I am going to take that as a compliment. There's a 'but' coming, isn't there?"

He nodded. "Is there going to be any sex?"

"Well, I'm writing about a woman who's in the middle of a divorce. She's not really going to want to date."

"She couldn't have a rebound boyfriend or a one-night stand? Hell, you could have a flashback of the better times in her marriage. You don't have to go explicit, but the readers will appreciate a little sex to go with their drywall-based violence."

"I don't even know if I'm going to be able to write a sex scene. It just makes me nervous, knowing that someone else would be reading it."

"Well, get the hell over it," he told me.

"Nice."

His tone softened a bit when he saw me blush. "Sorry. You asked for my opinion and here's my advice. Just sit down and write a sex scene. Even if it's a bad sex scene, just get it out of your system so you don't get blocked. You can go back and rewrite it. Come on, woman, you're a husband-humiliating, ass-baring Valkyrie! You can't be scared of a little sex. Where's your passion? Where's your fire?"

"Oh, well that's easy. I don't have either of those things."

"Do you have seizures?" he asked, nonplussed. "Do you drool? Experience uncontrollable arm spasms? What?"

"Oh, sweet Irene, this is just mortifying," I groaned.

"Oh, come on," he said. "I told you about getting shot in the ass; how much worse could it be?"

"That happened to you once," I said. "This is a lifelong problem. I just don't do well when it comes to sex with other people. I don't have orgasms, okay? I know I can, it's not an anatomical problem. It takes me a while to warm up and then by the time I get . . . enthusiastic, it's over. It's like I can't catch up in time."

Monroe chuckled and when I didn't smile in return, he blanched. "You're not kidding."

"Sadly, no."

"And let me guess who told you that's your fault," he muttered.

"I can provide you with a reference," I told him.

"No, I think I know who your source is. And I don't buy it. A frigid woman does not skinny-dip. A frigid woman would not have chased after me, naked, to tell me to fuck off."

"You're not going to forget that anytime soon, are you?"

"Not likely," he said, without pausing. "And when He Who Should Not Be Named hinted that you were no good in the sack, what did you do?"

My lips twitched. "I bought a vibrator." When Monroe barked out a surprised laugh, I added, "It has five speeds."

"And I'll bet you've used them all," he said.

I nodded. "Yes, I have."

"Frigid, my ass," he said, handing me my pages. "Now I want you to go home and write about sex. It's like X-rated homework. Write sex scenes until you're not embarrassed about it anymore. Be graphic, be dirty, and it won't be scary anymore, I promise."

"You will never see them, but okay," I said, heading toward the door. I stopped and turned back to him. "I don't want to have sex with you."

The color drained out of Monroe's face before he threw his head back and laughed. "That was really . . . straightforward. I haven't even kissed you yet."

"It's not funny," I said, smacking his arm.

"It is," he said, still laughing. "I've never been shut down so fast in my life. You're practically a cock-blocking ninja."

"Crude!" I shouted. I shoved at his chest. "No. This wasn't some coy, hard-to-get, I-want-you-to-respect-me game. I like you. I mean, I really like you. And I don't want things to be awkward between us."

"Did you just put me in the friend zone?" he asked, indignant as he backed me up against his front door. My hand raised instinctively against his chest and found that all that jogging had served Monroe quite nicely.

"Look, I don't have that many friends and you've been—well, you were an ass at first, but now, I think of you as a good friend and I don't want to—mmmph" I was cut off when Monroe wrapped his hands around the nape of my neck and crushed my mouth against his, taking my breath and any semblance of coherent thought right out of my head. It felt like every nerve ending in my body was focused in my lips, so I could feel Monroe from the roots of my hair to the tips of my toes. He released me, letting me settle rather unsteadily back on my feet. I blew out a shaky breath. "Okay, then."

"Do you feel awkward now?" he asked.

I bit my lip, wincing at how bruised and swollen it felt, and considered. "No, a little tingly, but not awkward . . ."

"Do you feel differently about me?" he asked. "Are you going to avoid talking to me or looking me in the eye because you're embarrassed that I just kissed you?"

Right now, all I wanted to do was kiss him again, so avoiding him really wasn't at the top of my list of priorities. "Er, no."

"So I think we'll be fine," he said, taking my elbow as I walked outside on wobbly legs. "Now go home and write some sex scenes. There's a game on tonight. Come over and have a beer, if you're interested. If not, I'll see you tomorrow."

Monroe winked at me and closed the door, leaving me to stare after him in stunned amazement.

What the hell had just happened?

I called through the closed door. "You know, there's a reason people don't *always* say exactly what they're thinking!"

• • •

At last count, it had been almost four months since I'd had any sort of sex. It had been Mike's birthday. He had too many drinks at his birthday party, and I guess he was too blotto to notice I was his wife, not his girlfriend. So it had been a grand total of one hundred twelve days, three hours, and forty minutes since I'd had even bad sex.

And it showed.

The first sex scene I wrote was basically porn. Monroe said to be as graphic as possible, so I was. I used every dirty word I knew . . . and some that I just made up. I didn't even give the characters' names or backgrounds or a plausible reason for having sex. They were just "he" and "she" and they were naked. There was thrusting, sweating, slamming, biting, pinching, and a lot of extremely clinical anatomical terms I will spare the kids at home.

"It sounds like I have Tourette's syndrome," I groaned, deleting it.

The problem, as usual, was that I didn't know what I wanted. I didn't know what I liked in bed, so how was I supposed to write about it? Obviously, I knew how to make myself . . . happy. But who wanted to read about that? Well, I'm sure there were people who wanted to read about it, but they weren't exactly my target audience.

Part of my problem was I was afraid of the penis—not the body part, the actual word. I didn't know what to call it.

Penis, I typed quickly. *Penis penis penis penis.*

The roof didn't cave in at this blasphemy, so I would begin at the beginning. With a nonthreatening penis euphemism.

Length. Length was a good word. It wasn't gross. It implied a healthy size. It was far more Nora Roberts than Violet Blue.

My hand snaked down his slick torso and palmed the hard length of him, I wrote.

"That's not so bad," I said, tilting my head like a sculptor observing a new clay shape. I continued typing.

> *I sighed, easing back to enjoy the sensation of his fingers gliding inside of me, stroking over the already sensitive nerve endings while I rocked against him.*
>
> *His hands splayed on the small of my back, anchoring me to him as he slid down my body, kissing the curves of my collarbone. Shivering for what I knew was coming, I watched him. I studied his eyes, the way they took in every detail. He knew what he was making me feel, and for him, that was half the fun. He caught me looking at him, and when I tried to close my eyes, palmed my cheek and brought me back to watch as he worshipped my skin.*
>
> *I couldn't seem to get enough of that first sensation, the entirety of my being holding its breath as I stretched to accept him. Knowing this, he pulled away from me and slid into me again. I flexed my legs, wrapping my arms around his shoulders as I rode him.*
>
> *His thumb skimmed over my lips. I caught it between my*

teeth, biting down gently. I could feel every ridge of his cool, wet skin with my tongue. I felt the warmth of his mouth against the lines of my jaw, his fingers clutching at my hips as the pace became frantic, desperate.

I opened my eyes and found him watching me, and that was enough to tip me over the edge. It was terrifying how easily I could reach my peak with him. The force of a good strong orgasm rippled through me, wave after wave, until I felt lost in the dark. He was my anchor, driving into me, keeping me from drifting away. Allowing him to have such an effect on me put a lot of power in his hands. At the moment his hands were more occupied with keeping me afloat as I threw my head back and screamed out my release. Monroe followed, digging his nails into my back, clutching me to him.

"Gah!" I cried, yanking my hands away from the keyboard and staring at the *Monroe* blinking back at me on the screen. Where did that come from? I went back and deleted the name.

It was perfectly natural, I told myself. Monroe was the only available man within screwing distance. He had recently seen me naked. He was the one who put this whole sex scene thing into my head. And he had recently pushed me against a door and kissed me. Really, really well.

"He will never, ever see this," I told myself as I continued typing.

19

Amending the No Penis Policy

In support of our budding friendship, Monroe and I decided to do something new: organized socializing. Instead of just spotting that the other person was awake or doing something stupid and life-threatening and coming on over, we actually agreed to meet at an agreed-upon time and make a meal that wasn't improvised.

I struggled with what I should cook for Monroe. He agreed to provide sides and dessert and do the dishes if I brought the main dish. As egalitarian as that sounded, I had a hard time returning to that homemaker role. For one thing, I didn't want him to think I was *trying* to impress him, some desperate attempt to lure a man through his stomach. And for another, I didn't want him to expect me to present him with spectacular meals on a regular basis. I'd already had a man who learned to take my efforts for granted and I wasn't interested in another one.

At the same time, it went against all of Mama's genes to serve a friend some Velveeta-based slop. So I raided my pantry and found the ingredients for chicken and dumplings. Informal, unsexy, and perfect for the weather, which was finally getting frosty heading into late September.

Unfortunately, Monroe's idea of side dishes was heated chili beans and raw baby carrots. And he forgot to add eggs to the brownie mix. No man is perfect.

"You need a mommy," I told him, sipping a Coke as he stood at his sink, washing dishes. "Or a very patient housekeeper. I am volunteering for neither job, but you need one or the other."

"Hey, I was subsisting just fine on chili beans and frozen lasagna, and then you came along with your homemade goodness and showed me what I'm missing. Now, when you move, I'm going to go into dumpling withdrawal."

"So you're kicking me out of the greater lake area already?" I asked.

"Well, you're not planning on staying through the winter, are you? I'm pretty sure I'm the only one around here who stays through the winter."

"Well, if I don't, how am I going to cut you off from the outside world and re-enact scenes from *Misery*?" I snickered, ducking when Monroe chucked a dish towel at me. "I don't know what my plans are. It all sort of depends on my lawyer and how quickly we can reach a settlement. You could be stuck with a quirky, dumpling-making neighbor for a long time to come."

"Eh, that wouldn't be so bad," he said, drying plates and putting them in the cabinet. "Once you scrape past that potty-mouthed, perversely perky exterior, you're not nearly as annoying as one might think."

"Wow, thank you. Really. I'm blushing," I muttered, swatting at his shoulder as I followed Monroe to the couch.

"So how are the sex scenes coming along?" he asked.

"I finally wrote one that I would be willing to show you," I told him.

"Which means there were very dirty early efforts." He

grinned. "So how many times have you used the word 'length'?'"

This time I did blush. "I hate you."

"You'll get over it; most of my friends do," he promised. "But really, how is your story coming along?"

"I'm getting ideas from the weirdest places," I told him. "Like, I was running the other day and I thought of all the different explanations for the house suddenly coming to life and eating Laurie's husband. Some of them were lame, like the house standing on an Indian burial ground or being haunted by the ghost of a wronged woman. But a few of them were worth writing down. And I was so afraid I would forget them, I turned around and ran back home so I could get to my computer."

"That's probably when your brain processes everything, when you're running," Monroe said. "You should get a pocket recorder so you can tape your ideas when you run. I get all my ideas in the shower. I started keeping a dry-erase board on the bathroom wall so I could write them down."

"You do not." I laughed. Monroe marched over to the bathroom door and flipped the light switch, illuminating a dry-erase board covered in scribbles. "I stand corrected."

"This is the benefit of my professional experience," he said with exaggerated pomposity.

I ignored his smug posturing. "Well, the bright side to this is that I'm learning a lot about the divorce process through life experience, and Sam is willing to let me pick her brain every once in a while when I run into a technical question. It's helped me structure the chapters. I think Sam's glad I've found a creative outlet that doesn't involve a mailing list. Or gasoline."

I flipped open the CD organizer that held Monroe's DVD collection. "You have a disproportionate number of Clint Eastwood movies in here. Honestly, I didn't even know *Every Which Way But Loose* was released on DVD."

"It's Clint Eastwood *and* an orangutan," Monroe said, obviously shocked at my naïveté. "What self-respecting man *wouldn't* own this movie?"

"I have so much to learn about men," I said, shaking my head.

"Well, my movie collection is a good place to start," he said. "*Dirty Harry, High Noon, The Dirty Dozen.*"

"I thought that was the one about the couple with too many kids . . ."

"You've never seen *The Dirty Dozen*?" he asked, clearly aghast. "Are you a communist?"

"I don't think nice girls from Singletree are allowed to be communists," I said as Monroe put the movie in the DVD player. "I think it's against the town charter."

I liked that it was just understood that I would be staying. There was no awkward thing where I edged toward the door while Monroe tried to convince me I was welcome. I was completely comfortable, even though *The Dirty Dozen* wasn't exactly to my taste. I asked a lot of stupid questions, like what crime was Donald Sutherland charged with, and how did half-literate felons manage to come up with such a catchy rhyming plan? But Monroe seemed to enjoy introducing me to an American classic.

Gravity and comfort eventually led to me cradling against him, my head pillowed against his shoulder. It was so comfy, a level of familiarity, of rightness, I didn't think was possible with anyone other than Mike. I lifted my head, really just to look and see if he was asleep. And found myself nose to nose with him.

"Hi," he rumbled. His breath was everywhere. His air was my air.

"Hi." I closed my eyes as he leaned closer. Three words blared against my eyelids in neon red. NO PENIS POLICY.

"Don't think about it," he said. "Just enjoy it."

He positioned my legs on either side of his hips. He wanted me to stay, badly. I could feel the evidence rubbing pleasantly through my sweats. He cupped my chin and pressed his mouth to mine. It wasn't roses blooming and fireworks, more like a long cool drink after crossing a desert.

"Nervous now?" he murmured. I nodded. He kissed me again, lifting my hands to his shoulders. His fingers snaked under my tank, circling lazily against bare skin. I lost track of time. I heard the movie credits roll and the TV click off.

"Nervous now?" he asked. I nodded again. He yanked the zipper of my hoodie down and tossed it aside. I've never had a man toss my clothes across the room. I didn't feel like a convenience. He was trying for me. That mattered a lot.

Should I suggest that he put on a condom, I wondered. He was a single guy living alone in the middle of nowhere. What if he didn't have them? Did I need to run back to my place and get one? It would probably kill the mood, but there was no way I was— *Hello,* what was that he was doing with his tongue?

He dragged me to the floor. It wasn't the comfiest surface, just a soft old rag rug and some throw pillows, but Monroe had a fire going in the big slate hearth. I let the heat soak into my bones, forcing myself to relax my toes, then my feet, then my legs. Legs that Monroe was settling between, skimming his fingertips along the waistband of my jeans just before unbuttoning them.

"Are you nervous now?" he asked, dragging his fingertips along the contours of my hip bones.

I closed my eyes and nodded. "Yes."

"How about now?" he asked, pressing his lips just under the curve of my belly button.

"Mmmm." I grunted in an unsure tone.

He eased my shirt over my head. "Now?"

My answer was lost as his lips closed over mine. I pulled Monroe's T-shirt off and ran my fingertips along his ribs. He was so warm, each muscle bunching as I brushed my fingers over his skin. Once I finally tangled my fingers in that thick dark hair, I didn't want my hands anywhere else, so I managed to push his jeans down with my feet. I happened to glance down as Monroe slid out of his jockeys. My eyes went wide. Wow. Mike had been exaggerating about what was considered average.

I had to slow down. Not to think, but to savor. I wanted this to work. I didn't want this to be bad. If it was going to be any good, I had to tell him . . . I had to tell him . . .

"Put your hands here," I blurted out, cupping his hands against my breasts.

Monroe drew back, startled. "Okay, then."

Well, at least I didn't tell him to turn them counterclockwise.

I laughed, nervous, but held his hands where they were. "I'm sorry! But, I just—I want you to know what I want."

"No. I liked it," Monroe said. "It's like Twister. Right hand, breast. Left foot, well, I won't go there, but—do it again." He kissed my smiling lips. "Tell me what you want me to do."

It took me a second to realize he was serious. He didn't mind being bossed around. He didn't resent me trying to "take over." It was a heady thing, to be handed that much power. I took a deep breath.

"Kiss me," I said, tapping the curve of my belly button. "There."

I guided his hands to the lines of my hip bones as he obliged. "Tell me," he murmured against my belly. The buzz of his voice against my skin had my nerve endings singing. A flash of heat zipped straight through me. I felt a trickle of warmth between my legs, soaking my panties.

"You can go lower," I whispered, unable to draw a full breath as Monroe slipped his thumb over the heart-shaped watermark I'd left on the purple cotton.

Monroe wriggled his eyebrows, kissing the inside of my knees. He reached into a desk drawer and pulled out a little foil packet, which solved the condom conundrum.

I hooked his fingers through the band of my panties. "Take them off."

Monroe's lips traveled the length of my body as he settled between my thighs, his "length" pressing against me. I was ready. I wanted him. And this was already so much better than any sex I'd had before. I had nothing to lose.

"Now," I told him, willing myself to relax as he started that long, slow slide into me. It had been so long since I'd felt so full, so potent. I breathed deep, enjoying the pleasant friction. I focused on that rhythm, the sound of Monroe's breathing. He grinned down at me, pushing my hair back from my face, running his fingertips along my browline. I was liquid, so relaxed and fluid I felt almost separated from myself, but still focused on every movement, every sound and scent.

I wound my ankles around his, tilting my hips up to his as an ever-tightening coil of pressure built inside of me.

"Don't stop," I whispered.

"Have to," he panted. "Fire."

"I'm on fire," I murmured dreamily.

"No, fire," he said, still thrusting, but now nodding toward the fireplace. While the haphazard manner in which Monroe had thrown my sweatshirt was damned sexy, it was also precariously close to the fireplace. My sleeve was burning, threatening to set the entire house up.

"Don't you stop!" I told him as my body thrummed.

Monroe tried to manage tamping out the flaming sleeve all the while moving over me. He could not do both.

"Just burn the thing!" I cried, tossing the hoodie into the fireplace as I fell over the edge into the dark spasms that shook my body. I screamed with each wave that ran through me, clutching at Monroe's shoulders. I fell back on the floor, my skin beading with sweat, as Monroe collapsed on top of me.

Even with the smell of burning sweatshirt filling the room, I was floating, blissful. I had almost nodded off when Monroe rolled and pulled me onto his chest. "No sleep just yet."

• • •

I'd expected it to be awkward. I mean, once you demand that a man burn an article of clothing in a midorgasmic frenzy, it's hard to go back to small talk. But later, when we were stretched out on Monroe's bed, chugging ice water like we'd just run a marathon, it was completely comfortable. I might as well have been fully clothed and watching a baseball game on the couch with him. Monroe propped my head onto his outstretched arm and blew a hard, pleased breath out as he smiled at the ceiling.

"If you don't show me those earlier, dirtier love scenes you wrote, I may weep openly. Obviously, you have some very interesting things going on in that head of yours."

"And the good news is that the bullet wound has only slightly affected your technique," I told him.

"Slightly?"

I shrugged. "It's nothing to be ashamed about."

"You want to see it, don't you?"

"No!" I cried before finally admitting, "Yes."

"It's okay, I don't mind," he said, looking smug as he rolled over onto his stomach. "It's not the first time this baby has bagged me a curious lady."

"Nice." I grunted, slapping his butt.

"Hey! Easy! I'm a wounded man," he exclaimed.

"Oh, you *were* a wounded man," I said, sitting up so I could get a better look at him. I'd expected an actual bullet hole, but what I saw was a long straight-line scar across one buttock. "Well, that's just sort of anticlimactic."

"I'm sorry to disappoint you," he said crossly.

I looked over his shoulder and saw the clock. It was almost 1:00 a.m. "Wow, it's late. I should get home."

Monroe's brows winged up to his hairline. "Really? You're not going to stay?"

Uh-oh. Had I broken some sort of friendly sex etiquette rule? It didn't make any sense for me to stay. I didn't have a toothbrush or contact solution there. I had both at my own cabin which was less than a hundred yards away. Plus, it took me so long to get to sleep these days, I didn't want Monroe to feel obligated to stay awake to entertain me . . . or realize what an insomniac mess I was.

"Is that okay?" I asked, wincing as I sat up. Athletic sex made you sore in new places.

He shrugged as I slipped back into my jeans. Thanks to the regular running and the thousands of calories we'd burned over the last couple of hours, they were fitting easily again. "Sure, I-I just never had a woman just get up and leave before. I think

I feel sort of cheap." He pulled the sheets up to his chest in a mock display of tearful vulnerability.

"Well, to make up for your emotional trauma, why don't you come over tomorrow and I'll make you waffles."

He gave me a suspicious look. "Wait, so I get to have sex with a beautiful woman . . . and waffles . . . and I get to sleep on my side of the bed?"

I nodded.

"You may be my favorite person ever," he told me.

"I aim high."

"So you're really fine with this?"

"Why wouldn't I be?"

"Because most women would want to stay over. In fact, most women would be hurt that I hadn't already asked them to stay over."

I pulled my shirt over my head, leaned over the bed, and kissed him. "Look, I've gotten used to sleeping by myself, right in the middle of the mattress with all the pillows piled into a little nest around me. You'd cramp my style."

Of course, it took me three or four hours to fall asleep that way. But he didn't need to know that.

"You," he said, kissing me and tugging me back into bed, "I really like you."

I grinned down at him, reluctantly pulling away as I slipped into my shirt. "You should."

20

Bitch-slapped by My Muse

Color me crazy, but I think I might have stumbled into a mature sexual relationship.

I didn't feel weird around Monroe. I felt great. Energized, relaxed, confident. I even danced around the cabin in my underwear. And even better, Monroe did not seem weird. It felt perfectly fine to get up in the dark cabin, slip back into my clothes, give him a peck on the lips, and go home at the end of the night.

He usually found me sitting on my porch in the mornings, working on a manuscript I was thinking of calling *Divided Property*. We talked about what we were planning on writing that morning. And then he kissed me on the top of the head and told me to behave myself. I would say that was unfair, but my last writing project did end up being re-enacted on YouTube, so draw your own conclusions.

We were still friends. Friends with benefits. Yay.

I didn't need him. I didn't depend on him for money or social standing. I just liked having him around. Monroe didn't care who my daddy was, or who I was married to, or how I could help him. He just liked me and he really enjoyed having sex with me, which considering how my last relationship went, was reassuring.

And when we did have sex . . . Wow. That's all I'm saying. No, that's not all I'm saying. When I was married, sex was just something we did on Wednesdays and Saturdays. It wasn't something I looked forward to, and afterward I didn't feel much better. I finally understood that my sex problems were not the result of me being frigid or inadequate or not knowing what the hell I was doing. And maybe it wasn't even Mike's fault. I was going to go ahead and blame Mike anyway, but it was much more likely that the two of us were just sexually incompatible. We didn't listen to each other. Neither of us knew what the other wanted. We were like two magnets with negative charges, whenever we tried to get together—well, the bottom line was repulsion.

Monroe didn't care whether I'd showered. He didn't care what time it was or whether he had something else he should be doing. He made me laugh before, during, and after. And it felt good. It made me feel good.

Nothing was expected. If we ate dinner together, great. If we didn't, okay. If we hung out together, but didn't have sex, it wasn't the end of the world. There was no pouting, no hurt looks.

One afternoon I was curled up on the sofa, reading *Drunk Tank Duets*. It was the kind of blustery afternoon you wanted to wallow in, to drink hot cocoa and wear fuzzy socks and do nothing but nap. I'd turned off anything that would make noise because I wanted to hear the patter of the rain on the roof.

There was a knock on my screen door. Monroe was standing outside, rain dripping from his hair and a smile stretched across his face. The afternoons were his usual writing time, so it was strange to see him out this early.

"You okay?" I asked, opening the door for him. "You're going to freeze wandering around in the rain like that."

He dug his fingers into my hair and dragged me against his cool, wet mouth. He tasted clean and spicy.

I dropped the book as he hitched my legs up over his hips and carried me, albeit slowly, into my room. I pushed his sodden jacket back over his shoulders and dropped it to the floor. His shirt followed just before he dropped me on the bed with a playful little bounce. It was at that moment I realized I was wearing my pajama pants with the little candy corns on them. And I just didn't care.

I reached for his belt buckle, but he pushed me back on the bed and stretched over me, pressing me into the old mattress. "Slow down. We're not in a hurry. We have all day."

This was different. This was slow, no urgency, no rush. Just the slip of skin against skin. Fingers brushing over my ankles. The curve of his smile against my belly as he peeled my shirt over my head. The good solid weight of him lying between my knees as he kissed my thighs and slipped on a condom.

I was warm and ready and when he was inside me, it felt so good I wanted to cry. He rolled over so that I straddled him, letting me ride him as my fingers intertwined with his. It was so odd to see this huge, "manly man" lying in the midst of my hot pink pillows. He released my hands to grip my hips and steady me.

I ground down, circling my hips in time with his thrusts. His breath quickened in his chest. He was close, holding on for me. He sat up, curving his hands up my waist and around my breasts. The clench of his teeth around my nipple sent me flying, a rainbow of colors exploding in my head as I quaked over him.

At the first shudder, he groaned into my mouth and toppled over the edge after me. I collapsed in a sweaty heap on his chest.

He cupped his hand around my jaw, pushed my hair out of my face, and kissed me. I rolled on my side, my arm slung over his chest. "So you will pretty much use any excuse not to work, huh?"

"Well, yes," he said, scooching down so we were eye-to-eye. "But that's not why I came over. I came over because when a guy has someone like you in his life and there's the opportunity to make love to her on a rainy afternoon, he should do it."

"If that's a line from one of your books, I will kick your ass." I promised him, stretching along the length of his body.

"No, but I really should write that down," he said, looking on my nightstand for a pen and paper.

I slapped lazily at him as I wrapped my arm around his waist. Every muscle in my body was relaxed and well used. My head felt so heavy against his shoulder. I yawned and closed my eyes. And I don't remember anything much after that.

• • •

When I woke, it was still raining, The quilt was draped across the small of my back as Monroe absently rubbed his hand along my spine. He was reading over my manuscript and making notes in the margins.

"I'm sorry," I mumbled, still so heavy with sleep that all I wanted to do was close my eyes again. "How long have I been out?"

"A couple of hours. Go back to sleep," he whispered, kissing my temple.

I laid my head back on the pillow and passed out again. When I came to, Monroe was sleeping beside me, his chin tucked over my shoulder, his hand flexed over my hip. It was very strange, sleeping with another man after so many years, to have some other person's body sprawled next to mine. For one thing, Monroe snored, a light, buzzing rattle out of his throat that reminded me of a hibernating bear. And I couldn't remember the last time I'd been touched in my sleep, held as if Monroe was afraid I would slip away while he dreamed.

I chuckled, rolling over to face him. I stroked a hand over his whiskers and he leaned into it, his eyes fluttering open. He grinned and kissed me.

"Hey."

He pressed a hand to the base of my spine, pulling me close to him. "Hello there."

"Sorry I fell asleep."

He shrugged, tucking my face into his neck. "You haven't slept a whole night since you got here. I figure you're due."

"So I wasn't able to cover up that insomnia nearly as well as I'd hoped, huh?"

He rubbed his palms along my jaw, running his thumbs along my cheeks. "I used to see in your window sometimes, when I looked up from my computer screen. You'd be all curled up on the couch, trying so hard to sleep. You were brave and strong and . . . really, really pissed off. Which I like in a gal. You'd pace and you'd prowl until you'd pass out. And for a moment your face would be still and you looked happy. I lived for that. Even when I wanted you to disappear and leave me in peace, I lived for watching you finally find the quiet."

"How closely were you watching me?"

"Pretty closely," he admitted. "Well, you're not hard to look at. Some perverse part of me wondered when you were going to break. But you never did. I think that's when I realized, 'That's a person I want to get to know better.'"

"You have strange standards for friendship," I told him, rolling onto his chest. I sat up; the sheets fell away and puddled around my waist. When he reached up to curl the ends of my hair around his fingers, I smiled down at him.

"Oh, no." He groaned.

"What?"

"That's the look of a woman who just realized I am completely in her power," he said.

"Really?" I arched my eyebrow in a sinister manner.

"Oh, don't act like you don't know you're a temptress," he said, rolling me onto my back and wrapping my legs around his waist. "Just look at you with your candy-corn pajama pants. You're irresistible and you know it."

"Yes, novelty pajamas are a key part of my reclaiming my feminine power agenda."

"I knew it," He groaned in false agony as he kissed me and began that long, slow slide back into loving me again. "I'm toast."

"Can I ask you something?"

He kissed the back of my neck, stroking his hand up my thigh. "Yes to outfits. No to third parties."

I snickered, but didn't respond to the imagery that conjured. "Do you think this would ever work in the real world? This thing with us? Is this the kind of friendship that could only thrive in isolation? No one to turn to but each other?"

"I think you should turn off that gigantic, somewhat frightening brain of yours, stop analyzing, and enjoy it," he said, tapping me gently on the forehead. "I am."

"So just don't think about the fact that I've been happy for an extended period of time? Just enjoy myself?"

He nodded.

"This is not a concept I'm familiar with," I confessed.

"Well, become familiar with it," he told me, rolling me onto his chest. "Now, let's talk about these outfits."

21

Tree-house Ladders

It came to my attention that Monroe and I rarely spent time over at my place unless we were having sex. Because Monroe pointed it out.

It was late one Thursday afternoon. Mr. Borchard had just packed up his tools for the day, leaving my half-finished replacement dock covered with a tarp by the shoreline. He'd had a brainstorm about using some of the wood salvaged from the old dock to build a couple of benches for the yard, and had spent nearly an hour discussing their construction with Monroe. When he finally left, we collapsed into my hammock, exhausted by a retiree with the energy of a kindergartner on Red Bull.

"So why don't we hang out here tonight? You know, with our clothes on," he suggested.

I frowned at him. "That's sort of random."

"Don't get me wrong," he said as we lounged, my feet resting on his chest. "I like having sex at your place just as much as I like having sex at mine. But is there a reason you don't ask me over for nonsexual reasons?"

I chewed my lip, considering. The truth was I was afraid of extending too many invitations Monroe's way because I didn't want to come across as one of those needy divorcées he was so afraid of. I figured letting him do the inviting kept me from overstepping his precious boundaries. And I liked having my own space. It was sort of like having my own little tree-house, when I wanted to be alone, I could pull up the rope ladder and hide out. Besides, Monroe had better DVDs at his place.

But letting him know that I'd put that much thought into this probably would have weirded him out. So, instead, I said, "Well, there is the chance you'll find that voodoo altar in my closet . . ."

"Nice," he snorted, flicking my ankle lightly, just enough to tickle.

"What happened to 'You may be my favorite person ever because you don't attach strings to sex'?" I asked, flailing my feet out of his reach.

"One, that's a pretty broad paraphrase. And two, maybe I would like to attach a string or two. Like a meal or a movie . . . or a meal."

I rolled my eyes. "You don't want to cook your own dinner, do you?"

He shook his head. "I'm not a proud man."

• • •

Since Monroe didn't give me a laundry list of ingredients, food groups, and regional cuisines he refused to consume, I decided to stretch my culinary muscles a bit with a Mexican feast of enchiladas with a three-pepper sauce. Judging by the way Monroe clutched at his throat and ran for my sink after taking his first bite, I may have overdone it a bit.

"Are you okay?" I cried as he downed his third glass of water.

A mile-wide grin split Monroe's sweaty, glistening face. "That was awesome! Hit me again."

"I don't know if I should," I said hesitantly, scraping the pepper sauce off of my own portion. Darn Mama and her unreliable "dash of this, pinch of that" recipes.

"I can't even feel the burn anymore. I think my tongue has gone into shock," he assured me. "I haven't had Mexican food like this since the roach coach that parked outside our precinct office got closed down by the health department."

"Have you stopped to think maybe comments like that are why I don't invite you over?" I asked him. "Would you do me a favor and take a preemptive Pepcid or something before you explode? They're by my laptop."

"You keep your antacids by your laptop?"

"That's usually where I'm sitting when I need antacids." I speared a forkful of nonsaucy enchilada and pointed my fork at him. "I've seen the bobblehead collection you keep by your laptop for inspiration, buddy. Don't judge me."

I heard Monroe shuffle around papers on my desk, looking for the illogically small medicine bottle. "Hey, Lace, what is this? 'My hope for this holiday season is for Tony to develop a debilitating case of ringworm.'"

Oh, crap.

Monroe was holding a stack of the sample newsletters I'd been putting together from Maya's case studies. He read aloud, "Jordan insisted that we both shower before we had sex, otherwise, he couldn't 'rise to the occasion.' And then, of course, we showered after we had sex. After a while I figured out that sex with Jordan wasn't worth all that showering. The environmental impact alone was shameful. Lacey, what are these?"

"It's just a . . ." I found that I was embarrassed to try to explain it to Monroe, which couldn't have been a good sign. I took a deep breath. "Maya, the girl with the cranial accessories, she thinks we can make a killing publishing newsletters like the one I wrote about Mike for angry divorcées across the country. People give me their information, I write the newsletters for them, they mail them out. Maya's already got enough orders to keep us busy for a while. The profit projections—"

"Have you lost your mind?" Monroe demanded.

"I'm not in love with your tone right now," I told him.

"Why would you want to do this?"

Monroe's voice seemed to rise in decibel level with every sentence. The mirth of just a few moments before had completely evaporated. I tried to choose my words carefully, keeping my tone as even as possible. "Because apparently I'm really good at it. And there are all of these women out there who need me. They're angry and humiliated and hurt and they need a voice. And that's something I can give them. I can help them and get paid handsomely to do it."

"And how much good did your newsletter do for you?" he asked. "Did it make you happier? Make you feel better? Did it do anything but make your situation worse?"

"It brought me up here. It brought me to you, so it couldn't have been all bad."

"What if some woman sends you information, you send one of these things out, and it turns out she's wrong? That her husband wasn't cheating and she's sent out an announcement calling him a 'dickless wonder'?"

"Maya has a legal waiver that would protect us if that happened," I said, realizing how lame that sounded even as the words left my lips.

"Well, I'm sure you'll sleep better at night, knowing that you helped destroy a marriage, but you're protected."

"Why are you so angry with me? Why the hell do you care so much whether I tinker with a stupid writing project? How is this so different from writing a book?"

"Writing a book doesn't drag other people down with you. You did your damage with your newsletter. You accepted it and I thought you'd moved on. But now you want to repeat the same mistake over and over again. How could you be happy wallowing in anger and bitterness every day, feeding into people's need to hurt the ones they used to love? What kind of person would do that?"

It was the disdainful look on his face that did it. The mad flutter of my heartbeat and my immediate instinct to make it right, apologize, take it back. The curl of his lip and tone in his voice that said I was "in trouble." I'd seen that look on my father's face, heard the tone from Mike. I did not need another man supervising me or protecting me from myself.

"I'm sorry, am I only supposed to write what you say I should write?" I asked, rising from my chair. "This is none of your business, Monroe. Who the hell do you think you are?"

"So what I have to say doesn't count?" he demanded. "It doesn't matter that I think it is a huge mistake?"

"I didn't say that. I just don't need you telling me what to do, what's an acceptable way to live my life and what's not. I've already had that. I don't want another husband. I don't even want a relationship. That's not what this is. This is— I don't know what it is. But what we're doing doesn't give you the right to boss me around."

"So this isn't a relationship to you?"

"No. This is great," I insisted. "This is exactly what I need right now. Spending time with someone who is funny and nice and *really* good in bed. No strings. No complications. You're a guy. I thought you'd be thrilled that I don't want to get all emotionally involved! I thought we had some sort of unspoken agreement."

As soon as the words left my mouth, I wanted to swallow my tongue. I sounded just like Mike, seeing the relationship the way I wanted to, damn the other person's feelings. Taking what I wanted and giving little back.

"How exactly is that not supposed to insult me?" he asked softly. He looked genuinely hurt, which made me want to apologize. But the damage was done. Anything I said now would just sound like I was placating him. Instead, I balled up my fists and concentrated on the pressure of my fingernails digging into my palms. "I haven't asked anything from you, Lace, because I know you're not ready to give it. But you can't just declare that this isn't real because you don't want to put a label on it. And you're only going to be able to use Mike as an excuse for so long. Don't make me pay for his mistakes." He shook a handful of the sample newsletters. "Don't make all of the men in America pay because your husband was a philandering idiot."

He dropped the papers on my desk and headed for the door.

"Monroe, can't we just sit down and talk about this?" I asked, gesturing to his chair, his empty plate. "Don't just walk out."

"I think I've lost my appetite," he said and slammed the door behind him.

22

Flashing the Harvest Moon

The Harvest Moon Festival was the only truly community-oriented event in which the citizens of Buford participated. There were plenty of summer events for the tourists: the Strawberry Festival, the Fourth of July Jamboree, the Annual Redneck Regatta. But the Harvest Moon party, held on the second Saturday of October, was something the locals did just for themselves. I suspected it was to celebrate the departure of the annoying summer people.

The festival stemmed from an annual effort to help the community's poor prepare for winter. Only now, instead of hunting deer and turkeys to stock underprivileged pantries, local residents helped charities by funneling them cash through carnival games, rides, and truly unhealthy food.

One silence-filled week after our disastrous dinner, Monroe stuck the flyer for the festival on my screen door as a sort of apology gesture, along with my own little pocket recorder for taking notes while I ran. I know that a crumpled, badly formatted sheet of neon orange paper and an electronic gadget shouldn't bring a grown woman to tears, but being released from my own personal guilt-hell was so much better than getting flowers or jewelry.

When I speculated that the world wouldn't end just because someone was mad at me, I was wrong. It did feel like the end of the world knowing that Monroe was angry with me. I was more depressed, more emotional, than I had been after leaving Mike. Food had no taste. Nothing I read, nothing on TV appealed to me. All I could do was write and sleep. I wrote pages and pages about Laurie's heartbreak, her hope at meeting Mac, the sheriff of the tiny town where she settled. I felt like I had damaged something important, and somehow writing it down would keep me from losing it entirely.

I must have started for my front door a hundred times, holding the knob and trying to find exactly the right words to tell Monroe that I was sorry. But some unlikely combination of shame and pride kept me from opening it. Yes, I felt bad for making Monroe feel unappreciated or cheap. But I couldn't help but resent the idea that he was practically commanding me not to write the newsletters, even if he thought he had my best interests in mind. I'd fought too hard to start making my own decisions. I wasn't ready to hand over proxy votes just yet. I was afraid of ending up right back where I started.

That ugly orange flyer was like a pardon from prison. The minute I found it, I practically ran across the yard, even though I had no idea what I was going to say. How exactly did this work? Did I speak first? Did he? How did you apologize for half of an argument? Before I could knock, Monroe opened the door.

He cleared his throat. "I'm sorry."

Well, that was easy.

"I'm sorry, too," I said. "I shouldn't have—"

"I'll go first," Monroe said.

"No, I should go—"

"Lacey, just let me," he said. "I shouldn't have come down so hard on you. I can't tell you what to do. I want you to find your voice as a writer and . . . I guess I took it a little too personally when you started working on something else. I still think the newsletters are a horrible idea and that you could do so much more with your talents. But I could have said so without hurting your feelings—"

"Well, you had a point and sometimes, obviously, I don't see things unless I'm smacked over the head with them," I admitted. "I'm going to rethink the whole letter thing. If it's going to cause problems between us . . . I think I just got overexcited at the prospect of something I could do well. There aren't a whole lot of tangible things that I'm good at—"

"I don't want you to think that way," Monroe said, interrupting me. "I'm sorry if I've been coming off as condescending or overbearing—"

"I'm sorry I called you all those horrible, vile names," I told him.

His brow furrowed. "You didn't call me names."

"Well, you weren't here for it, but, trust me, I did. And I'm sorry. Right now, besides my brother, you're the best friend I have."

"Same for me. If sex is going to complicate that, maybe we can cool down for a while."

"Whoa, whoa," I exclaimed, holding my hands up. "Let's not get crazy."

A wide grin split Monroe's face, his relief palpable. "Oh, thank God, because I was totally bluffing."

We spent most of the evening apologizing. In a baby step

toward a more normal relationship, Monroe suggested we go to the festival. He said it combined his two great loves, deep-fried Twinkies and Tilt-A-Whirls.

He was a deep and complex man.

The truth was, I needed to get out of the cabin. Even without the Monroe-based guilt weighing on me, I was spending so much time on the computer, I was starting to get a laptop-shaped burn mark across my thighs. It wasn't just the manuscript marathons. Despite my assertions that I would rethink the letters, I was still tinkering with Maya's case studies. She sent me a new batch every few days, each time offering me increasingly attractive salary packages.

The stories made my experience seem like a particularly bland episode of *The Brady Bunch.* There was a woman named Alice whose husband had moved out of their house one T-shirt at a time for a month until there was almost nothing left of him in their home. He'd moved in with a co-worker who he'd been working on "projects" with for the last six months. Alice had even called her his work wife. What embarrassed Alice the most was that she hadn't noticed anything was wrong. Her husband had removed everything that was important to him out of the house, and she'd missed it. So I wrote a "change of address" announcement for the husband.

Please forward all mail to Carl Finley at his new residence at 3379 Jackson Street, where he will be living with Robin, the woman he's been sleeping with for the last six months. Most of you will be relieved to know that you don't have to help Carl move because he slowly but surely moved his stuff out of the house over the last month so his darling wife wouldn't notice anything was amiss. While Alice was busy calling hospitals to see if her husband had been injured in a car accident, Carl sent his mother to tell Alice that her marriage was over . . . and that she wanted her heirloom china back.

On an unrelated note, Alice will be hosting a bonfire this weekend.

Carl left behind his precious collection of Elvis memorabilia.

I'm not going to say the money wasn't a motivating factor for me. But frankly, it was easier to vent on unfaithful husbands than to keep building my story. And it made me feel helpful, I guess. Like I was doing some sort of service for these women, helping them. And it made me feel a little less crazy for doing what I'd done.

On the other side of my professional conundrum, Monroe was already preparing me for "selling myself" as a writer, which sounded uncomfortably similar to prostitution. He said the most important step in getting published was finding a good agent. He'd offered to send my stuff to people from his agency, but that made me uncomfortable. I didn't want people in the publishing industry doing me favors just because I happened to be sleeping with a bestselling author. That felt like something Beebee would do. I wanted to know that my writing was genuinely good, that it might sell. So I refused his help. Monroe lovingly called me "a stubborn pain in the ass," but he also gave me the address of an internet database of literary agencies so I could find my own. He said it took him a year and forty-nine rejections before he found an agent. I hadn't even finished the damn thing yet and it seemed like it was going to be more work to sell it than it was to write it. The thought of it exhausted me. And I just wasn't sure if I was up to being rejected again and again.

Monroe talked about writing as if it were something that just happened, like he sat down at the computer and the words just appeared somehow. He acted like he didn't have anything to do with it.

"It's like these people are living in my head, telling me their stories," he said as we traversed the festival fairway.

"Some people consider that a mental illness," I told him, sipping homemade apple cider, which I suspected might have been made in an old oil drum.

As much as I enjoyed my little hermit's retreat, it was nice to be out among people, even if most of them were five-year-olds whining for balloons. I liked walking through the crowd with Monroe, his hand at the small of my back, making me feel linked, but not led. Nobody seemed to recognize me with my Wildcats cap pulled low over my face, and if they did, they didn't care enough to say anything. The air had just enough nip to it to make me appreciate the smell of churning peanut oil and woodsmoke. I had eaten my weight in kettle corn, lost five dollars at the dart booth, and had bought a ridiculous frog-shaped paperweight made of painted rocks. Overall, I considered that a productive afternoon.

"And lately, my antagonist doesn't seem to be speaking to me," he said. "I want the reader to be creeped out by her actions, but I don't want to make her a caricature. I want her to be human, but not sympathetic."

"So basically you're afraid of alienating your female readers with psycho crushes on you," I mused.

He nodded. "Yes."

"Well, the best way to get a woman to dislike a character would be to give your cop a nice, normal girlfriend, then have your crazy girl do something that endangers her, but doesn't actually hurt her. Girlfriend is separated from cop either because she's afraid or he breaks up with her to protect her, then by chapter twenty, they're reunited."

"You're trying to make me into a romance writer, aren't you?" he said, narrowing his eyes at me.

"It wouldn't hurt to chick-ify your books by about ten percent."

"I'll take that into consideration," he said.

"It's flattering that my opinion matters to you, despite the fact that I've only read one of your books," I told him.

"Wait, I thought you were reading *Drunk Tank Duets*?"

"I knew you'd catch that." I grinned.

"You're not nearly as funny as you think you are," he told me. "Well, what about you? How goes Laurie's search for personal-fulfillment-slash-personal-renewal?"

"It's progressing. I'm still having a hard time reconciling the idea that other people might read this. There are things that I want to say about marriage, about husbands, about sex, but I keep editing myself because I'm afraid of offending people or grossing them out."

"Lacey, I'm pretty sure you've already crossed that bridge," Monroe said. "I don't think there's much you can write at this point that would shock people."

"Good point," I admitted, frowning at him when he dug his hand into my kettle corn. "Hey, hey, popcorn thief!"

"You need to learn to share," he said, popping the oversweet popcorn into his mouth.

"You need to learn to ask," I told him, giggling as he reached around my back to take another handful from the bag.

Over his shoulder, I saw Hap Borchard coming our way,

sipping from a large blue bottle of homemade root beer. He saw me, smiled, and waved.

"Okay," I breathed and tried to talk without moving my lips as we approached. "Be polite, but not your normal engaging self. If he starts to tell a story, I will fake an anaphylactic reaction to the cider and you carry me to the infirmary tent."

"You're assuming I can carry you after all that kettle corn," Monroe muttered, dodging when I reached out to smack him.

"Nice to see you out and about, Miz Lacey," Hap Borchard said.

"Mr. Borchard!" I exclaimed in a sweet tone that had Monroe double-taking. "It's nice to see you, too. Is Mrs. Borchard here with you today?"

"She's over at the craft booths, buying some geegaw for the yard. Lord knows we don't have near enough concrete critters on our lawn."

"Well, the good news is you don't have to clean up after them," Monroe said.

Mr. Borchard gave a loud, hooting laugh. "I'll have to remember that one."

An awkward silence fell over the three of us. Mr. Borchard was looking at me, expectantly. Clearly, I was supposed to say something here, but what? It had been so long since I'd socialized with anyone but Monroe, I felt out of practice. I wracked my brain, trying to think of the appropriate conversational volley. What would my mother say in a situation like this?

"Oh, I've been meaning to tell how much I appreciate you finishing the dock so quickly," I told him. "It's just as solid as the old one. I'm really very happy with it. And the benches are great. Gammy would have loved them. I've told everyone I've seen what a great job you've done."

Okay, the only person I'd told was Monroe, but he was the only person I'd seen for a while. So it was just a small lie, necessary to maintain the delicately balanced scales of small-town politics.

"Good to have something to keep my hands busy," Mr. Borchard said in a pleased, proud tone. "Have you thought about those other improvements to the cabin?"

"Improvements?" Monroe asked.

Mr. Borchard smiled beatifically at me. "Yeah, she's thinking about staying up here for the winter, becoming a local. If she's going to do that, she's going to need some new windows, some new insulation. We don't want her freezing to death, do we?"

Monroe shot me a speculative look. "No, we don't."

"Then again, from what I can see, you two do what you can to keep each other warmed up," Mr. Borchard said, winking at us. Before either of us could respond or protest, he raised his hands like he was making a benediction and said, "The missus and I think it's a good thing. We couldn't be happier for you, Miz Lacey. Never took much to your husband. If this fella here treats you right, he won't have to worry."

"Is that a not-too-subtle threat?" Monroe asked, grinning good-naturedly.

Mr. Borchard shook his head, all innocence. "Not from me. I meant, if you treat her right, she won't send an e-mail to all and sundry, calling you everything but a nice Christian boy. You've got your hands full, I'd say." My eyes must have looked like saucers, because Mr. Borchard winked at me again and said, "The missus just got a copy from one of the gals in her quilting group. We laughed our heads off. Always knew you had your granny's backbone."

"Thanks," I said. "I think."

"Well, I better get going," he said. "I promised the missus a corn dog. Don't want her getting cranky with me."

"Tell her I said hello," I said. "See you around, Mr. Borchard."

"I'll call you next week. We'll talk about those improvements."

"I will."

"You've been holding out on me," Monroe said, turning on me the minute Mr. Borchard was out of earshot.

"You're right, I should have told you a long time ago. I hope one day to have a relationship based on foods on a stick, just like the Borchards."

Monroe quirked his lips. "Were you going to tell me you were thinking about staying?"

"I haven't made any definite decisions," I told him. "I want to be prepared, just in case. It's not a big deal."

"For you, maybe, but what happens to me when my winter girlfriend shows up?"

"Nice," I said, rolling my eyes. "Is this the sort of charm that drew her to you like a moth to a flame?"

"No, I think it's my resemblance to Hugh Jackman."

I gave him my patented confused look.

"You talk in your sleep sometimes," he said, shrugging.

"Sonofa—"

"Oh, it's adorable. And you say some other very interesting and dirty things. Where do you think I get half my ideas?"

"Well, this is weird," I muttered.

"No, this is us out in the world," he said. "Plagues and pestilence have yet to pour forth from the sky. I haven't forgotten your name or turned into a toad. We have managed to have a real date out in public."

"This is not a date," I told him. When his brow furrowed,

I quickly said, "I'm wearing a baseball cap. I'm eating from a brown paper bag."

He grinned. "You're right. It won't be a date until we have funnel cake."

"No, it won't be a date until you demonstrate your manliness by winning me something plush and inanimate through ring-toss ability."

"Well, let's go make it a date, then," he said, slipping his arm around my waist and leading me to the games.

"I have news for you," I told him. "You just became the girl in this relationship."

23

The Bottom Line of Booty Calls

Mike's lawyer, Bill Bodine, finally ran out of legal reasons for not showing Samantha the credit card records she'd demanded. I did not want to know what sort of unholy power she'd called upon to obtain these records. I was just glad she was on my side.

"Do you really want to see this?" Samantha asked, sliding the manila envelope across the desk. "This can prove upsetting for a lot of people."

"I can handle it," I promised, taking a seat on her couch.

"Well, just in case . . ." she paused and reached into a mini-fridge and pulled out a pint of Häagen-Dazs and an airline-size bottle of vodka. "Pick your poison."

At the sight of my raised eyebrows, she said, "This is not my first rodeo."

I refused the liquor and the ice cream, instead ripping open the envelope to survey the neatly typed pages.

True to Sam's estimation, there were several charges to Leo Goote's jewelry store. No wonder Leo had seemed sorry for me. He knew exactly how much Mike had spent on his mistress. Mike had bought a tennis bracelet, a gold locket, and several crystal figurines, none of which I received.

"Sadly, one of these charges is for me," I told her, taking a little red pen and crossing it off the list. "Mike had my engagement ring cleaned and inspected six months ago, for insurance purposes. But everything else, he bought for Beebee. In fact, I'm pretty sure I admired that locket when I stopped in at the office a few months ago. She said it was a gift and I said she was lucky to have someone who was so thoughtful."

"Ow," Samantha said, wincing.

I sighed. "I think I'll take that ice cream now."

Samantha put a spoon in my outstretched hand and served the ice cream with a flourish. She took out a pint of coffee ice cream for herself, kicked off her rather stylish tan heels, and joined me on the couch. She put her feet up on the coffee table, dug her spoon into the ice cream and stayed silent as I read over the charges.

Being anesthetized by mocha chip didn't quite dull the shock of seeing thirty pages of itemized adultery expenses. Beebee was definitely a high-maintenance girlfriend. There were, of course, several charges to Cherry's floral shop, at least once a month for the last year. There were receipts to restaurants outside of town on nights when Mike was supposedly attending Lions Club meetings. Some of the places Mike hadn't even taken me, but all of them were romantic, out-of-the way restaurants where people went on special occasions.

"I had no idea he was spending this much," I said, shaking my head.

"Well, having an affair is expensive," Samantha said. "Generally, you're trying to impress your girlfriend. You're insecure about your ability to hold on to a younger woman—"

"Watch it," I warned.

Samantha grinned cheekily, dishing up more ice cream. "You

wine her, you dine her. You buy her special little presents for no reason. You end up treating her better than you're treating your spouse. And you feel guilty, so you end up throwing a little money your spouse's way, too."

"Not really, I mean, Mike gave me flowers once a couple of months back, but—oh, crap." For Valentine's Day, Mike had given me a silver bracelet with a monogrammed heart charm, a rare departure from his usual "practical gift" MO. I checked the page listing February expenses and saw that Mike had purchased two of them from Leo Goote. So basically, he purchased something nice for Beebee for Valentine's Day and threw me a bone by doubling the order. "I think I'm going to need the vodka, too, Sam."

"I told you, this part can be upsetting," she said.

"Yeah, yeah, make with the liquor, woman."

"I see those lovely manners diminish proportionate to the amount of sugar you consume."

"Oh, look, he took her on a tour of the Missouri wine country," I said, tilting my head as I held up the April page. "He told me he was going to a tax seminar in Nashville."

"I wasn't aware Missouri has a wine country."

"Well, it does, and it's home to the Dew Drop Inn, which I'm guessing is some sort of bed-and-breakfast."

Samantha wrinkled her nose. "Gag. Some people have no sense of irony."

"Or decency." I muttered. "Seriously, hasn't he ever heard of using cash?"

"Well, you can't get the frequent-flier miles that way," she said. When my eyes went wide, she shrugged. "I've been at this awhile. I've heard every possible rationalization you could think of."

I tried and failed to tamp down the now-familiar little flashes of anger and embarrassment. Why was I mad? I knew that he'd taken her out, bought her things, sent her flowers. Why was I so pissed off now that I knew exactly what he'd bought her?

Samantha cracked open the vodka and poured a shot into each of our cartons. When I made a face, she told me, "Think of it as a flavored White Russian."

"Speaking of rationalizations," I muttered.

"Look, I've noticed that—while you have a healthy sense of justice when provoked—you have a tendency to kick yourself pretty hard. You're going through perfectly normal stages, blaming yourself for what you didn't see. You're kicking your own ass for taking the easier route in your marriage, which is normal. Most people take the easy route. That's why it's called the easy route. If it appeals to your sense of self-flagellation, you're paying for it now. So learn your lesson, spank your inner child, and let it go."

After offering me a few more platitudes, Samantha said she would request a mediation session with Mike's lawyer sometime over the next month.

"Mediation sounds a little scary," I admitted.

"Oh, it's no big deal. Your lawyers get together and talk about what your issues are."

"I think it should be abundantly clear what my issues are," I deadpanned.

"Ha, ha, Jokey Jokemaker. I mean, your financial issues, division of property, maintenance, if you and Mike had kids—"

"Let's not even joke about that."

"If you'd had kids, we would discuss visitation and child support. It's basically a starting-off point for negotiations. Most cases actually resolve themselves in mediation. Depending on

Mike's shame level, we might be able to wrap it up before we go to trial."

"Mike has no shame."

"Well, in that case, we'll be scheduling a pretrial conference sometime in the next six months."

"Six months?!" I cried. "I can't be married to Mike for another six months. I don't want to be married to Mike for six more minutes. He's moved another woman into our house, Sam. Isn't there some sort of special asshole divorce law exception that could speed the process along?"

"I'll try to make it as quick as possible, Lace, but you don't want to rush it. We're going to need time to iron out a financial settlement that works the first time. It's not like we can go back and ask for more money if you figure out you can't live on what we get. Have you thought about what you're going to do for money after the divorce is final?"

"Oh, you mean, like a job?" I asked.

"Yes, that's what the large majority of the population does for money."

"I have thought about it. This probably won't make you happy, but I have the chance to do some writing, the kind of writing I have some experience at, for a living. And it would be enough money for me to live on, but it might mean that I would be retaining your services for a while longer."

"So that explains the e-mails Maya Drake has been sending me." Realization spread across Samantha's features. "Oh, not good."

I shrugged. "Apparently there's a lot of money to be made in the revenge business."

"Lacey, let me look around. You have other options. Give me a few more weeks," she said. "If I don't have you single and gainfully employed within a month, well, I don't know what to offer you. Just take some time and make the right choice before you do anything drastic . . . again."

• • •

That Saturday I woke up in Monroe's bed, which was becoming a common occurrence that neither of us commented on. He was lying on his back, one arm thrown over his eyes and the other resting on my stomach. This was his deep sleep before the dawn position and meant he would be in a near coma for at least another hour. Even though I had a few things in Monroe's closet, I slipped into one of his LPD T-shirts and a pair of panties. I shuffled into the kitchen to make coffee and tried to remember whether we had the makings for chocolate chip pancakes.

Monroe's coffeemaker was one of those old-fashioned percolators that made more noise than a jet engine. As the water hissed and roared, I wondered how the hell he was able to sleep through it. I thought cops were supposed to be hypervigilant and jump out of bed at the slightest noise. But clearly, if we ever had a break-in after bedtime, I was going to have to face off the burglar on my own.

I sat at the kitchen table and read over Monroe's latest revisions to *Two-Seven-Zero*. This book was definitely funnier than his previous ventures, I mused as I sipped that ambrosial first cup of coffee. I liked to think I had something to do with his getting in touch with his inner smart-ass, particularly the creation of the sassy, smart female police dispatcher who mocked the main character through most of the book.

I'd just poured myself a second cup and was taking another back to bed for Monroe when I heard the tumblers of the front-door lock turn. I turned to see an older couple come through the door with grocery bags, the wife singing "Happy Birthday" in an exaggerated falsetto. I shrieked, flailing one arm, sending boiling hot coffee splashing across my chest.

"Ow! Shit! Shit!" I hissed, pulling the scalding shirt away from my body.

And that's when I remembered I wasn't wearing any pants.

I yelped, dropping both cups and pulling the hem of my shirt as low as it would go.

"Lacey, what's going on?" Monroe ran into the living room, pulling on a pair of sweats, to find me doing the third-degree-burn dance half naked in his living room while *June and Ward Cleaver: The Golden Years* looked on.

"We came to surprise you for your birthday," the woman said weakly. "Surprise . . ."

Monroe skidded to a stop in front of me. He looked from the couple to me, and back again. "Um . . ."

"Well, son, aren't you going to introduce us?" the man asked, smirking.

Of course, now that I'd seen the smirk, I knew. I should have recognized the man as Monroe's father right away.

"Mom, Dad, this is Lacey Vernon, my neighbor. Lacey, Doctors Frank and Janice Monroe."

Two tall, dark-haired men in their early thirties appeared in the doorway, both of them cleaner cut versions of Monroe. I'd seen them in the photo he kept on his bookshelves. These were Monroe's brothers.

Shit.

"Nice," the younger one said, offering his own smug grin as he took in my bare, coffee-splattered legs.

I straightened, pulling the T-shirt as far down over my

thighs as I could as I backed into the bedroom. I smiled way too brightly, my cheeks hot and flushed. "Well, if you'll excuse me, I'm just going to . . . go die of embarrassment."

"Thanks a lot, guys," I heard Monroe say as I closed the bathroom door behind me. I pressed a cold washcloth over the reddened skin on my chest. And then I put another on my cheeks. I leaned my head back against the bathroom wall and murmured, "Lord, I know we haven't talked in a while. I'm Lacey Terwilliger, soon-to-be just Lacey Vernon. You've smote me pretty good this year, what with the cheating spouse and the public humiliation and all, so if you could just move on to someone else, I'd really appreciate it."

"Lacey," Monroe said, appearing at the bathroom door. "I am so sorry. I had no idea they were coming. Their schedules are so crazy, I usually have at least two weeks' notice."

"Why can't I meet anyone in your family while wearing pants?"

He shrugged. "I met you without pants and I like you just fine."

"Not helping."

"You have to admit, it's a little funny," he said, chuckling. "I mean, of all the ways they could have met you. You're going to look back at this and . . ." He stopped that conversational train wreck in its tracks when I scowled at him. "You're right. It's too soon to even think about laughing. Levity is dead to me."

I turned toward him, leaning against the bathroom counter and burying my face in my hands. "Oh, come on, sweetheart," he said, lifting me up on the counter and wrapping his arms around me. "It's not that bad."

I groaned into his chest.

"It was memorable," he offered, reaching around me to run

the washcloth under the tap. He wiped the cool cloth down my legs, clearing away the sticky drying coffee. He swirled it up over my knees, up my thighs, sweeping between my legs. I moaned a little, and he captured the sound with his mouth. He hitched my newly clean legs over his hips and ground against me.

"I know a way to make you feel better," he murmured against my lips as he slowly slid the damp shirt up my body. I broke away from his kiss, and pushed him halfheartedly.

"I am not doing this with your whole family in the living room," I told him, finally able to laugh. "They already think I'm some trampy T-shirt thief."

"Yes, so, the damage is done. Might as well take advantage." He ghosted his fingers across my breasts, gently tweaking the nipples. My ankles flexed around his hips, pulling him closer.

"You're insane!" I laughed, as he nuzzled my neck. He cradled my cooling cheeks in his palms, and kissed me tenderly. I smiled up at him. "Why didn't you tell me it was your birthday?"

"Because I'm not a woman?"

"Seriously, this is important stuff. Birthdays, food allergies, the location of tattoos I may have missed so far."

Monroe shrugged, lacing his fingers through mine. "I just didn't want to make a big deal out of it. And I know you, Lace, me casually dropping it into conversation would make you think you had to make a fuss."

"You're right. Your whole family surprising me while I'm running through the living room commando, that's the very definition of low-key."

"If I agree that I should have told you, can I unwrap my present?" he asked as he pulled the shirt over my head.

"You are just not giving up on this, are you?"

As he shook his head and kissed my neck, I slid my hand in the bathroom drawer, searching around for condoms. He lifted my butt, securing my legs around his hips. I braced my hands against the counter and thought that this was something I would never have done before meeting Monroe.

"You are a very bad influence on me," I whispered as he slipped into me, inch by inch.

• • •

Monroe went out to smooth things over with his family while I showered. I reeked of spilled coffee and hurried, quiet sex, and that just wasn't the way I wanted to spend the morning. By the time I emerged from the bedroom, fully clothed in a very modest turtleneck, Monroe's mother was sliding cinnamon rolls out of the oven and reminding her youngest son, Andy, that setting the breakfast table didn't mean tossing the dishes in the middle of the table and walking away. Monroe's father was looking through the bookshelves for titles he hadn't read yet. And Monroe and his oldest brother, Matt, were arguing over the most efficient way to get kindling started in the fireplace, which sounded remarkably like a scene from *The Great Outdoors.*

I walked into the kitchen and handed Janice Monroe a trivet for the hot pan and dragged a bunch of mismatched juice glasses out of the cabinet. "I'm so sorry about earlier, Mrs. Monroe. Or I guess, it's Dr. Monroe, isn't it?"

"Call me Janice, sweetheart," she said, patting my shoulder. "We're all Dr. Monroe, so it could get confusing otherwise. And don't worry about earlier. I raised three boys. There's not much you can do to shock me."

"Oh, good. But, for the sake of my conscience, I should probably say I'm sorry I flipped out and cursed in front of you. Not the best first impression, I know. I just never imagined meeting Monroe's parents."

"You didn't think he had any?"

I pursed my lips. "I'd imagined some sort of hatching scenario."

She laughed. "Someday I'll tell you about the time I came into Franny's room early one morning to find his homecoming date—"

"That's not a story we need to share," Monroe said, striding into the room and giving his mother a warning glance. Janice glared right back and pushed a carton of juice into his hands.

"So early-morning raids are habit with you?" I asked. "Wait, did you just call him Franny?"

Monroe groaned. "Mom, we've talked about this. I'm not Franny, especially in front of other people."

"Well, his father was already Frank. He refused to go with Francis or Bernard," Janice said, turning her attention back to the stove, where she was heating a pan for eggs. "It's a perfectly acceptable nickname."

"Did people call you Franny in high school?" I asked. He scowled at me. "So much of your personality makes sense now."

"Do you see why I went with Lefty, even if it took getting shot in the ass?" he asked as his mother swatted at him with a dish towel.

"You get out of here so we can talk about you," she said.

"Actually, I think I'm going to head on home, give you guys some space. I don't want to intrude on a family thing," I said.

"Don't be silly!" she exclaimed while Monroe practically barred my escape route with his body. "I've seen you half-naked. You know about my son's embarrassing, effeminate nickname. Franny likes you enough to declare an embargo on certain stories from his adolescence. You're practically family now, anyway."

"You have strange standards for family membership," I told her.

She grinned, her eyes twinkling just like her son's, and handed me a mixing bowl and a carton of eggs. Monroe hesitated for a total of two seconds, shot me an apologetic look over his shoulder, and then abandoned me like a rat running from a sinking ship.

Coward.

"I should apologize to you, Lacey," she said in a softer, more serious tone. "Franny didn't tell us he was seeing anyone. Otherwise, we would have had the sense to call. Don't take that personally, he doesn't tell us about anyone he's dating. Ever since Sarah, he hasn't made a habit of . . ."

"Making friends with ladies?" I suggested helpfully.

"Yes, thank you," she said, chuckling. "It's obvious my son likes you very much if he lets you invade his inner sanctum. I don't remember the last time someone besides family was allowed in his home. So I want you to know—"

"Mom?" Monroe called from the living room. "Don't forget that it's Matt that likes fried eggs. The rest of us like scrambled."

"Like I could forget something like that!" she called back.

She smiled at me. "Ten minutes together and it's like the boys are kids again. Lacey, I want you to know—"

"Hey, Mom?" Monroe called again. "Are you making toast? Because I have a new jar of strawberry jelly in the cabinet."

Janice frowned. I rolled my eyes and said, "I'll get the toast."

"Anyway, Lacey," Janice started again just as Monroe yelled, "Hey, Mom! There's grape jelly, too, in the fridge."

"I know exactly what you're doing, Francis Bernard Monroe!" she said, storming into the living room, hands on hips. "Don't for one second think you can keep Lacey and me from having a civilized conversation."

I laughed as Monroe insisted it was worth a shot and tried to convince his mother to declare a moratorium on all stories about him that did not extend from events of the past year. His mother ignored him and turned back toward the kitchen.

"It was a little ham-handed, son," Monroe's father told him, shaking his silver head in disdain. "You should know by now the best way to distract your mother is by breaking something semivaluable in another room."

"Or pushing one of your brothers down the stairs," Matt muttered in a resentful tone that labeled him as a "pushee."

"Or hiding the incriminating wrappers from her secret chocolate stash in your brother's room," Andy suggested.

"I knew that was you, you little bastard," Monroe griped.

"I don't know whose children they are," Janice told me. "They're the product of terrible parenting, obviously. They just showed up on our doorstep one day and we took them in."

By this time I was leaned against the counter, laughing so hard I had a stitch in my side.

• • •

We finally got breakfast on the table, after Janice insisted her sons and husband "get off their chauvinistic asses and help." I suddenly understood where Monroe got his unique grasp of the English language. There was quite a bit of plate shuffling, tossing of cinnamon rolls across the table, and fights over the "good" strips of bacon, but eventually everyone was leaning back in their chairs and moaning about eating too much.

"So what exactly do you do when your family comes to visit?" I asked Monroe quietly as his brothers loudly argued over the last cinnamon roll.

"Well, my dad comes up with a big itinerary for the day. Hiking, renting a pontoon boat, visiting that apple orchard off County Line Road. He usually ends up falling asleep right after breakfast and napping through lunch. My brothers watch basketball games. I spend most of the day fighting Mom off of my laundry hamper. We play a couple of board games while my dad snores. Mom makes a big dinner, we eat, and they all go back to their motel room, leaving me to appreciate the silence of my little home."

"Wow," I marveled. "Still sounds like more fun than Christmas with the Terwilligers."

He snickered and tugged gently on my hair. I looked up and found that Matt was staring at me.

"Do I have jelly on my face?" I asked.

"No, it's just you look really familiar. Where do I know you from?" Matt asked.

"I just have one of those faces," I said, shooting a covert glance at Monroe.

"No, I saw you somewhere, like on TV or something. Were you on one of those reality dating shows?"

I tried to play it off with a laugh, while the blood drained out of my face. "Yes, I must confess, I was that girl who threw up while making out with Bret Michaels on *Rock of Love.*"

"No, that girl was a redhead," Andy said. "But now that you mention it, Lacey does look familiar."

"Drop it, guys," Monroe warned.

"Oh, my God, you're that crazy e-mail chick!" Andy exclaimed.

I froze, with an expression akin to Bambi caught in headlights.

"Andrew, the family policy is that we don't call people crazy until we've known them at least twenty-four hours," Janice said sternly.

"What is he talking about?" Frank asked.

"Nothing," Monroe growled, shooting his brothers a face-melting death glare. "They have Lacey mixed up with someone else."

"No, crazy e-mail chick's name was Lacey, too. I remember now," Matt said. "You know, the nurses at my office printed that out and taped it to the refrigerator in the break room? You're like a role model to them. I can't wait to tell them I met you. I will admit that while the actual letter scared the crap out of me and my Y chromosome, I thought it was pretty awesome that you nailed your husband like that. He sounded like a scumbag."

"What are you talking about?" Janice demanded.

When Monroe opened his mouth to protest again, I put my hand on his arm. "It's not like they can't go home and google me," I said. I closed my eyes and took a deep breath. "A few months back, I found out my husband was cheating on me—"

"And she sent everybody he knew an e-mail busting him out as a 'spineless, dickless wonder'!" Matt exclaimed. "It was hilarious!"

"Actually, it was 'spineless, shiftless, useless, dickless wonder,'" I mumbled, unable to look up at the elder Monroes' faces.

Andy picked up my hand and pressed it to his chest. "You made me laugh until coffee came out of my nose; therefore, I pledge my undying loyalty to you. In fact, if you and Franny break up, I'd be glad to be your shoulder to cry on—"

Monroe cuffed Andy on the back of the head. "Keep your shoulders, and all your other parts, away from my girlfriend."

At the use of the word "girlfriend," I stiffened, particularly given Andy's big announcement. Monroe's parents probably weren't going to be thrilled that his new . . . "special lady friend" had recently been featured on David Letterman's Top Ten Women Who Make Your Wife Look Better list.

"I remember reading something about that. Your husband cheated on you?" Monroe's father asked. "Left you for another woman?"

I nodded, mentally calculating exactly how much time I would allow to pass before succumbing to embarrassment and bolting for the door.

"Well, he's obviously an idiot," Frank said dismissively, before sipping his coffee. "Now, I'm going lie down for a minute to rest my eyes, and then we are going to take that scenic trail around Cosgrove Point."

"Right," Matt snorted.

"We'll see you around dinnertime, Dad," Monroe said.

"Not this time!" Frank said. "This time I've set the alarm on my watch."

"You don't have an alarm on your watch, honey," Janice said as Monroe's dad made himself comfortable on the couch.

"Scrabble or Trivial Pursuit?" Andy said.

"Surprise me," Matt responded.

"Not Trivial Pursuit, guys. You always end up fighting over obscure Civil War trivia and then my coffee table ends up broken," Monroe moaned.

"Wait, that's it?" I asked, as Matt and Andy took their plates to the sink. Janice picked up the dirty cutlery and started loading the dishwater. "That's the sum total of your parents' reaction?"

Monroe shrugged. "Yeah. My dad worked in an ER for thirty years before going into family practice. Mom works in a state-run psychiatric hospital. Short of bloodshed, not much you can do will shock them. Also, you may have noticed that my family places a lot of value on an effective insult. In fact, your stock has probably just gone up, as far as they're concerned."

"Then why did you keep telling your brothers to shut up?"

"I didn't want them to embarrass you. I know you don't like talking about the newsletter. I figure today's been uncomfortable enough for you."

"This feels like a trick," I told him. I pursed my lips. "Your mom isn't going to ambush me in the kitchen and tell me my crazy, damaged ass has no business near her baby boy?"

He shook his head. "She may ask you to do a reading of your newsletter, but other than that, no."

"I wouldn't mind reading it if you have a copy," Janice said as she came back to the table. "Andy only shoots coffee out of his nose for high comedy."

"Oh, no." I gave an uncomfortable little laugh. "It's not that funny. Andy's just exaggerating."

I looked up to find Monroe silently mouthing, "It's on my desk," and poked his shoulder. "You're no help at all."

Janice leveled me with those sharp, hazel eyes. "You know, I see a lot of desperate, damaged women in my work. Women who let the hurts and disappointments push them down until they can't find the will to go on living, much less stand up for themselves. As a psychiatrist, I'm supposed to say that indulging a desire for revenge isn't healthy, that it would be better to focus on healing and rebuilding your own life. As a woman, I say that well-executed payback is an important ingredient in healing and closure is required before you can rebuild anything. If you managed to do that without slandering or hospitalizing anyone, I say good for you."

The approval in her tone had me blushing—a pleasant, warm sensation spreading through my chest that suddenly flushed cold. I wasn't ready for this. I wasn't ready for family breakfasts and inappropriate stories from Monroe's adolescence. I didn't want to have to work to get another mother's approval, to make sure her expectations were met and her birthday gifts had appropriately sappy cards attached.

I felt a panic akin to claustrophobia. I wasn't ready to be anyone's girlfriend. Even though I was having the tender, green beginnings of those feelings toward Monroe, I wasn't ready to love someone else. I couldn't think about him in the long-term, whether it was a month from now or a year from now. I just wanted a simple, uncomplicated relationship with my companionable, sexy neighbor. And if he became more than that, a sweet guy with smartass brothers and a tragically feminine first name, I wouldn't be able to manage it. I recognized that these were selfish, shallow thoughts, but I also recognized that they were true. And I wasn't going to be getting around them any time soon.

I needed to leave, to run, to get back to my own space and breathe for a little bit. But I wouldn't embarrass Monroe in front of his family, not because I wanted to keep up appearances, but because it would hurt him. So I released my death grip on the table, smiled at his mother, and started clearing dishes.

"How about we leave those until after the first round of Trivial Pursuit?" she suggested. "Maybe we can keep them from beating each other bloody over the Sports and Leisure questions."

"I don't make any guarantees," I told her. "I fight like a girl."

"And I can't tell you how nice it is to have another girl around," she said, putting her hand on my shoulder as we joined the boys at the coffee table. When Monroe looked up at me with that content expression, mixed with familial exasperation, I couldn't help feel a twinge in my stomach that had nothing to do with overeating.

24

Happy Endings Gone to Hell

I was stuck.

I was lounging in my hammock, enjoying what would probably be the last tolerably warm day before the temperatures took a dive toward winter. I was reading over some of Monroe's notes on my chapters. He'd drawn little smiley faces next to the lines he thought were funny and written "ew!" next to the particularly bloody scenes, which I found to be very helpful. He also wrote "bowchikawawa" next to a particularly well-written flashback love scene, which made me giggle.

When Monroe's family had departed the week before, I'd scrambled to find some sort of personal equilibrium. If he was hurt that I basically shut myself up in my cabin and didn't come out for three days, he didn't say anything. I told him I was writing, that I'd hit a groove, and he gave me this understanding smile that made feel that much worse. I knew it was a jerk move. It was something a guy, something Mike, would do. But I had to feel like I had some control, independence. And he seemed so pleased when I showed up with pages and pages of new material to critique. It helped me feel like things were getting back to normal, or at least our version of normal.

Given that I didn't have a job and spent every spare minute at my laptop, it wasn't a surprise that I was rounding the corner toward the last third of the book. The problem was I had no idea how it was going to end. On one hand, I wanted to give Laurie a happy ending because, let's face it, I wanted a happy ending for myself. But did that mean helping Laurie find love? If anything, I'd learned that a relationship doesn't necessarily mean permanent happiness. And every time I sat down to try to suss it out, or just make notes about possible endings, I froze.

And, yes, I recognized that finishing the book meant proofreading, editing, and the very scary agent search, so the fear of failure was a rather large brick in the wall that seemed to have built itself inside my head. I'd hoped that maybe seeing some encouraging notes from Monroe would help, but mostly it just made me feel guilty for not writing.

When I heard a car door slam, I assumed it was my favorite grumpy crime writer returning with the ingredients for Margarita 'n' Fajita Night.

I didn't bother looking up from my manuscript as I heard footsteps approach. "Just let me finish this thought and then I'm all yours for the night."

"Sounds good to me."

I flinched. That was not Monroe's voice.

I looked up to see my soon-to-be ex-husband smirking down at me. I scrambled to sit up, nearly spinning myself out of the hammock. "Mike! What the hell are you doing here?"

Mike advanced, his hand outstretched to help me stand. "A man can't visit his wife at his own lake house?"

I slapped his hands away and righted myself. "I'm not your wife and this isn't your lake house, jackass. You have a house. You live there, with your secretary, remember?"

It's very difficult to appear dignified while teetering on the edge of a hammock. I swayed there, trying to maintain my seat and a level gaze with Mike. At the mention of our home, Mike's face softened. He looked tired, older and tired. There were circles under his eyes and the slightest hint of expression lines around his mouth. "You look great . . . just great. You've done something new with your hair. It's—"

"Spare me," I told him. "You've got about five seconds to tell me what you're doing here before I go inside and call my lawyer or animal control or whatever it takes to tranq-gun your ass."

Mike gave a sad little smile. "You're not going to make it easy on me, are you?"

"I stopped making things easy for you a while ago. How's that working out for you?"

"I made a mistake with Beebee," Mike admitted, scooting a white plastic lawn chair over to sit in front of me. "It's just not working out the way I thought it would."

"So you were thinking you could just replace me with another woman without any snags or inconveniences?"

Mike shrugged, managing to look the slightest bit guilty. "Well."

When he saw the expression on my face, he said, "I wasn't thinking! I-I made a mistake. I went through a selfish phase and I didn't think it through. And I'm man enough to admit it. After all our years together, I think you owe it to me to recognize that and give us another chance."

In the eternity between those words reaching my ears and my tongue's productions of the words "hell" and "no," the thought that kept bouncing around in my head was, "His mama probably wrote that speech for him." Instead of saying so, I laughed my ass off.

"Are you kidding me?" I threw my hands up, making Mike take a step back.

"Lacey, please. She doesn't get any of my jokes," Mike said, his brown eyes as sad and lost as a homesick kindergartner. "She hates action movies. I can't take her to Scrabble night over at Tina and John's because she hates board games. Anyway, Tina and John stopped inviting me because the wives don't like Beebee. I took her to a dinner party at the McClarens'. She went on and on about some lemon juice and cayenne pepper thing that would help Jolene McClaren 'take all that extra weight off.'"

Amos McClaren was one of Mike's biggest corporate clients and his wife, Jolene, was very sensitive about her weight. I bit my lip to keep from laughing, because laughing would bring Mike to his senses and make the funny stories stop.

"I'm lonely," Mike said. "I miss telling you about my day. I miss you scratching my back before I go to sleep. I miss the way you turned the toast over so the sides with the butter faced each other. I wasn't thinking. I just— I shouldn't have treated you like that. And I just want to go back to way things used to be, Lace. I want you to come home. I was blind, Lace. I took you for granted. And Beebee made me— I mean, the sex was—"

"I don't want to hear about it!" I cried.

Mike threw up his hands, whether it was a conversational gesture or an effort to shield his face from oncoming blows, I had no idea. "I'm just saying, that's all it was, sex. I can't make a life with Beebee. Not the kind of life I had with you. If you want to come back, the door's open."

I just stared at him. He missed the way I buttered his toast? My purpose in his life was to laugh at his jokes, scratch his back, and butter his toast? I was vaguely sick to my stomach, but mostly, really, really sad. That was my marriage? Not once had he said he was wrong or that he was sorry. He was just telling me what he wanted. Nothing had changed.

"I just need some hope that there might still be a chance for us."

"Mike, there is no us," I told him firmly. My voice lowered to a less harsh whisper when I said, "There is no you and me. That's all over now."

"It doesn't have to be," he insisted. "Everything can go back to where it was. We can have it all back."

Wait a minute. This was all pretty proactive for a man who used to have me prepeel his fruit for him. I narrowed my eyes at him. "So how did Beebee take it when you told her it was over?"

He gave me a sheepish look.

"So you're going to do to her what you did to me?" I yelled and started toward the cabin. When I heard Mike's footsteps behind me, I whirled around and stuck a finger in his chest. "You can't even stay loyal to your mistress, Mike! What kind of degenerate does that make you? Why would I even consider being with someone who can't stay faithful to the person he cheated on *me* with?"

The shift from kicked puppy to wounded martyr happened so quickly, it was like a ripple under the skin. Mike's eyes narrowed, his lip curled, and he looked at me like I was something he scraped off of his shoe. "I'm trying to give you, us, another chance. You could at least give me that much credit."

"You're trying to get out of the mess your hormones made."

"I can't believe you're talking to me like this!" he shouted, his face flushing red. "What's wrong with you, Lacey?"

"I'm a wild woman. I skinny-dip. I have orgasms that don't require heavy equipment."

"I can't believe you're sleeping with someone else!" he cried.

"How exactly do you have the balls to get angry with me about that, Stinger?"

Mike looked like he might take a swipe at me when something he saw over my shoulder made his face melt back into a more "social" mode. I turned to see Monroe's truck pulling into his driveway and felt both relief and annoyance. This was not an introduction I needed to make at the moment.

Monroe stepped out of his truck and looked from Mike to me and back. From the look on my face, he must have thought that Mike was a door-to-door evangelist or a census taker or something. "Everything okay, Lacey?"

"I'm fine, Monroe. This is Mike." I huffed.

Mike's back stiffened. He sucked in his stomach and glared at Monroe. "Who is this, Lacey?"

I sighed. "This is my neighbor, Monroe. He's renting the McGee place."

Monroe gave Mike an appraising once-over and offered his hand for a shake. Mike reluctantly accepted and I could see the tension in their hands as they each squeezed far harder than was socially necessary. The message could not have been clearer if there had been telegraph wires stretched between them. Monroe was letting Mike know "I'm sleeping with your woman now." I was being marked, like territory. I was being peed on. Wonderful.

"If you don't mind, my wife and I are having a private discussion."

Mike's prissy tone was enough to break the tension. I had to bite my lip again to keep from laughing. Monroe and I shared a look that made Monroe smirk. Mike saw this and scowled. "How well do you know my wife, Monroe?"

"Why the hell would you care?" I asked him.

"Oh, come on, Lacey, what's the point of hiding it?" Monroe asked, slipping his arm around my waist. "Very well. You know, it's not every day that a woman so spontaneous and open-minded and well, flexible, moves in right next door. Am I the luckiest guy you've ever seen or what?"

Monroe leaned in and gave me a long, loud, smacking kiss. As Mike's face drained to paper white, Monroe gave him a cheeky grin and slapped me on the butt before walking away. "Nice to meet you, Mark," he called over his shoulder as he ambled to his front door and walked into his house without so much as another look.

"Right." Mike began to roll his sleeve up, stomping toward Monroe's door.

I rolled my eyes. "Oh, what are you doing?"

"You think I'm going to just let him put his hands on my wife in front of me?" Mike demanded.

"I'm not your wife anymore."

"So this is why you won't come home?" Mike snarled. "We hit a rough patch and you shack up with the first ex-con you meet?"

I spluttered, "Wha—what—? Yeah, Mike, this is why I'm not coming home. My reluctance has nothing to do with the fact that your mistress is living in my house now. It would have to be because of another stud in the corral, right?"

"I told you I made a mistake! Why do you keep harping on me when I've said I'm sorry?"

"Actually, you haven't said you are sorry. You said you made a mistake. It's not the same thing," I told him.

"I tried to give you another chance," Mike said rather snottily. "If you're not willing to take it—"

"Just leave, Mike."

"You're not going to get another chance," he warned me.

"I don't need one. Tell Beebee I said hello."

Mike stormed off to his car and peeled out, flinging no small amount of gravel my way. Monroe stepped outside and waved at Mike's departing car. He grinned at me.

"What on earth has gotten into you?" I demanded as I marched up his front steps. "I thought you had this whole 'divorce drama' phobia."

"You wanted him to stay?" Monroe asked.

"No, definitely not. But I didn't need for you to step in. And there was no reason for you to manhandle me in front of him. I did not like that."

Monroe snorted. "Right, why make him think that you're unavailable?"

"Don't do that," I ground out. "Don't make this into a you-versus-him thing. There's no contest. Why would I care what Mike thinks? I do not want Mike back. I am not still in love with him."

"And you're saying you didn't enjoy that just a little bit, making Mike think you might spare him a lifetime of alimony?" Monroe asked.

"I'm not taking alimony from Mike. I don't want anything from him. Hell, if Maya keeps throwing money at me, I'm not going to need it anyway."

Oh, double damn it. From the look on Monroe's face, I immediately wanted to change the subject back to my ambiguous feelings toward my soon-to-be ex-husband.

"What are you talking about?" he demanded. "I thought we agreed you were going to drop the newsletter thing? You said you were going to rethink writing the letters."

"Well, I did rethink it," I said. "And I decided, for myself, that it might not be such a bad idea. I could make a lot of money writing the newsletters. And I could help people. Mostly it would be about making money, but I would have a lot of satisfaction in my job. I've never had that before. Even your mom said that writing that e-mail was what I needed to move on. I could do that for someone else."

"My mom said it made sense for you to do that. She wasn't writing a blanket prescription for everybody," he insisted. "And you've been making so much progress on your book. Why stop now?"

"I don't have the dedication that you do when it comes to writing," I told him. "I don't know if I'm going to finish that book. And let's face it, even if I finish it, I have a better chance of getting hit by lightning *while* scratching off a million-dollar lottery ticket than getting that thing published."

He followed me as I turned to walk away. "You want to know why your life hasn't turned out? Why you're not going to finish what you've started? Because you take the easy way out. Whenever something's hard or doesn't just fall into your lap, you give up or you let someone else do the heavy lifting for you. You're just waiting for someone else to hand you the answers, to make the decisions for you. Mike, your parents, Maya."

"Well, if I'm so lazy and immature, why did you even bother with me?"

"Because you have the potential to be this amazing person. You're smart and you're funny and you can be so brave. You've grown so much since you've come up here and you're just going to give it all up."

"Who the hell do you think you are?" I yelled. "Who appointed you the great determiner of personal growth? And stop trying to pretend that you're mad about the newsletter thing when you're really mad about Mike being here. I can't help that he managed to remember the way."

"This is about you, Lacey," he said, taking my arms in his hands with just enough force to hold me in one place. "This is about you being unable to just move on and let Mike go. Stop letting it fester. It would really suck, forty years down the road, to look back on a lifetime of being petty and resentful, and think, 'Well, at least I took him down with me.'"

I jerked away from his grip. "I don't have to stand here and listen to this."

"Right, because I don't get a say. I mean, it's not like we're in a relationship or anything. You've made it loud and clear we're just two people having friendly sex, right? Fuck buddies?"

"Don't," I growled stalking toward my door. And damned if he didn't follow me, his voice growing louder and angrier with every step.

"I mean, I guess I should be grateful that some divorcée just wants to jump me and then walk away like I'm some anatomically correct prop. But somehow it hurts my feelings a little bit. I'm not stupid, Lacey. I see you pull back at every chance you get. I know how much this freaks you out. You made it pretty clear when you turned into Howard freaking Hughes after you met my parents. I just don't understand why. We're good together. I've made it clear how much I care about you. You know I wouldn't hurt you. Why are you working so hard to keep from calling this what it is?"

"And what is it, exactly?" I asked, fighting the tears flooding the corners of my eyes. "Are we going steady? Are you going to give me an ID bracelet and a box of conversation hearts? Do you want to get married? Because I've been there, done that, and I don't know if I'm ever going to be ready to do it again. So what's the point, Monroe? "

"The point is that I love you. And it really pisses me off that you don't want to hear that."

"Because it's got to be on your terms!" I yelled. "It's got to be on your timetable, your way. You know, maybe it's not that I don't want to be in a relationship, maybe it's that I don't want to be in a relationship with *you*. You're always pushing and judging and trying to make me change into the person that—I don't know—is worthy of you? I mean, you wouldn't even talk to me until I proved that I was low-maintenance enough for you. I don't want to be your pet project. I've already tried living with a man whose standards I couldn't meet and I'm not going to do it again."

"Stop making this about Mike. I am not your husband."

"You're right, you're not."

"Grow up, Lacey."

"Fuck you, Monroe."

25

A Step Back

When everything imploded with Mike, I prided myself on the fact that I hadn't shown up at anyone's door crying hysterically and looking for a sympathetic ear, despite the fact that such a juicy piece of gossip would have made me welcome in any home in town.

After my fight with Monroe, I felt that I was due.

"Honey, what happened?" Emmett cried, opening the door to find me tearstained and disheveled.

"Monroe . . . fight . . . labels!" I sobbed as he took my suitcase.

"She had a fight over Marilyn Monroe and labels?" a low voice sounded from the dining room.

I opened my eyes and realized that there were three men sitting at Emmett's dining room table, sipping wine and staring at me like I had an extra head. The table was sumptuously spread with dim sum, rice noodles, and a couple of Asian vegetables I didn't recognize.

"Em, I'm so sorry!" I gasped. "I didn't know you had company."

"Oh, sweetie, you just made a rather bland evening that much more interesting," he whispered, tucking his hand through my elbow. "Seriously, Kirk just finished his fourth retelling of his entire cruise to Alaska . . . with his mother. Can you imagine? I mean if he'd gone somewhere interesting, that would be one thing. But he spent fifteen minutes describing whales surfacing. You've saved us all."

He wrapped his arm around me and said in a much louder voice, "Now come in and have a good cry, and we'll sympathize."

"I'm sorry about this," I said to the guests, only one of whom I recognized—Emmett's on-again, off-again boyfriend, Peter. Emmett made the introductions. The guys stood and helped me to my chair as if I were the walking wounded. Thomas, a whippet-thin man with three earrings and a healthy head of silver-blond hair, poured me a glass of white wine and patted my head.

"Emmett told us all about you," Kirk gushed. He seemed very young and still had a bit of the baby-fat look around his chin. "You are so brave. I just don't know if I could ever hold my head up if something like that happened to me—"

Thomas cleared his throat and shook his head. "So what's got you so upset, Lacey? Emmett told us you were doing so well."

"Post-divorce stress disorder?" Peter suggested. "I know I only met Mike once or twice, Lace, but I just did not like that man. It's okay to be uptight and it's okay to be boring, but not at the same time."

"No." I sniffed. "Mike had nothing to do with it, really, even though he technically started the fight and then ran off, as usual. Monroe was just being such an asshole, telling me how great I could be if I would just change. I'm really tired of people telling me what about my personality needs fixing."

"So we're *not* talking about Marilyn Monroe, then," Thomas said speculatively.

"Monroe's my . . . I don't know what to call him, which was part of the problem, really. He's upset with me because I refuse to put a label on us."

Peter nodded. "That makes more sense than what I had in mind."

"It's her neighbor up at Chez Divorcée. You should see this guy," Emmett said. "Legs that go on forever, biceps the size of my head, and his ass—"

I frowned. "Let's just say he's doable and move on."

"Sooo doable." He sighed. When he saw my face, he flinched. "Crossing a line?" I nodded. "Sorry."

"So how long did you two date?" Will asked, seeming nonplussed by our "doability" sidebar.

"We didn't really date so much as just hang out all the time, talk, and make each other meals."

"Sounds sort of perfect," Thomas said, tilting his head.

"It was. It was kind of perfect. I mean, I was fortunate to have two functioning brain cells after the e-mail thing, although I suspect those cells spend most their time arguing. And I met this guy, and he was all prickly and mysterious, but I dug that."

"Prickly could work," Peter conceded. "As long as it was paired with hot, prickly could work."

"We ignored each other completely for a while, or at least I ignored him, while he tried to figure out why I was ignoring him. And then he just started being nice to me. We became friends. We hung out, talked about stuff we were interested in. We had athletic, spontaneous, no-strings-attached sex."

"Baby's first booty call. I am so proud," Emmett said, wiping a mock tear from his eye.

"We continued to have the friendship. Then I met his family, he met my ex, and everything got weird."

"Emmett, you said she sucked at relationships!" Kirk exclaimed. "That doesn't sound so bad."

"Emmett!" I yelled. "That's not fair! I've only had two relationships in the last decade!"

"Sounds healthier than my last three relationships," Peter said.

"I was at least one of those relationships," Emmett said. "Ass."

Peter shrugged. "I'm just saying."

"So what went wrong, Lacey?" asked Thomas, who seemed to be the group moderator.

"He found out that I'd been offered a job writing e-mail newsletters for other woman like me, and he told me he thought it was a bad idea. He got really upset about it, thought it would damage my soul or something. I told him I'd drop it, but I was still considering it. I mean, the woman who offered me the job kept upping the salary—"

At that, the tribe winced collectively, making a unified "ooooh" sound, as if they'd been kicked in the gut.

"So you, basically, lied to him," Peter said.

"Well, it sounds really bad when you put it that way," I protested. "Don't I get a say in how I'm going to make my living?"

Thomas poured more wine. "Sure. Claim your personal power. Be the master of your destiny. But expect some fallout when a man tells you that it's really important to him that you don't do something and then you go behind his back and do it anyway. Whether it's going after a job you want, or say, cheating, when you use deception, you have to accept the consequences."

I frowned. This conversation was not going the way I'd expected. I thought Emmett's friends were morally obligated to fuss, ply me with regional wines, and make me feel better. This whole mirror of truth exercise was not as fun.

"So how did Mike play into all this?" Emmett asked.

"He came up to the cabin in his usual way, trying to bluster his way through and act like nothing happened. He had the nerve to get pissy and territorial with Monroe."

"That must have been hilarious," Emmett hooted. "Like a Pekingese going after a pit bull."

I chuckled. "Mostly it was just sad. I didn't like Monroe acting like he owned me now and when I told him that—"

"Oh, honey, no." Kirk shook his head. "Even I know you're not supposed to do that. You don't defend the old flame to the new flame. Even indirectly."

"You know that because I told you that," Peter retorted. "So let me guess, Lacey, you started arguing about ownership. You brought up the job issue. He exploded because you lied to him."

Emmett interjected, "He told you a bunch of stuff you didn't want to hear about being a grown-up and a better person, and then you flounced away."

"I wouldn't use the word 'flounce . . . '" I grumbled.

"Fail," Kirk said. "Epic Fail."

"Kirk, we've agreed that you do not tweet during polite conversation," Emmett warned him. "It dates you. And it's obnoxious."

"Fine." Kirk huffed. "It was a fail-ure."

"What is going on here?" I cried. "I thought you said you would sympathize!"

"That was before we got all the details," Emmett said dismissively. "He introduced you to his family, Lace. That means something. Do you know how long it took Peter to introduce me to his family?"

"Don't bring that up again, Em," Peter sighed, sinking back on the couch and crossing his arms.

"Two years!" Emmett exclaimed. "And I had to pretend to be his roommate."

"I dated a guy who didn't care what I did for a living as long as it meant he could sponge off of me and write *Grey's Anatomy* fanfiction all day," Thomas said, his lips twisted into a wry expression.

"I still live with my mother," Kirk said. "That should tell you about the kind of guys I date. So I think it's safe to say that any of us would have killed to be in your position."

"Wait." I sipped wine to fortify myself before ranting. "So, according to you guys, I was wrong, then followed it up by being more wrong. Then I finished up by being unreasonable and unappreciative of what I had?"

After a moment's consideration, they all nodded. "That just about sums it up, yes," Thomas said.

"This has not been helpful, at all."

Thomas took my chin in his hand and made me look him in the eye. "Sweetheart, if you want someone to cuddle you and stroke your ego, get a dog. But we will always tell you the truth, which is why a lot of people don't spend time with us. You've screwed up. And you've screwed up big. Own it, apologize for it. Either make up with him or move on."

I frowned, draining the last of my wine. "Can I get a second opinion from a panel of lesbians?"

"No," Emmett told me. "All verdicts are final, no appeals. Who wants dessert?"

• • •

Emmett was never one to let me dwell. The bastard.

Instead of being a decent brother, he allowed me only two days of wallowing in the intensely cheerful comfort of his guest room before forcing me to come in to work with him.

"Come on. Up and at 'em, kid," he called as he poured himself a cup of coffee at his kitchen counter. "There are no free lunches in this house—what the hell are you wearing?"

I looked down at my usual daytime ensemble of yoga pants and a hoodie. "What? This is what I've been wearing during the day."

"Well, then, my darling sister, it wasn't luck that landed you Monroe. It was a miracle."

"Keep the gloves above the belt, Em," I muttered. "You're the one who's told me for years that I dress like a Junior League fembot. I've just taken your advice and relaxed a bit."

"You left 'a bit' behind a long time ago, Lacey," he said, dragging me into the guest room and going through the dresser drawers. "We need to find you a happy medium."

I flopped down on the four-poster canopy bed, wallowing in the mussed white eyelet spread. Emmett's guest room was a 1950s teenager's dream come true. Candy-striped pink-and-white wallpaper, the princess bed, and a picture of Elvis in his army uniform on the refurbished nightstand. He didn't even like Elvis. He just loved a good theme. Emmett's own room was a little less innocent, a lot more Pier 1 Imports. I loved my brother, but he was a throw-pillow junkie. I'd been planning on an intervention before Cherry Glick came along and derailed the course of my existence.

That seemed so long ago now, like it had happened to someone else. And yet, the idea of going into town with Emmett was exhausting. So far I'd managed to dash into town to visit Sam's office without encountering any of my former Singletree friends and neighbors. Once people knew I was helping Emmett at The Auctionarium, they'd make up any excuse to come by for a chat, just to get a look at me.

I could probably deal with being a sideshow attraction if I wasn't busy throwing myself a big Monroe-based pity party. At the moment I just wanted to go back to bed and pull the covers over my head.

"Come on, Lacey, out of bed, this stopped being cute about five minutes ago," he said, tossing dark jeans and a tomato-red sweater at me. "If you're going to stay with me, you're going to pull your weight, which means coming into the store and humoring the cranky technophobic geriatrics who insist they could get ten thousand dollars for their mothers' china if they took it to Sotheby's."

"Well, you make it sound so attractive," I snarked, tossing the sweater back at him. "Why do you even have women's clothes here?"

"Merry Christmas," he said, opening the guest room closet to show me several color-coordinated, accessorized outfits in my sizes. "When you left Mike, I figured there would be a makeover at some point. Though, I'll be honest, I thought it would be sooner. I like to be prepared."

"Emmett, were you not listening last night when I was drunkenly ranting about men who keep pushing me to do what they want?"

"Yes, but I don't count, I'm family," he said, frowning.

"Bullshit!" I exclaimed. "Being family means you count twice. I don't want a makeover. I don't want you laying out outfits for me like I'm six years old. I'm perfectly comfortable in what I have on, thank you, and old enough to pick out my own damn clothes."

"Fine," he said icily, dropping the sweater on the bed. "You have ten minutes to do something with your face and get your poly-blend-covered ass in the car, woman, or I'm calling Mama and telling her you chose to stay here instead of with her."

I gasped. "You wouldn't dare."

"Try me," he said, before sweeping out of the room. "No. No dramatic exits this time. I have something to say to you. So your life didn't turn out exactly as you expected? Well, boo fucking hoo, sweetie. You think this is how I saw my life turning out? Despite dating every eligible man between here and New Orleans, I don't know if I'm ever going to have someone to share my life with. Dad doesn't have anything to do with me. Even though I have plenty of acquaintances, including that coven you met the other night, my baby sister is my closest friend, which is just fucking sad. The only thing I have going for me is my keen eye for breakables made fifty years ago and the fact that you occasionally let me boss you around, even if it's just about your hair. But that's my life. It's what I make of it."

"I'm your closest friend?" I asked. "That *is* fucking sad."

He ignored me. "But you want to know what pisses me off more than anything? That in the end, Mike gave you something most of us would kill for."

"A vulnerability to STDs?"

I made an "uhhf" sound when he threw a pillow at me. "A second chance! Thanks to his boffing the secretary, you found a man who loves you and is just waiting for you to stop being a moron so you can make a life together."

"No, I have a man who thinks I'd be great if I just tweaked my personality a bit here and there to suit his needs," I countered. "Look, I opened myself up to someone completely. And I got burned for it. I'm afraid now that I won't be able to love anybody else. And part of me thinks that's okay, that maybe it's worth it if I don't have to hurt like this anymore."

Emmett sighed. "Lace, let's not romanticize your time with Mike. We both know—"

"I'm not talking about Mike; I'm talking about Monroe."

"Oh." Emmett chewed his lip for a moment. "Well, then, that was a valid and well-constructed argument."

"I'm sorry, Em. I do appreciate what you do for me. Maybe I just need a little less of it. I'll be in the car in five minutes," I said, squeezing his hand.

"Take seven," he said, patting my leg as he pushed up from the bed.

"I'm wearing the sweats!" I called, flopping back on the bed. "I do not know who won that argument."

• • •

A cold strawberry Pop-Tart and a colder Coke later, I was sitting at the computer at Emmett's desk, cataloging a set of milk glass pitchers.

"I do not know how you drink that stuff so early." Emmett shuddered as I took a long pull from the frosty red can. "It can't be good for you."

"Says the man drinking three hits of espresso mixed with overheated milk and four sugars," I said, searching through the tangle of spreadsheets on his hard drive for the appropriate tracking number.

"It's *low-fat* milk," he said.

I shook my head and ignored him. Emmett's office/storeroom was a sort of cross between Ali Baba's cave and Grandma's creepy attic, filled with old bicycles, old framed movie posters, kitschy cookie jars, and the odd antique wooden dressmaker's form. Emmett had a special case to protect the books, magazines, and comic books from humidity and dust. There were dozens of china dolls lined up on Lucite cases on the shelves, like an imprisoned evil doll army. I had a hard time turning my back on them.

Emmett had remodeled the former Faber's Hardware Store so that the storeroom took up the majority of the real estate. He'd walled off the reception area to create a cozy space where he could greet clients at a refurbished Queen Anne table, appraise their valuables for a reserve bid, determine a commission, and sign their paperwork.

While Emmett was willing to sell online for anyone, there was also a small showroom for the items Emmett had gleaned from estate sales and auctions. Emmett sold direct to select, discerning clients who drove hundreds of miles for the privilege of picking through his private collection of antique glass and furniture.

It was that special collection that was giving me fits at the moment. My brother might have been obsessively protective of the condition of the items entrusted to his care, but he sucked at tracking where they ended up. It was some sort of miracle that he managed to ship the items to the buyers. I guessed the "in the now" quality of eBay sales helped him stay on top of those items, but anything that stayed in the store long-term was in danger of being lost in the shuffle. There were half-finished address spreadsheets, spreadsheets that used abbreviations that might have been Sanskrit, and a list of names Emmett had just titled "Nuh-uh."

"Hey, Em, what does 'dep. R. dais. 4-set,' mean?" I asked, thumbing the so-called inventory book while I walked into the reception area. Tansy Moffitt, our pastor's first cousin, was sitting at Emmett's desk while he looked over a collection of old *National Geographic* magazines.

"Oh, sorry, I didn't realize you had a customer," I said, backing away.

Suddenly I wished that I'd shut the hell up and put on Emmett's stylish sweater and jeans ensemble.

"We're just finished," Emmett said, smirking. Tansy Moffitt had the biggest mouth in four counties. The minute she left the store, she would activate a phone tree that would bring every busybody reachable by Ma Bell to Emmett's door.

"Lacey!" Tansy cried, springing up from the chair. "I didn't realize you were here! How have you been? We haven't seen you in such a long time. Let me get a look at you. Oh, I just love that new haircut. It's so . . . interesting! Now, I know that things are hard for you right now, but I'd really like to see you in church this Sunday. Your church family misses you, shug!"

"I think that would be sort of awkward, with Mike's whole family being there," I told her. "But thank you."

"Oh, honey, I think you all just need to put this whole thing behind you. You know, the reverend is preaching a whole series on forgiveness this month and I couldn't help but think last Sunday how much it would help you and Mike to just let the past be the past. You just set it before the Lord and forget it."

"You set it, and forget it," Emmett said, grinning at me, daring me to laugh at his inappropriately Jesus-based Ron Popeil–Rotisserie joke.

"I appreciate the thought, Tansy," I told her, trying to tug my hand out of hers, but she just wouldn't let go. The woman had a grip like a teamster. "I just need some time."

"Oh, sure, shug," she said. "You give me a call if you need anything at all. And I'll see you this Sunday, right?"

"Still too soon, Tansy."

"Well, I'm not going to give up, I'll be stopping by every week until we see you there," she said cheerfully, waving to Emmett as she walked out the door.

Through tight, smiling lips, I said, "I believe you."

"I think I know someone who's going home at lunch to cha-ange," Emmett sang.

"Yes, okay?" I cried, burying my face in my hands. "I will submit to your Machiavellian fashion machinations. Clearly, I was wrong to choose this particular area to make my stand."

He snickered. "Come on, you have to face your public at some point; consider this a safe space."

"Hmmph," I snorted. "My public face aside, could you please explain your organization system, which I suspect isn't so much a system as a series of brain games designed to drive me insane à la Jigaw the serial killer?"

He frowned and I showed him the entry marked "dep. R. dais. 4-set."

"That means depression-era daisy glass, four-piece set. It's in a red box on the third shelf from the bottom in the special collection."

"Well, it's supposed to be on a FedEx truck on its way to Augusta, Georgia. You promised delivery by Friday, which is in two days. You put a reminder on a Post-it note that somehow ended up on the bottom of my shoe. How has eBay not put some sort of skull-and-crossbones disclaimer on your sales profile?"

He sniffed. "There have been a few missteps along the way, but I always manage to keep the customers happy."

"Well, those missteps are costing you a fortune in overhead, like the overnight shipping fees you're going to have to cough up to get the daisy glass to Augusta," I said.

"Since when did you become little miss office manager?"

"If there's anything I learned from serving as an unappreciated part-time serf at Mike's office, it was compulsive, anal-retentive control over paperwork flow. Your books are a mess. Just this morning I found a dozen payments missing on items you shipped months ago. You're charging just enough to make an itty-bitty profit after shipping, the mortgage on the store, and overhead. And from what I could see, most of that comes from your direct antique sales to special clients."

"You couldn't have seen all that in one morning—okay, fine, it's a mess. So, you think I should start charging more?"

"No, I think you should start keeping your books in order and cut some of your waste. Like the overnight fees, which I should mention, you probably want to run over to FedEx now if you want to make the afternoon delivery run."

"Be my unappreciated part-time serf and run it over for me?" he implored. "There's a shiny nickel in it for you."

"No, you procrastinated your way into this bed, buck-o, you handle the shipping," I told him. "But I will go through the rest of your quote-unquote files to make sure you don't have any customer approval rating bombs waiting to go off."

"You're going to reorganize the whole thing, aren't you?" he said, his voice fearful and small.

I thought about it and found that I sort of liked the idea of having somewhere to go every day, at least for a while, somewhere I could forget about Mike and Monroe and just devote myself to someone else's mess. "Yes, I am."

"But I won't be able to find anything," he whined.

"Do you know the alphabet?" I asked. He nodded. "Can you use basic reasoning skills?" He nodded again. "I think you'll be okay."

"Lacey!" Vanessa Whitlock, a friend of our mother's, came through the door, lugging what looked like a standard Black and Decker bread machine. She must have whipped it off the counter in her rush to get out of her house and to the source of fresh gossip. "It's so good to see you!"

"Maybe I will go to the FedEx office for you," I said quietly, peering down.

"Oh, no," Emmett said. "I have to learn my lesson. You can mind the store for a while. Oh, look, more ladies coming into the store. It looks like they're forming a line."

"I hate you," I muttered.

"You love me," he said, turning on his heel to the storeroom. "New client paperwork is in the top drawer on the left. It's called tough love, Lace. I'm ditching you because I care."

"Emmett!"

But he'd left me, with a pack of gossipmongers gathering in the waiting room. And I was still wearing the damn yoga pants.

26

Hidden Piercings

Emmett had thrown me in the deep end of the pool. And that pool was filled with sharks.

The Great Whites came in the form of church ladies, my mother's bridge club friends, and wives of Mike's clients. And they weren't after my blood, just delicious bits of information about my appearance and overall mental state. They were all on my side, they assured me, and just came by to lend their support during my "trying time." My mother's golf partner, Mimi Becket, just couldn't believe Mike was bringing "that awful woman" to country club events and expecting everyone to just accept her like one of their own. Jenna Upwell swore she and her husband only went out to dinner with Mike and Beebee to be polite, and that she was thinking of me the whole time. I emerged from this gauntlet of strained social interaction exhausted, with very little to add to the stock but a bunch of gently used kitchen appliances.

After ducking home to change into Emmett-approved office attire, I avenged myself in many, many ways, starting with a complete overhaul of Emmett's "filing system." I dumped his banker's box of invoices onto the floor and used a hand-carved ivory walking stick to shuffle them around. Emmett was both incensed and horrified by my abuse of the stock.

By the time we closed, I'd almost gotten the invoices near some sort of order. Mama came barreling into the shop, clutching her handbag like a Spartan shield.

"Oh, crap," Emmett muttered.

"Would you like to tell me why I had to hear from Betty Vogel that you're back in town?" she demanded, stopping to give Emmett a quick kiss before continuing her tirade. "And why the whole of the Ladies Auxiliary seems to think you have a tattoo of a snake around your waist?"

Emmett snickered.

"Mama, I don't have a tattoo," I said, the picture of innocence. "But Emmett does."

Emmett gasped right along with Mama. "How could you?" he spat, unconsciously rubbing at the little yin-yang symbol he'd had put on his hip in a drunken spring break debacle. "I swore you to secrecy!"

"You will never leave me in charge of reception again," I told him.

"Agreed," he ground out.

Mama exclaimed, "What is wrong with the two of you? Emmett, I didn't spend fifteen hours in labor, passing your pumpkin of a head, for you to do that to your body! And Lacey, how could you move back to town without telling me?"

"I haven't moved back, Mama, I'm just staying with Emmett for a few days while I figure some things out. Emmett, on the other hand, was drunk, and an art student from Atlanta convinced him it would seal their love."

"Shut it," Emmett warned. "Or I bring up the public yoga pants."

I shuddered. "Agreed."

"I thought you went to the lake to figure some things out," Mama said, running her fingers through my hair, fluffing it up.

"Her problems followed her," Emmett said. "Lacey is now dodging phone calls from men in two counties."

"Monroe called?" I asked, my brow furrowed.

"Who's Monroe?" Mama asked.

"Your voice mail was full, so he starting calling my cell," Emmett said. "I assumed that since you let your voice mail fill up, you didn't want to talk to him. I told him I didn't know where you were."

I pulled my cell phone out of my purse and saw that the battery was completely dead, which happens when you don't charge it for three days. Monroe had called. And when he couldn't reach me, he tracked down my brother. He cared enough to find me, which was more than I could say for Mike in the last days of our marriage. I didn't know whether to be happy or annoyed. I settled for ambiguous and confused, with a teeny little spark of hope wriggling the weight loose from my chest.

"Oh, that's good," I muttered.

Mama took my face in her hands and forced me to focus on her question. "Who's Monroe?"

"The man Lacey owes a big apology," Emmett said.

"Oh, honey, you didn't write something about him, did you?" Mama asked, shaking her head and clucking her tongue.

"No," I mumbled. "It's a normal relationship apology."

"Relationship!" Mama exclaimed. "When did you have time to start a relationship? And how did you meet someone? You've been living in the middle of nowhere."

"Well, she didn't have to look far," Emmett said, smirking.

"Hidden piercings," I said in a warning tone.

"Shutting up now," promised Emmett.

"I'll never understand the two of you," Mama sighed. "Well, Emmers, it's sweet that you put your sister up, but it would be best if she came on home. It would give her more time to tell me about this Monroe character." She gave me a pointed look.

"Mama, I can't come back to your house. I'm not staying at Emmett's place permanently either. I'm just there for a few days and then, I don't know what. I'll figure something out."

"Lace," Emmett protested. "There's no need to—"

"No."

Mama sighed, "But if you would just—"

"No," I repeated. "You two can't keep passing me back and forth like I'm some emotionally handicapped tennis ball. I love you guys, but I've managed to dress myself, and feed myself, and live on my own for the last several months without withering away and dying. I know I came down here looking for help, but sometimes that means 'Just listen to me while I vent,' not 'Please take over my whole life.' Now, I'd like to keep working here, Emmett, if it's okay with you, but I think we can agree I need my own place, whether it's up at the lake or here in town. Mama, don't argue. I need my own space, and my own things, and room to make the huge mistakes I know you're going to try to protect me from." Emmett frowned, but seemed mollified when I added, "But I am keeping the clothes, though, because they're really cute."

"Will you at least let me make you an appointment with Dorie, honey, because this needs work," Mama said, gesturing to my head.

"Hey, I did that!" Emmett explained.

"Oh . . ." Mama said. "It's lovely, really."

"In Emmett's defense, it's grown out a little since he cut it," I said. "And I didn't put much effort into grooming this morning."

Emmett cleared his throat.

"Fine, this week."

My head ached dully at the thought of going to a salon, a public place, filled with women who would have dissected and discussed every little detail of my divorce. Face-to-face, they'd put on sweet smiles and make polite small talk and act like nothing had happened. The minute my back was turned, the whispering would start. But I'd put off dealing with this for long enough. I was going to have to deal with it eventually. Better to jump headlong into the icy pool than slide back into Singletree's social circle one toe at a time.

I told Mama, "Please make an appointment with Dorie. Not because either of you told me I need it, but because I'd actually like to have some input into my haircut and not just wake up with a new one." I scowled at my brother, who seemed more miffed than ever.

Mama smiled triumphantly and whipped out her cell phone. Our shared stylist's number was on speed dial, between Daddy and poison control. "Dorie, hi, honey, it's Deb. I've got a bit of a hair emergency here. Lacey's in town and she could use a cut if you have a spot open." Mama's grin faltered a bit. "Oh, I see."

Emmett shot me a confused look. I shrugged.

"Well, I suppose that will be fine," Mama said, somewhat stiffly. "I understand that you're booked up. Yes, that will be fine." She hung up the phone. "Dorie says you can come by tomorrow at four."

"Okay," I said. "You seem a little upset about that."

"Dorie's never made me wait before," Mama said. "She's kept the shop open late for me when I needed a last-minute appointment. She opened up at the crack of dawn that morning I woke up with orange hair because the chlorine in the Terwilligers' pool—" Mama gasped. "Wynnie got to her."

"Mama, Wynnie doesn't even go to that salon," I said, laughing.

"No, but Dorie's husband works for your soon-to-be former father-in-law," Emmett reasoned. "This could be her subtle way of showing where her loyalties lie."

"In the Great Hair Wars?" I laughed. "Mama, has Dorie treated you any differently since the e-mail?" Mama shook her head. "Then I'm sure she just didn't have room for me on the schedule. I'll go tomorrow and it will be fine. There is no mass salon conspiracy or darker purpose at work here."

• • •

But from the moment I walked into the Uniquely You salon, I knew I was wrong. The salon was packed with the usual Friday afternoon primping-for-the-weekend crowd, and the moment I walked through the door, everyone stopped talking. Plump, pleasant Dorie Watkins blanched at the sight of me, her mouth set in a grim line as her baby-doll blue eyes flicked to the peach and chrome shampoo station in the back.

"Hi, Lacey," Janey Radner ventured. "It's nice to see you."

I smiled politely, plucking at the long-sleeved red jersey dress Emmett insisted I wear, with a red-and-jet-bead lariat and killer heels. It had been so long since I'd worn a skirt or heels, it had felt almost alien to slide them on, like a skin I'd shed a long time ago. But now I was glad I'd slipped into one of the nicer outfits Emmett had purchased for me. I wanted to combat those insistent "dumpy sweatsuit and snake tattoo" rumors.

Dorie cleared her throat nervously. "Um, Lacey, I'm running a little behind on another appointment. It will take me a little while to finish up. Do you want to maybe have a manicure while you wait? Judy's free. Or we could just reschedule."

Judy Messer, a sweet girl I'd gone to high school with, waved at me from the rear of the shop. "Sure, my hands are a wreck. Are you okay, Dorie?"

Dorie insisted she was fine, but I couldn't help but notice the way she kept angling me away from the shampoo station, pushing me to the rear of the shop. When Shelly, the shampoo girl, gently raised the chair up and began toweling the client in question's hair, I realized it wasn't just another woman, it was *the* other woman. Beebee, in all her bronzed and lacquered glory, shot me a triumphant look as she was led to Dorie's station and seated. I felt like I'd been punched in the stomach. The scent of perm solution roiled across my nostrils, making me dizzy and nauseous. The roar of the dryers grated on my eardrums. My grip on my temper was getting more tenuous by the second.

"What the hell is she doing here?" I demanded.

"Getting a trim," Beebee said, smirking at me. "You might consider it, honey, you've got some split ends showing. Now, exactly who the hell do you think you are, showing your face around here again?"

I smiled and stretched my hand out as if to offer a friendly shake. She flinched dramatically, as if I'd taken a swing at her. I rolled my eyes. "I know it must be difficult for you to keep track of all of the wives of the married men you've slept with, so I'll help you out. I'm Lacey, Mike's wife. You're living in my house, sleeping in my bed, oh, and, driving my car."

Over Dorie's shoulder, I saw Pam Hamilton watching our exchange with glee. Behind her, Felicity Clark was pretending to read a magazine, but was obviously memorizing every word and expression.

"Someone doesn't like being replaced," Beebee singsonged in a silly Betty Boop voice that made me want to smack her.

Distress raised Dorie's voice by two octaves as I took a menacing step toward her rack of scissors. "I'm so sorry, Lacey," she whispered, pushing me away from Beebee toward the manicure station. "She started coming here right after you left town. Her usual appointment is on Thursdays, which is why I booked you for today. But then she came marching in ten minutes ago and demanded a shampoo and updo for some fancy dinner thing Mike's taking her to. I thought I could squeeze her in before you got here."

"What the hell, Dorie?!" I exclaimed. "I've been coming here for years! You did my hair for the junior prom, for God's sake!"

"I know," Dorie said, chewing her lip. "But with Mark working for Jim, I need to keep the Terwilligers happy, Lacey. I can't make a fuss."

"Lacey, I think you need to calm down," Felicity told me. "You're making everybody uncomfortable."

I whirled on Felicity, and it was on the tip of my tongue to tell her that she'd be just as upset if her Karl paraded Margie Wannamaker through the salon. Or to tell Pam that everybody knew her hubby, Larry, and Bruce Gibbs don't really go "camping" once a month, unless you count shacking up at the DeLuxe Inn for two days as "roughing it." Emma Powell, who was smirking at me from under the dryer, had the bad fortune to have married a man who gave a stripper at Tassles more than five thousand dollars from his 401(k) and a used Honda. And he paid to have some of her tattoos removed. I could wipe the smug expressions from their faces with just a few well-chosen words, just like I was knocked off my own smug little pedestal all those months ago.

Hell, I could tell Beebee that Mike came crawling back to me, begging me to butter his toast and scratch his back again. That little tidbit would be circulated on the kitchen circuit by dinnertime.

But just as my lips parted to launch my opening attack on Felicity, I remembered feeling that sick, queasy sensation of my world spinning off its axis. And I tried to imagine going through that with other people around, with a room full of women I knew. And I couldn't do it.

"Why don't we all just admit that we have problems?" I asked, shaking my head. "My ex-husband is nailing this bimbo. He moved her into our house, gave her my car. Hell, I'm pretty sure those are my shoes she's wearing. And how exactly is that my fault? I didn't do anything to encourage it. I wasn't a bad wife. I had a bad husband. Why don't we just admit that we married the wrong men? Hello, my name is Lacey, and I married an asshole. Why is that so hard? Whatever happened to sisterhood? Why can't we just be honest and support each other? Well, obviously Beebee's out. But why can't we just admit to each other that our lives aren't perfect? That's all I did when I wrote that newsletter. I admitted that my life, at the moment, sucked. And if that scares you, or sickens you, I'm sorry. But you might want to ask yourselves why.

"Dorie," I said, turning to her. "Finish Beebee's hair. I'll come in the same time next Wednesday if you're free. That should keep us from any unpleasant passing encounters."

Dorie smiled shakily. "That should be fine."

I walked out of the salon with my chin up, my heels clicking on the floor as the silent patrons watched me. The moment

I stepped out the door, the buzz of voices rose like a swarm of angry bees.

I'd almost made it to my car when I realized I'd actually walked over to my old Volvo, the car Beebee was now driving. Crap.

"Don't you touch my car!" Beebee shrieked, scrambling out of the salon door with a wet head and a nylon cape tied around her neck.

"I wasn't going to," I sighed and spotted a half-dozen faces pressed against the salon window, watching us. "I just forgot you were driving it now."

"Don't you play dumb with me," Beebee hissed. "What do you think you're doing, just waltzing around town after what you did to me and Mike?

"Beebee, I know you're upset. I mean, after all, I did call you a whore in a public forum. But I would just like to point out that you did sleep with my husband. So, really, I think that makes us even. So if you don't mind, I'm going to climb into my car and leave with some dignity intact."

"Oh, spare me, you wives always climb up on your high horses, getting all righteous and offended, like it's not your fault your husbands sleep around. You know, Mike wouldn't have come after me if you were keeping him happy! That's why men leave women like you for women like me. You're dull. You're uptight. You're so worried about keeping Mommy and Daddy happy that you can't keep your man happy. You're useless in bed. And then you're surprised when he goes looking for something else." Her eyes narrowed and she smiled nastily. "He told me you're so frigid, you would just lay there like roadkill."

Okay, that did sting a little bit.

Even with grinding teeth and my fingernails biting little half moons into my palms, I managed to smirk at her. "So how many times have *you* had to fake it for him?"

"That's none of your—" she hissed before she caught herself. "You're never getting Mike back. Do you hear me?"

"I don't want him back!"

"I don't believe you!" she yelled.

"I don't care what you believe. That's the crazy thing about having your life derailed. It means you have nothing left to lose. I'm not even that angry with you anymore, Beebee. If you're happy with my hand-me-downs, more power to you. If anything, I owe you a big fat thank-you for showing me what kind of man my husband really was. I'm not going to thank you, because, again, I think you have no redeeming value as a person, but the temptation is there."

"I love him," Beebee said simply, in a voice that made her sound so much younger. "I know that probably doesn't matter to you, but I do. And I don't want to lose him."

I stared at her. This was a different Beebee than the unnaturally colored, husband-stealing she-beast I'd come to picture in my head. Her face was clean. Her hair was damp and slick against her skull. There were actually tears shimmering in her eyes. She looked . . . bare, somehow, vulnerable. And scared.

Of all the emotions bubbling through my chest at the moment, the one that caught me by surprise was pity for Beebee. She really did feel something for Mike, and he had already given up on her. He'd made it clear that afternoon at the lake that he was moving on, whether it was with me or the next receptionist, cocktail waitress, or dog shampooer that took his interest.

Wait a minute.

"I don't care!" I cried. "I don't care if you love him. I don't care if you tattoo his name on your eyelids! If you came to me looking for forgiveness or some sort of blessing, you're even dumber than I thought you were."

Beebee's lip curled back over her teeth as she snarled, "Fine, if you want to be a bitch, be a bitch. But you stay away from us."

"Fine!" I exclaimed, climbing into the car. As I backed away, I could see the salon patrons scooting away from the window as Beebee stomped through the door. But I managed to get out of the parking lot without running her over, and I gave myself a little pat on the back.

The drive home seemed to take longer than it should. I used the time to stew. Was this the way it was going to be for the rest of my life? Would every trip into town result in some sort of public scene? Would I have to sneak into town for holidays with my family, assuming that my father was speaking to me? Was I going to have to enter some sort of shamed small-town divorcée witness protection program?

I'd been evicted from my whole damn life. Mike had replaced me with the kind of woman that could engage in a catfight in a beauty salon parking lot. Someone who he could lavish with stupid, thoughtful, impractical gifts that had no value other than making Beebee happy. He had time to take Beebee on long weekends at bed-and-breakfasts. Her gifts weren't bought with the intention of impressing our neighbors. I'll bet she didn't get a damn robot vacuum for Christmas.

Just when I thought I had moved on and wasn't angry at Mike anymore, I got pulled back in. It was like I was in some sort of petty mafia. And I wanted that righteous anger, that feeling that I'd been wronged. It was clean, clear, like a gas flame that helped burn away my more jumbled emotions, like guilt and doubt and regret. But I couldn't find it. I wasn't even angry with Mike anymore. I just didn't want to know him. I wanted him out of my life, to cut him out like a cancer. I wanted . . . why was this drive taking so long?

I finally focused on my surroundings and realized I was about a mile away from the cabin. I must have driven the car there on autopilot. I'd wanted to go home, and here I was. The light sprinkling of rain that had started to fall just a few minutes ago picked up to full gale-force winds and sheets of water over my windshield.

"Shit," I muttered. "Emmett's going to love this."

I pulled the car into the gravel driveway. Monroe's truck wasn't parked outside his cabin. For a panicky moment, I worried that he'd moved out. That he was gone and I'd never see him again. I jumped out of the car, shucked the needle-thin heels, and trudged across the wet, muddy ground in my stocking feet. The porch light was on, a beacon in the growing darkness of late fall. I peered in the window and saw his laptop open on the desk, his running shoes thrown in the corner, as usual. The place was a mess. There were dirty dishes piled on the kitchen counters. Stacks of papers were strewn over every available surface. It looked like he'd started reading a half-dozen paperback novels and then just dropped them when he was finished.

I shivered, touching the cold glass with my fingertips and thinking of Miss Havisham and her moldy wedding dinner. It didn't seem like the same house anymore, the place where I'd spent so many happy hours. I backed away from the door, worried that Monroe would come back and find me staring into his window like some creepy stalker. I ran back to my car and grabbed my purse, thankful that I'd left some stuff behind when I bolted to Emmett's.

I took out my cell phone and called him. After he shrieked at me for a couple of minutes about being worried sick and checking the emergency rooms because he'd heard Beebee had whipped my ass in the Uniquely You parking lot, he calmed down enough for me to tell him that I'd just driven up to the cabin to pick up a few things.

"Well, it would have been nice to let me know," he huffed. "Are you staying up there for the night? It looks like the weather is supposed to get pretty nasty."

"It already is up here," I told him. "I will probably stay. But I'll come back first thing in the morning."

There was a long silence on the other end of the line. "Actually, Lace, there's an auction I wanted to check out in Sikesville. I'll be gone all weekend anyway; why don't you just stay up there?"

There was a casual nonchalance to Emmett's tone that I just didn't trust. I chuckled. Emmett had always been a terrible actor. "Emmett, if you and Peter are getting back together, all you have to say is that you need some privacy."

"Um, sure, you got me," he said, laughing awkwardly. "Remember, we're closed on Mondays, so no need to rush back. I'll see you soon, Lace."

I listened for Emmett's line to go dead and shook my head. "My brother is weird."

I shrugged out of my wet dress and into some warm flannel pajamas. I spied my laptop, open and in hibernation mode, at the kitchen table. I hadn't even thought to grab it in my exodus to Emmett's. I clicked the touchpad and the screen roared to life, showing me the chapter I'd been working on before my fight with Monroe. The police had just questioned Laurie about Greg's mysterious disappearance. Greg's new girlfriend,

Patricia, had stormed into the house and demanded that Laurie tell her where Greg was. Behind her, Laurie saw the sliding pocket doors twitching in the entryway to the dining room, as if any second they would snap together, closing on Patricia like the jaws of a steel trap. I'd been in *Gladiator* thumbs-up or thumbs-down mode, trying to decide Patricia's fate, when I'd left the computer.

Part of me wanted to write Patricia's death in brilliant, blood-soaked detail, the sound of the doors crunching through bone to meet in the middle, the look in her eyes when she realized that Laurie was making this happen. The more rational part of my brain realized that as long as I wanted Laurie to punish Greg or his mistress, she wasn't going to be a bigger, better person. She was going to be the same person she was at the beginning of the book. And she'd be stuck in an evil house that ate people.

As long as I was mad at Mike, I wasn't going to be able to finish this book. As long as I was unsettled on my future, I wouldn't be able to give Laurie the ending she deserved.

"Okay, I get it!" I shouted at the ceiling, at some invisible writing god. "It's a metaphor!"

I chewed my lip, staring at my cell phone. I dialed Samantha's cell number. She picked up on the first ring. "For future reference, when we talked about 'not having contact with Beebee or Mike,' that includes not beating the tar out of one of them with your car antenna on a beauty salon lot."

"I did not do that," I promised her.

"I know, I'm just messing with you," she said, hooting. "The antenna thing seemed a little too mafioso. You're more of a fists-and-fingernails kind of girl."

"Thank you," I muttered. "I need to come see you next week. There's some paperwork we need to talk about."

"Has Mike filed involuntary commitment papers?" she asked.

"It's likely, but that's not what I need to talk to you about," I muttered. "What would be the fastest way to wrap up the divorce proceedings?"

"Off the top of my head, you could ask for what you brought into the marriage, a fair share of your savings-slash-gifts, and promise not to come after more later if he drops the lawsuit," she said. "He might go for that, or he might laugh in your face and threaten you with the Sizzler again."

"Could you have that drawn up for me this week sometime?"

I could almost hear her smiling through the phone. "What are you up to, Lacey?"

"Growing up," I told her.

"Sucks a little bit, doesn't it?"

"You aren't kidding," I snorted.

After settling a few minor details and asking Sam to keep an eye open for decent rentals in the area, I hung up, closed the blinds, turned off my phone, and refused to acknowledge the outside world until I'd finished the damn book.

Eventually, I lost track of time and the cartons of Coke I'd consumed.

I didn't know if Monroe was paying attention to the lights in my window or how late I was staying up. Frankly, I was glad he couldn't see me pacing in front of my computer, dancing to Gloria Gaynor to try to make words come out of my brain . . . eating chocolate fudge icing straight out of the can. Using an Oreo as a spoon.

I wrote until my eyes drooped and I thought my head would explode from staring at the screen. I fell asleep with my head against the keyboard on more than one occasion.

In a gesture I preferred to think of as hope, I did not let the house eat Patricia—or Laurie, for that matter. In the end, Laurie burned it to the ground, destroying her past, banishing the bloody specter of her former husband. But because this was a horror novel and I wanted the ending to be somewhat ominous, I wrote a little scene in which Laurie is moving into her new apartment. Her handsome male neighbor comes over to introduce himself while she's moving in, and romantic sparks fly. Behind her, where neither of them could see, the stairs rippled just the tiniest bit.

"The end," I muttered as I typed out the last line.

And now, according to Monroe, the real work began. Editing, writing query letters to agents, surviving the rejections. As intimidating as it was, I wanted to see if I was good enough, if my work was good enough to actually get published.

"And now, the editing," I muttered, returning to page one. When the overwhelming smell of, well, me, wafted up from my T-shirt, I shuddered. "But first, a shower. Blech."

• • •

When I'd read the manuscript, once and then again, taking most of Monroe's advice into account, I printed it out and sneaked it over to his cabin in the dead of night. Well, I thought it was the dead of night. By the time I came out of the cabin, it was 4:30 p.m. on Monday. And I was still in my pajamas. Well, let's face it, Monroe had seen worse from me.

I padded across the lawn, my paper baby cradled in my arms. I laid it on Monroe's steps and almost made a clean getaway when I heard the door open behind me.

"Crap," I muttered without looking back.

"Well, hello to you, too," he said in a tone far more pleasant than I'd expected. "So we're just leaving manifestos on each others' doorsteps now?"

"It's not a manifesto," I protested. "When I stalk you, you'll be aware of it."

"Good to know," he said.

There was a long awkward pause. "I'm sorry." I said. "I'm sorry for the things I said and for taking the easy way out again. You said some pretty horrible things, but they were accurate, which was probably why they hurt so much."

"Lacey—"

"I'm not saying this because I'm looking for an apology. I just wanted to say I miss you and not just because you're the closest thing I've had to a functional sexual relationship. I miss my friend. And I'm hoping that we'll eventually find our way back to being friends again."

"Lacey, don't—"

"Let me finish," I told him. "But for now, I'm moving out. I'm sorry we left things the way we did. Thank you being my friend and the voice of reason I so desperately needed. If you ever base a crazy-woman, scorned character on me, please be kind. My brother's right; I've hidden out up here too long. And if you ever tell him I said that, I will deny it to my dying breath.

"But I did want to leave this for you," I said, handing him the manuscript. "It's an extremely rough draft. But I'd like to know what you think."

"You finished it?" he asked, flipping through the pages.

"Well, what did you think I was doing when I was avoiding you?"

He pursed his lips. "I pictured something involving ice cream."

"Well, you weren't wrong there."

"So did you do this just to spite me for saying you wouldn't?" he asked.

"What? No!" I scoffed. He stared at me. "Okay, yes. That had a little bit to do with it."

"I'm sorry I said that," he told me. "And all of the other mean, horrible—"

"Incredibly hurtful, yet accurate?" I added.

"Yeah, those things I said. I didn't mean them," he promised. "Well, I meant it when I said I love you. But the rest was just my being an ass. Could we go back to the way things were before? I don't care if we don't put a label on it. We were happy and that's all that—"

"Let's just take things slow, okay?" I asked. "We'll start with you reading that."

"Well, I'm looking forward to it," he said. "So does Laurie find love with a brooding, far more handsome man in the end?" He blanched. "Wait, did you make the house eat him, too?"

"You're just going to have to read and find out for yourself."

27

Blah, Blah, Blahdy Blah

I'd like to say that my newsletter ruined Mike's life, that his clients were so disgusted with his extracurricular activities that they abandoned him. But if anything, the newsletter and the ensuing drama gave the firm more cachet, like having your taxes done by the cast of *Melrose Place.*

The employees in the lobby of Terwilliger and Associates froze when I walked in. A couple of clients were sitting on the couch, their jaws unhinged and a gleeful anticipation shining in their eyes. Libby Hackett, Beebee's younger, blonder replacement, widened her eyes to an even more doe-like state when I approached the desk. Dexter and Dave, the junior associates, snapped out of their stupor first, dropping their coffee mugs on the floor with a clatter and scrambling for the video function on their cell phones. I smiled sweetly, which seemed to frighten the receptionist even more.

"I need to see Mr. Terwilliger, please," I said.

"I'm supposed to call the cops if you show up," Libby whispered.

"Would you mind giving me a five-minute head start?" I whispered back.

She let loose a nervous laugh. "Okay."

"You know I'm kidding, right?" I told her.

She shook her head. "No, I don't."

"Libby, honey, if you feel you need to call the cops, you go right ahead. I won't hold it against you."

"Really?" She sighed in relief. "Thanks."

"No problem. I'll just pop into Mr. Terwilliger's office before the sirens get close, okay?"

Libby nodded. Behind me, I heard Dexter and Dave follow me into the hallway. Over my shoulder, I saw them holding up their phones.

"Mike," I said, knocking on the frame of his door, something I'd never bothered with before.

Beebee was in his office, demanding his opinion on fabric swatches. The bitchy part of me wanted to tell her that they were all hideous, but the whole point of this visit was emotional growth and that wasn't a good start. (But seriously, they were all butt ugly. We're talking a lot of pink. Mike was going to be living inside of a Pepto-Bismol bottle.)

Somehow, that made it easier when Beebee sprang up off the couch and yelled for Libby. Mike looked up and, for a moment, it looked like he forgot we weren't married. His first instinct was to smile. Then I'm sure he remembered, just as soon as he saw the thunderous look on Beebee's face. I could tell by the flinching.

"Don't make me call my lawyer," he said, sounding tired.

"Oh, I'm not going to do anything; sit down," I commanded. Mike looked unsure. "Sit down."

I turned to Beebee, who was sending a poisonous glare Mike's way. "I just want to tell you that I hope you're everything he deserves and more."

"What do you mean by that?" Beebee demanded.

"If you think about it for a while, you'll figure it out," I told her, winking. "Would you mind if I spoke to Mike alone, please?"

"Like hell!" she cried.

"Beebee, please." Mike said.

"No, Mike." She glowered at him. "We've talked about this."

"Beebee," he pleaded.

"Fine," she huffed. "But I'm waiting right outside. This door stays open and I'll be listening to every word!"

"She's a . . . lovely girl," I told him, sitting across from him. "You caught me off guard the other day. There are things I need to say to you, without lawyers . . . or witnesses present."

Mike looked so hopeful for a moment, but his face fell when I said, "You're a jerk, Mike Terwilliger. What you did to me was just shameful, wrong, despicable. But what I did was sneaky and spiteful and immature. I was a good wife to you. I may not have met all of your needs, but I never set out to do anything to intentionally hurt you. You can't say the same thing. But I forgive you for what you did, because I don't want to carry this around with me for the rest of my life, screwing up everything else that I touch. I don't want you to have that kind of power over me. And I hope that one day you'll forgive me for what I did."

I took a manila envelope out of my shoulder bag and slid it across his desk. "I had my lawyer draw these up. It's a settlement. It lists all of the assets I brought to the marriage, plus a request for the equivalent cash value of my car, the equity I have in the house, my part of our savings—enough to get me started. I don't want to hurt you. I don't want anything from you that I didn't earn. I've already signed them. I'd appreciate it if you signed them and we could get this over and done with."

I'm pretty sure all Mike heard was "Blah, blah, blahdy blah, I'm going to make this easier for you." But I didn't say all that for him. I said it for me. If one of us was going to learn from this, I'm glad it was me.

I stood and offered Mike my hand. "Good-bye, Mike."

He pursed his lips and grasped my fingers. I had been holding that hand since I was nineteen years old. I knew every ridge, every scar. It was warm and solid in my hand. And it might as well have belonged to a stranger. I shook it. He smiled sadly. "Good-bye."

"Lacey," he said as I walked out the door. "I'm dropping the lawsuit, and so will Beebee."

Beebee gasped. "But—"

"So will Beebee," Mike said again, giving her a stern look. "A clean split, okay? I'll tell Bill we want to do this as quickly as possible. No more fooling around."

I smiled and nodded. "Thanks."

I was pretty sure that was the closest thing I was going to get to an apology.

I walked out of the office with a clear conscience.

Somewhere in my heart a little door closed with a clean, quiet "snick." I was through with Mike Terwilliger. And he had moved on to a woman who, while she obviously didn't make him entirely happy, was still better suited to him than I was. Whether he stayed with her or left her within a year, I knew it wouldn't affect me either way. Instead of waiting for them to collapse on themselves, I would be living my life. I may not have wished them well, but at least I wasn't devoting precious energy to wishing they would spontaneously combust.

Surely that had to be a sign of emotional development.

• • •

As I hauled in the bags of groceries I'd bought in town I found another package from Maya on my doorstep. It contained very subdued, expensive-looking letterhead for Season's Gratings. It listed both Maya and me as owner/operators. "Okay, final offer time," Maya's note read. "Full partnership."

I'm not going to say it wasn't tempting, especially when I saw what my share of the profits would be as a full partner in Maya's company. But I'd finally made a clean break from Mike and Beebee. Even though it had some, let's say, negative aftereffects, I couldn't say the newsletter was a mistake. I'd taken a stand. The newsletter had shown people that I was more than my father's daughter or my husband's wife. I made my own choices, even if those choices had the potential to get me in a lot of trouble. And it had brought me to the lake, to Monroe. And even if things with Monroe had taken a turn toward the end, his friendship had helped me figure out what sort of person I wanted to be.

Still, somehow it seemed like a step backward to write more. The newsletters were my way of standing up for myself. As much as I wanted to help these other women, they needed to do the work for themselves. They needed to find their own way of striking back at their exes, or not, if they managed to cool down.

I opened my e-mail and composed a new message for Maya entitled, "You may find this hard to believe . . ."

28

Moving On

Mike had provided everything I had asked for, plus some family Christmas decorations and an heirloom rocking chair I'd forgotten in my flight from the house. He even agreed to replace my iPod, which had mysteriously been run over by Beebee's car.

It was the nicest present he'd ever gotten me.

In return, I was giving Mike the skeleton of his boat, unscathed. He'd sent movers for it the week before I planned to move out of the cabin. It would have felt like a hostage exchange, if not for Wynnie Terwilliger's glowering at me from the front seat of the moving truck. She made it a little less friendly than a hostage exchange.

Samantha felt bad for taking my retainer, but not taking my divorce case or my lawsuit to trial. It looked like Mike and I were going to be able to wrap everything up in mediation now that we'd agreed to start acting like adults. She didn't feel bad enough to repay my retainer, but she was helping me move, so I guess it was a wash.

I had elected not to move into the Pheasant Hollow apartments, no matter how nice they were. Because the only unit available had recently been abandoned by Beebee and that would just be weird. So I was using my first month's paycheck to put a deposit on a rental house Sam found. It was just a few blocks away from Emmett's, close enough for the occasional visit, but well outside of smacking range.

I was toting the last of my bags out of the cabin when I ran into Monroe and a giant basket. We'd been carefully maneuvering around each other for weeks, afraid to broach the subject of our relationship, now that I was finally ready to call it one, or what my moving out would mean for us. Conversations were short, superficial, and unsatisfying.

I chuckled. "Funny, I didn't order a big manly man bearing chocolate . . ."

"Maya sent this for you," he said, hefting the basket onto the porch railing.

Maya's basket was full of various chocolate products and a specially printed card with avenging angels dancing around the border. "'I still love you even if you don't reconsider (PLEASE, PLEASE reconsider). Call me,'" I read.

"Creepy and yet resourceful," I said, handing it to him.

Monroe seemed pleased and surprised by the contents of the little card. "So you couldn't pull the trigger, huh?"

"No, I don't think it would have made my life mean more or make me feel better. I don't think it would do any of those women any good. What worked for me probably isn't going to work for most women. Someone told me I'd make a pretty decent novelist. So I think I'll give that a try."

"No, you're going to be a great novelist. I finished the book, and there are some rough spots," he said. "But there's some seriously scary stuff going on there. For a day or so, I was honestly a little leery of my bathtub because I was afraid the shower curtain would try to smother me."

"Thanks," I said, laughing. "Emmett hated that bit, too, when I told him about it. I'm still editing, and will probably start submitting it to agents in the next few months. But, in the meantime, I've been offered a position working for a pathologically disorganized antiques expert who can rat me out to our mother if I don't reach my performance goals."

Monroe watched Emmett huff and puff as he loaded my suitcase in the car. "I would say he wouldn't do that, but I know I'd be wrong."

Emmett draped himself dramatically against the frame of my car. "Honey, I told you, I don't lift things," he groaned. "Nice to see you again, Monroe."

"Hi, Emmett, how are you?"

"Peachy freaking keen. So are you two finally going to kiss and make up or what?" Emmett huffed, with his usual amount of tact. "I don't know if I can stand any more of this romantic tension. Or lifting. I can't emphasize the lifting enough."

"We're working on it," Monroe told him. When Emmett didn't take this as a hint to leave, Monroe gave the front door a pointed look.

"Emmett just says things sometimes. We're having him tested," I said, adding, "I'll get everybody out of here as quickly as possible."

"You don't have to." Monroe's face softened. He reached out and stroked a hand along my arm to take my fingers into his. "You could stay up here. Stay with me."

I smiled sadly, my mouth tilting at the corner. "In a parallel universe, where I met you first, I bet we're the kind of couple that makes all their friends sick with how happy they are. I'll bet we have two-point-four kids, a golden retriever named Max, enjoy smoking hot sex on Wednesdays, the whole bit."

"Nobody has smoking hot sex on Wednesdays," he said.

"That's why all our friends hate us." I giggled when his serious expression broke into a grin. "I can't. I can't hide up here anymore. I have to go out and face the world, learn to be a grown-up. I'm not sorry, not for coming here or being with you. But I'm just not ready— Oh, what the hell."

I grabbed him and kissed him, pushing him against the truck and swallowing his startled grunt. Vaguely, I could hear my sibling, and possibly Sam, wolf-whistling from behind the window glass.

"Stay," he said when we came up for air. "You can do all that. Figure out who you are, what you want to do, just let me be there while you do it. You can have all the space you want, write as much as you want, do whatever you want. Just stay."

I leaned my forehead against Monroe's. Here was a man who didn't want control. He just wanted me. I could choose to be with him and still do all that growing stuff. I just had to choose. I leaned back and narrowed my eyes at Monroe's painfully earnest expression.

"I don't have to entertain your friends," I told him.

"I don't have any friends."

"I don't have to join certain groups or clubs. I don't have to host anything or plan anything or do anything remotely beneficial for the community."

"These seem like oddly misanthropic rules, but I'm willing to agree to it if it means you'll stay."

"Well, actually, I was thinking, what if you moved in with me?" I asked. Monroe's eyebrows shot up to his hairline. "Not right away. But maybe in a couple of months or so, we could work toward you sharing the house with me. I know you like solitude, but Emmett says my new place is surrounded by married couples. There are no crazy divorcées, well, except for me. You'd still have the whole day to yourself to write while I'm at work. I just think we need to rejoin the world, or it's going to pass us by."

"But when will you write?" he asked.

"At night, when things are slow at work, weekends," I said. "I mean, people don't start out as full-time writers, right? I have to start somewhere."

"Just to be clear, you're not asking me to be your roommate, are you?"

"No," I assured him. "This offer is for strictly nonplatonic cohabitation, possibly leading to long-term commitment." He quirked his lips. "I've spent a lot of time with Sam this week," I told him.

"Is she going to make me sign contracts?" he asked, shooting a wary look at the door.

"Possibly," I said solemnly. "Come make a home with me, Monroe. Please?"

He nodded and then the kissing started again. Samantha came out and saw us mashed against the truck. She sighed, but was smiling as she said, "If you tell me that you're not moving after all, I'm going to throw this very heavy box at you," she huffed. "You know, I don't do this for my other clients."

"Don't worry; your manual labor has not been in vain," I said. "But you might have to come back in a while to help me move Monroe."

Samantha managed to conceal the beginning curve of a smile. "Good, then you might want to get into your bedroom, Lace. Emmett's going through your closet, muttering something about 'ridiculous novelty pajamas' and throwing a bunch of stuff into a box marked *Goodwill.*"

"Emmett, leave the candy-corn pajamas alone!" Monroe barked. "There's sentimental value there."

"Then you get your happy-ending-having asses in here and pack your own damn boxes," Emmett yelled back.

"I think I finally understand why my brothers didn't faze you," he said as we walked back into the cabin. "You've been dealing with your own irritating sibling for years."

"I heard that!" Emmett called.

"Matt and Andy say hi, by the way," Monroe said. "In fact, they want to make sure you have their e-mail addresses, just in case I screw up and you feel the need to send out another newsletter."

"Well, if that doesn't keep you on your toes, I don't know what will."

Monroe grimaced. "I was thinking maybe we'd close your e-mail accounts, at least for the first couple of months."

"Very funny," I said, grinning up at him. After a beat, I made my face go serious and still. "You should know that I've added your mother to my contact list."

Monroe kissed my temple and said in a low, sober tone, "I'm hiding your laptop."